CTHULHU'S COUSINS

AND OTHER WEIRDNESSES

CTHULHU'S COUSINS

AND OTHER WEIRDNESSES

W. PAUL GANLEY

WILDSIDE PRESS

To my wife, Terry Rose, with all my love. Without her encouragement, these manuscripts and other sources would be decaying hunks of old paper buried in a cellar, to be destroyed by floods or the tides of time.

Published by Wildside Press LLC.
www.wildsidepress.com

CONTENTS

W. PAUL GANLEY: MODESTY AND ACCOMPLISHMENT

Pay attention to syntax, Dear Reader. Precision of language matters. I am not writing about the "modest accomplishments" of W. Paul Ganley, because they are actually quite considerable, but the fact that he is not the sort of person who trumpets his own accomplishments. Instead, he merely *accomplishes* them, and has been doing impressive things in the horror/fantasy field for longer than many of you have been alive.

Paul first came to my attention in 1968, when there was an ad in *Amazing Stories* offering a *free magazine* to anyone who wrote for it. This proved to be the first issue of *Weirdbook*, a (then) 32 page, but nicely printed publication which described itself as "a literary vitamin pill" designed to fill some of the void left by the collapse of the venerable *Weird Tales* in 1954. 1968 was a low point for weird fiction, but *Weirdbook* managed to lure some of the old-timers—notably H. Warner Munn and Joseph Payne Brennan—back into the game. The first few issues also contained stories by writers I'd never heard of before, including Walter Quednau and one Oliver Ward, whose "I Am Human" I remember enjoying. Both are pseudonyms for Ganley. Only later did I learn that at the outset he actually had difficulty getting material and was doing what editors have always done, filling the pages by any means necessary. Later on, *Weirdbook* would feature writers as illustrious as Stephen King, Tanith Lee, Brian Lumley, Dennis Etchison, and Michael Bishop.

I could go on for great length about the importance of *Weirdbook* and W. Paul Ganley as a publisher. Both changed my life. Here I was, 15 years old, desperate to see my name in print as 15-year-olds of a certain type are, and I figured that, realistically, I wasn't ready for *The Magazine of Fantasy & Science Fiction* or *Galaxy* yet, but maybe, if *Weirdbook* was publishing unknowns like Quednau and Ward, it might be slightly more of a pushover. So, filled with youthful hubris, I sent Paul a story. He, with unfailing good sense, sent it right back, but he showed both his generosity and his editorial talent when he explained to me what was wrong with it, as he did with several more stories I deluged him with in an attempt to break down his resistance. I don't think he cracked. I think I learned something, and I just barely squeaked by with a marginal poem in *Weirdbook* 3 and a marginal story in *Weirdbook* 4. Paul Ganley mentored me, and I remain enormously grateful for that. He was a pillar of my career, not only at its beginning, but in its middle, as I had a very long and fruitful relationship with *Weirdbook* that lasted until the magazine's end, almost thirty years later. He also published (or co-published, since the last was done with the assistance of the late George Scithers) three of my story collections, including the World Fantasy Award nominated *Transients* in 1993. He was the sort of editor who would back writers he believed in. He published volume after volume of Brian Lumley, but also books by Jessica Salmonson, Nancy Springer, William Scott Home, and others.

It is not as if this went entirely unnoticed. Paul was made Publisher Guest of Honor at the World Fantasy Convention in 2003. He won the World Fantasy Award, for *Weirdbook*, Special Award Non-Professional, in 1987, and again in 1992.

Meanwhile, with little fanfare, he was also a *writer.* He has published a good deal of serious poetry (and has always maintained an interest in poetry as a publisher of the work of Joseph Payne Brennan, for whom he created an entire new imprint, New Establishment Press), not to mention the time he got bitten by the limerick bug and the result was *Limericks for the Midnight Hours*, a chapbook I myself brought out under my Zadok Allen imprint (named after the town drunk in "The Shadow Over Innsmouth") in 1999.

None of which attracted much attention to the fact that he has, over the years, over the *decades* been publishing the occasional story here and there. I also remember enjoying his "Others, Who Are Not Men" when I read it in Meade and Penny Frierson's festschrift *HPL* in 1972, where it appeared alongside, among other things, a considerably less substantial contribution by myself. This was not his first appearance in print by any means. He actually started out as a letterhack in the pages of science fiction pulp magazines in the late 1940s. His first fiction appeared in fanzines in the early 1950s, including one story, "The Old One," published under the byline "Toby Duane," which took up an entire issue of a tiny booklet publication called *Space Trails* about then. Later, Paul let me reprint that story in my own fanzine, *Procrastination.* In 1953 the elusive Toby Duane was involved in something more substantial, contributing a chapter to a round-robin sword-and-sorcery novel, *Shanadu* (SSR Publications), along with Robert Briney, Eugene De Weese, and Brian McNaughton.

Of course literature has never even been Paul Ganley's main calling. In real life he has been a physics professor (now retired). In the early 1960s he spent five years as an Assistant Professor at Bryn Mawr College, teaching part-time and working as the Assistant Editor on the *American Journal of Physics.* He has always written fiction and verse as an *amateur* in the very best sense. Recall that the word derives from the Latin word for "love." An *amateur* in the sense that, for example, H.P. Lovecraft held up as an ideal, is someone who writes purely for the satisfaction of having done so, out of love of the act of writing and of literature itself.

Over the years, Ganley's publications have been accumulating, in mostly small-press journals such as *Crypt of Cthulhu* and *Eldritch Tales.* A lot of his stories have a decidedly Lovecraftian feel to them, a fact which is by no means concealed by the title of the present collection. Now, after having brought his limericks together inside one set of covers, I am glad to have a bit to do with something more substantial:

Here is a collection of *stories* by W. Paul Ganley, award-winning publisher and editor, poet, fan, a friend for decades, and also, quite simply, a *writer.*

—Darrell Schweitzer
Philadelphia PA
December 21, 2015

ANCIENT EVIL

A LOST MEMOIR BY OLIVER WARD

I

As to where I was—somewhere within our own solar system was my first guess. Probably the planet Pluto, farthest that we know of from the sun. A few odd cultists call it Yuggoth.

On the other hand, would my weight not have felt lighter on a smaller planet? It didn't. But I still thought I was on Yuggoth!

At one time, I decided to climb as far as I could in this three-dimensional maze that engulfed me. And I reached a great domed room with a queer crystalline ceiling that impressed me as totally transparent. There, shining above me with the very same splendor I had witnessed on many a winter's night in snow bound Connecticut, was the shape of Orion, the Hunter, sharp and clear. The tiny belt stars gleamed steadily. Sight of this familiar constellation of earth's skies lifted me for a moment out of the depths of a dark depression. Off to the upper right, I noticed a brilliant star, out-rivaling in magnitude even Venus as seen from the earth on a clear spring evening. I finally realized its identity after only a few moments of wonder. That star had to be the sun, as it would appear from a vast distance, a gulf almost inconceivable to a simple warm-blooded mammalian creature such as myself.

How I came to be in this queer place I shall tell in some detail, though I shall omit information that is unfit for dissemination to the general public.

My training is in engineering with an emphasis on applied physics. The occult is not my field—that is the business of the historian, the antiquary, or the student of religion and mythology. As one of my physics professors once said, our business is the study of natural phenomena, with a view toward widening the boundaries of the natural to such an extent that eventually they will cross and obliterate those regions at one time thought to be supernatural.

My encounter with the bizarre stemmed directly from President Richard M. Nixon's decision to reduce government support in various areas of pure and applied science, including the space program and research on military projects. This produced a surplus of engineers and scientists and a deficiency of opportunities. In short, like many others (including steelworkers as well as engineers), I was out of work.

Despite my Ph.D. in computer engineering (not to mention my M.S. in nuclear physics), employers whose offers I might have sneered at a few years earlier suddenly closed their doors when I approached them; they had, in some cases, 200 applicants for one opening. But after six months of searching, I finally received an offer to teach computer programming and physical science at Bridgehaven College in Connecticut. It was only a temporary position, but I accepted it at once (I was getting hungry). It was particularly felicitous because I was born and raised in nearby Fairfield, and I looked forward to going home again, if only for a while.

The college was rather small, with considerable interaction between faculty members. In a large university one gets to know the members of one's own department, but scarcely anyone else. In a small college, life is considerably more interesting and varied, as I discovered when I became friendly with psychologists, political scientists, classicists, and all sorts of academics in fields far removed from my own. In this way I came to know Bruce Matheson. Bruce was a medievalist, by which I mean nothing more arcane than the fact that he was an expert in medieval customs and history. However, his professional interests had led to a less academic pursuit, namely, a rather unhealthy interest in the magical and mystical beliefs of the past. I refer to this interest as unhealthy because it was not a scholarly interest in the professorial sense, but a practical one. He believed (as he told me after too many manhattans at a faculty party) that magic had actually worked, at one time, but today most of the key knowledge had been lost or distorted beyond recognition.

A few weeks before the end of the school year, when I still had not located another job for the following year, Bruce and I were talking in the faculty club after our afternoon classes had ended. Upon listening quietly to my common-sense debunking of the occult, smiling a little in obvious disagreement, he said something like the following:

"You know, Oliver, not all scientists have refused to investigate these phenomena. People like Sir James Jeans and Sir William Crookes studied spiritualism a long time ago, and lately I have come across some evidence that even that giant of physics, Sir Isaac Newton, may have dabbled in the supernatural." He paused for a moment. "Though the physicists at the university, across town, deny the possibility of this."

"Well, they're wrong," I told him bluntly. "Newton apparently spent more time studying the supernatural and the writings of the ancients on such subjects as alchemy than he did working out the calculus and inventing basic sciences like mechanics, not to mention the Newtonian telescope."

Bruce's eyes bulged out and he gasped.

"You mean, all this time you've known all about this?!" he exclaimed, pounding the table with one fist. "Damn. What can you tell me about this work. Where are his papers?"

I put my cocktail glass to my lips and took a long, slow sip, while I tried to gather my thoughts.

"As far as I can recollect," I replied at last, "the Newton papers stayed at his university until early in this century. Most of the scientists who have looked at them just backed off in horror. When the head of Trinity College took a look into Newton's papers, I read somewhere, he turned pale and ordered the box sealed against intrusion forever. Though some say," I went on in my most pedantic manner—which I carry off best when slightly under the influence—"it was merely because Newton, in some of these papers, expressed his belief in the unity of the deity and proved conclusively, through careful references to original sources, that the concept of the Trinity was a later corruption of the holy works."

"To Hell with the Trinity," Bruce blasphemed, "where are the papers today?"

"The scientific papers were separated out and given to the library at Trinity College. The rest were sold at auction. I don't know who bought them or where they ended up, but they may very well be right here in the U.S."

"Well, find out!"

"Bruce," I pointed out, "you know I don't have time for games like that. I'm busy with end-of-semester chores and job-hunting."

"H'mm…any luck?"

"Very little."

Bruce cogitated for a moment, then said:

"You know, Oliver, I don't need this job to support myself. I had a rather nice legacy from my great-uncle just last year. (And nobody in the family ever guessed he had made so much money back in the twenties…we thought he was broke!) Anyway… I want to see those papers, and I want to hire you to find them and go through them, make copies if possible. If they are housed in a university library, it may just be easier for a physicist than an historian to see them. At least, that's what I was told when I tried to see the scientific papers in Oxbridge. How do you know all this?"

I explained that one of my close friends had done a thesis on the Newton manuscripts, and that I could probably find out more about the situation from him. As to the job offer…if I couldn't find anything in my line for next year, I'd consider it.

He offered not only to match my current salary, but pay all expenses. And in the end, nothing else in the way of an offer appeared. So I took Bruce up on his proposal, and he immediately paid my full year's wages (about $12,000) into my bank account.

And I started off on my journey to Yuggoth.

II

Originally, of course, my journey was not to Yuggoth (about which I knew nothing, not even the name). It was to California and my friend Bob Blumstein at Stanway University. I explained part of the situation to him, and he was very obliging about the entire matter. Some of the papers in the Newton collection had been dispersed far and wide as a result of the auctions, but had afterward been gathered together by Sir Geoffrey Keynes and presented to the library at Trinity College, Oxbridge. The remainder of the collection had ended up in America, where it had gone to three universities in the United States. An effort had been made to bring these papers together in one collection, but the plan had failed, and the three collections were currently housed in three separate libraries—at Miskatonic University, the University of California at Riveredge, and the Platte Institute.

My friend Bob—as he explained further—had only been able to obtain permission to see the collection at Cal at Riveredge, having been denied admission to the others, but he did arrange with his friends at that institution to allow me to have access to their holdings. He, himself, had only actually read a small portion of the manuscripts; there were, after all, more than a million words in Newton's own handwriting in the entire set. I'm afraid that I abused everybody's confidence, for I took along a small camera disguised as a nylon-tipped pen, and proceeded to make microfilms of the lot.

Getting in to Platte was not difficult, for I had friends of my own there to pave the way. As for that odd place, Miskatonic, Walter Quednau was at that time Chief Librarian He was a friend of my father's and arranged the entire matter. Again, an abused confidence, together with a lot of microfilms, was the result.

Bruce was elated at my findings. While he began his extensive study of the microfilms, he sent me off to examine the manuscripts in Oxbridge. The British were extremely polite, and, after checking my bona-fides, agreed to permit me to view the manuscripts at some length.

These matters required a considerably greater span of time than the telling has indicated, and well over a year had passed when we finally managed to enter the Platte's "inner sanctum" and abscond with microfilms of their part of the collection.

In betwixt traveling and other work for Bruce, I had continued to hunt for a job more in my own line, finding absolutely nothing at all. (The year 1974 was even worse in this respect because of the incipient recession.) So I was amenable to an extension when Bruce suggested that I help him collate the papers with other background material that he had assembled. During my tenure as his assistant, I had as a matter of course begun to acquaint myself with various fields of the occult—all the way from astrology and the tarot to alchemy and modern witchcraft. I balked at first when Bruce insisted I delve into the fiction of H. P. Lovecraft, a kind of latter-day Poe, who had apparently wearied of the same old ghosties and beasties of traditional supernatural fiction and invented his own pantheon of horrors, called the Cthulhu Mythos after one of its more abominable deities (though all were abominable, to be sure). But I found myself enjoying the stories on their own merits.

"Great entertainment," I responded to a question from Bruce. "But are these stories relevant? Surely this so-called mythos is pure fantasy."

"Maybe, maybe not," said he.

"Lovecraft himself says so," I pointed out.

"A lot of it is indeed pure fiction—especially most of the balderdash invented by the other writers who have tried their hand at the Mythos. But there may be a germ or two of truth behind the fantasy. I'll tell you what, Oliver, I never took the stuff seriously until what you told me a few months ago."

"About Miskatonic U—getting some of the Newton papers?"

"Right. They are kind of a strange crew, those folks at Miskatonic. Have you read what Barron's has to say about them?"

"Nonsense! None of the college 'blue books' lists them at all."

"Not today, but they did once. Listen: 'Miskatonic University, 6 acres of campus on the Miskatonic. Exact year of founding uncertain, but claimed to be very early. Student body: 4220 males, 1180 females, 13 others.' What the hell they mean by that, your guess is as good as mine. 'Library: 780,000 volumes, including several famous collections, such as…'—get this—'the Lovecraft Collection, the Whateley collection, and the Upton manuscript collection. The science laboratories are completely modern, and the campus is serviced by a modern IBM 650 computer system…' Well, in those days I suppose an IBM 650 was modern, was it, Oliver?"

"A 650? Certainly, if you're quoting from a book published around the late fifties. Well. I'm not convinced about any of this, but I'll keep on reading."

I shan't belabor the point. I had begun (as you may have perceived) to become interested in the entire subject, not from the "practical" aspects of it, as Bruce would say, but rather simply from the overall amusement to be derived from studying what I liked to think of as one of the more foolish damn-fool aberrations of mankind. I, myself, had very little time to do more than skim over the Newton manuscripts themselves. Bruce spent almost his full effort concentrating on these.

"Newton's scholarship is immense, just beyond belief," he remarked once, "and even where he does not have evidence or information he makes his own connections from what he does have, and the connections seem to me to be right."

I spent more time traveling. Now that the Newton papers were in hand, I was sent after information concerning the early Miskatonic expedition to the "cold waste," as Bruce liked to call it. I also was sent after inside data on some of the recent expeditions to

South America; Bruce seemed particularly interested in the South American data after the material I brought back from the Platte Library. A report concerning an expedition to the "Plateau of Leng," touched on in a kind of mimeographed magazine that Bruce had picked up somewhere, turned out to be a hoax, as far as I can tell, much like those tongue-in-cheek expositions about the true biography of Mr. Sherlock Holmes, written by fanatical devotees who almost persuade themselves (and perhaps some do!) that their favorite literary characters really existed. Indeed, there is an active coterie of Lovecraft aficionados both in professional and amateur publishing who keep alive the concept of the Cthulhu Mythos and the related horrors of time and space that fell so agilely from the pen of Howard Phillips Lovecraft. But as far as I can tell, these individuals only pretend to believe. I found little to interest Bruce in this direction. Although I must in fairness to these folks add that Bruce did take their so-called Leng Expedition a little more seriously than I did.

It was the South American expedition that proved to be the single most important source of useful information for Bruce. How Newton obtained the information that dovetailed with those facts retrieved from the South American Jungles is hard to say. Such information may very well have been available in the European world of that era, brought back by Spanish Conquistadors, but how a secretly-unitarian professor of Trinity College could have prised such information from the confines of the Spanish Church Archives, I fail to comprehend. At the time he wrote these works, Newton was a recluse and a scholar; later on he blossomed out into a financial wizard and something of a politician, and was very successful at all these endeavors; still there seemed something almost supernatural about his possession of such information.

Clearly I am not making very much sense at this point, and this is not by accident, for I insist on keeping back pertinent data in several areas. Still, I do not mind mentioning that part of the information I refer to consisted of what uses one may make of a peculiar trapezoidal niche often seen by those who have excavated the ruins of the Inca civilization or who have seen photographs brought back by that possibly spurious Leng expedition. Newton described a similar niche (only he called it a window) as occurring in a ruined church of his acquaintance; a church built upon the ruins of a much more ancient site.

I did not know even as much as I have now described at the time when Bruce and I embarked for the Andes Mountains of South America. Nor did I regard any of this information as more than an amusing coincidence regarding a strikingly parallel bit of absolute nonsense.

Of our journey to the ruined city recently unearthed by the Lawson Expedition I shall say little. They believed it to be a prototype—one of the earliest Inca cities, and possibly *the* earliest, destroyed fairly recently as if by a monstrous earthquake and still only partly uncovered.

Equipped with a pack train and several assistants, all paid for from Bruce's convenient legacy, we entered the jungles and reached the mountains where the unnamed city was located. Indeed, it was partly built into the side of a mountain, which at some time had collapsed, crushing most of the buildings.

Carrying electric lanterns, we entered the inner building of the gods, wherein lay the trapezoidal niche. We had no fear of being disturbed, since our guides and assistants were Indians or part-Indian, and while professing no superstition about these long-lost regions of their putative ancestors, in actual fact they were quite nervous about being too near to these ruins after dusk.

Bruce had never really explained to me in detail what he planned to do, here, but I had figured it out to some extent. Newton had called these "windows," and therefore presumably there was something to see on what I shall call the "other side." Bruce proposed to search for that other side, whatever or wherever it might be.

I had long ago given up expostulating. Bruce was paying his way and I was having a fine time as an explorer. I had found that playing physicist or engineer was not the only way to excite the cells of one's mind, and I was enjoying the whole thing hugely. My only problem, as far as I could see, was how to console Bruce when his experiments did not work.

Those were, indeed, my very thoughts as Bruce set out to follow the ancient ritual which he had resurrected from the scattered writings we had both studied. But a sudden end to these thoughts came—there was a great explosion, a feeling that I was sinking into oblivion, and then a loss of consciousness...

...but not before I saw what I saw. Not before I saw the figure of Bruce Matheson limned in a blue glow—not before I saw him disappear bodily from his place within the niche. The explosion was apparently caused by the gases of the atmosphere suddenly rushing into the vacuum left by his vanished body. I saw it and automatically figured out the physics of the situation even as my brain descended into a soothing, cool darkness and I fell limply to the floor.

III

I awoke numbed, realizing what had actually happened. Perhaps Newton's trapezoids were indeed windows, but this one wasn't a window at all—it was a doorway…a doorway that had swallowed up Bruce almost instantaneously.

My friend was trapped—somewhere—without food or water and possibly without a means of returning. He had not expected to travel anywhere, bodily. He had been right, after all, about the practicality of the ancient writings, and I had been wrong. And yet, as it had happened, he had not been altogether right in every small detail, and was therefore in grave trouble.

My first thought was to obtain provisions and possibly, also, weapons (although we all carried hand guns on the expedition). Bruce would also need his notes, voluminous notes, on the occult procedure he had followed, for this would probably be necessary if he were ever to figure out how to return.

I therefore stood up, shakily, and returned to camp with the intention of fetching a supply of food and several canteens of water. My appearance in camp, well after midnight, somewhat disheveled and with a rather frantic gleam in my eyes, panicked the men beyond all belief. No doubt they had heard the noise of the explosion I have described (technically, it was an implosion), and had spent the ensuing time imagining all kinds of dire happenings. But I doubt whether their imagination extended to the reality.

As I gathered the supplies together, I picked up an extra hand gun and a good supply of spare cartridges. Manuel Osaban approached me warily, with a questioning gaze.

"Accident. Keep the men ready for departure in the morning. I'll be back in an hour or two." My Spanish was poor but I could make myself understood as long as I kept the sentence structure simple. Osaban backed off, watching me with caution, and muttered something I did not immediately understand. Then I hurried back to the ruins of the city.

As I went, I heard noises behind me, as if a couple of men were following, stealthily. Suddenly what Manuel had muttered began to make some sense to me. I realized that he thought I had either murdered Bruce or that we had encountered some sort of demon in the half-buried city. If it was the former, he was a brave man, to follow me at all; if the latter, he was doubly brave, in view of his background.

Suddenly, another idea hit me with the force of a blow! Indeed, I almost staggered. How could I possibly explain to anyone from the outside what had gone wrong? What would I have thought, only a few hours ago, if someone else had carried such a tale to me? Murder. Murder at the very least. I would be arrested for murdering Bruce and somehow concealing his body in the ruins or in the jungle.

Now panic came and I hurried, almost running, to get to the entrance of that trapezoidal niche. Panic, exhaustion, and a kind of resignation all combined to make me behave foolishly. I had planned to try to send Bruce the supplies I had fetched. Now I was determined to bring them myself.

Hurriedly I prepared the niche, went through the pattern of the ritual (about which I propose to describe nothing whatsoever), and then felt my heart bound uncontrollably as the whole world seemed to be pierced by mists of liquid blue fire. A thunderclap sounded as, for the second time that day, I lost consciousness.

IV

My swoon, this time, was momentary. I felt my feet strike a solid floor and I crouched on my hands and knees, shaking my head and swaying from side to side for several long moments. Then I forced myself upright and stood staring about me.

The sight that greeted me was one of horror. I was standing in a spacious chamber with a ceiling that curved overhead a distance of forty or fifty feet above. There were no lights. The walls themselves emitted a soft, steady glow that seemed (to my eyes that were accustomed to lanterns in a dark ruined city) bright as daylight.

Bathed in this soft effulgence was the body of my friend, his limbs literally torn from his torso and his head twisted awry. Blood spattered the stone floor. Its smell was in the air, together with the smell of cordite. Bruce had used his hand gun. I looked for it and found it clutched tightly in Bruce's hand. Even the force that had rent that arm from his body had not loosened his grip on the gun.

I stared at the scene, eyes bugging from my head. The blood belonged to Bruce, as I saw clearly, but surrounding him were other shapes—amoeboid hulks, sprawled in puddles of some noxious ichor, not blood but a liquid of a different sort—black slime, still oozing from the slug-like things. There were several of these disgusting corpses. Bruce had clearly been attacked and had defended himself. He had evidently shot these creatures. And, as I saw on further examination, he had then shot himself, using his last cartridge. The greater portion of the blood near him had come from that fatal head wound.

I pried the empty gun from his still-warm fingers. The entire scene was now clearly delineated in my mind. He had appeared, been attacked, defended himself, and then at the final moment had killed himself rather than be taken by the rest of the attackers. Then, in a fury, they had torn him to shreds, almost literally.

But—if so—if I were right—where were those other attackers?

In much less time than it requires to write down my thoughts, I had reached these conclusions. Warily I searched the room, my own gun ready for use. But I saw no one and no thing living. Bemused, I reloaded Bruce's weapon and stuck it in my belt, keeping my own gun in my right hand.

There was no sign of the things that had attacked Bruce with such apparent fury, other than the corpses and their ichor. Perhaps they had learned to keep clear of men with guns. Perhaps the survivors had gone to seek reinforcements. Perhaps I was still unconscious and dreaming.

I pinched myself, shook my head to clear it of cobwebs. The corpses remained.

I searched Bruce's body for spare cartridges (there were none), but I found some of his papers and stuffed them into my knapsack. I had nothing to blame for my predicament but my own fuzzy thinking. I must have gone temporarily insane to have come here like this. And yet the last thing I had expected to see was Bruce, dead; I had the idea that between the two of us we would be able to make it back home again, sooner or later.

Well, there was nothing else to do but explore. I must find out where I was. I still had some hope that I was on the earth, somewhere, perhaps in another part of that ruined city, perhaps underground, although I knew full well that those black shapeless blobs never evolved on earth.

Taking care not to make any appreciable amount of noise, I moved to one corner of the large room, where I saw a staircase. Exploration would help me to orient myself properly and it would also help by removing me from the vicinity of the recent carnage. The sooner I left that room, the better for my peace of mind and stomach. Also, it seemed to me, there was considerable danger in remaining. Weren't they bound to return, if only to pick up their dead?

I climbed the staircase. The steps were huge—perhaps twice or thrice the usual size of a normal stairway—and the treads were narrow. Going up those ponderous stairs was rather like climbing a long ladder. The stairwell went both up and down from the floor on which I had made my entrance, and I chose to go up rather than down for no logical reason at all—unless I really felt I was somewhere underground. Perhaps it was a deeply submerged feeling of claustrophobia, an old trace of an instinct first developed by my tree-climbing ancestors. Because of the shape of the stairway itself, and the long distance up to the next flight, I was thoroughly exhausted and aching in every limb when I finally reached the landing.

At that instant it seemed to me that I heard a sound—the sound of a movement, below me, possibly at the bottom of the flight of stairs.

Now you must keep in mind that I am a rather sedentary type— a scholar more at home in a library or in a laboratory than in the midst of a pulp-magazine adventure story. For two or three hours, now, I had been the recipient of a series of shocks, each worse than the last. I was not thinking as clearly as I thought I was thinking (if that remark makes sense). In fact, I was suffering in a mild way from shock. Suddenly I was oppressed. I felt hungry, thirsty; I needed a bathroom; I was frightened and disoriented; I seemed to be pursued by the demons that had murdered Bruce; I felt lost in a place beyond time and beyond space; and I was not enough of a coward or a weakling to faint. So I ran.

My instinct chose a direction where the illumination seemed fainter, almost shadowy. Dimly lit alcoves and corridors at one side of the stairwell landing beckoned me. Twice in the next few minutes I ended in a cul-de-sac. Every time I turned about, I expected something to launch itself at my back. I must have been screaming something at the top of my lungs as I fled, for I remember hearing with utter consternation the echoes of my own voice, but at first I was unable to stop. Then I pulled the trigger of my gun.

Thank heaven the gun was aimed away from me! The shot brought me back to my senses. (I hadn't even realized the gun was in my hand!) Good god, I was doing the worst thing in the world if I was trying to hide. I was telling this entire world where I was. I fell exhausted, moaning and panting under my breath, berating myself for my stupidity. But my outbreak was over. I was an animal run to ground as though by a pack of shadowy hounds (like the Hounds of Tindalos, I thought crazily). And yet nothing had actually pursued me, save for the miasma of fear. That fear was self-defeating. Its very senselessness now gave me the incentive to control myself and to keep calm, analyzing my situation as best I could. Did I call myself a man? An intelligent man? I vowed by my own particular gods (the gods of knowledge and truth, that I thought I had always served) that I would not again run shrieking through strange corridors under any provocation. If I met something to fear I would stand and fight to the death, as had Bruce.

As the great poets have always understood, but psychologists found it harder to grasp, the true story of man is contained in his language. In my own case I cannot help but be struck by the similarity between two common words: relive and relieve. To relive is to relieve—and there is the whole concept of psychoanalysis wrapped up in a tiny linguistic truth accessible to anyone who speaks English. It is certainly true in my case. Despite the labor necessary to etch these words on this incredibly tough metallic leaf that passes in this place for paper, I am gaining new insights into myself and my position merely by recording it. You, my reader, lacking the immediacy of my emotions in this bizarre situation, will no doubt comprehend my position long before I, in the heat of discovery, was able to do so. So much the better for you: you may thus avoid the shock of the sudden discovery of alien concepts. In my situation, all discoveries were shocks and all shocks seemed sudden ones.

When I had grown calmer, and had begun to look about, I discovered that I was lost. Then I laughed, quietly. I had been thoroughly lost in this place from the very beginning, and could be no further lost than that!

I found myself within a maze of small alcoves and rooms, served by a series of long narrow hallways—it reminded me of nothing so much as an old college dormitory given over to a number of single rooms and an occasional bathroom. The architecture was dissimilar, to be sure. The walls were of smooth stone, and all yielded that soft glow in brighter or lesser hue. I wandered from room to room, noting as I did that several of the rooms contained trapezoidal "windows." My back pack had grown heavy, but I dared not do more than adjust it in minor ways. Should I misplace my food and water, then I was lost indeed.

Beyond these small alcoves, a transverse corridor led me to a series of more complex rooms, some of which looked like a combination of laundromats and automats. Indeed, if the other rooms were dormitory rooms (or rooms at the local version of the "Y"), then these might well be kitchens and laundries. I laughed, again, to myself. Where was the desk clerk?

The temperature seemed normal for human comfort, although my skin was by this time perspiring from my efforts. I was still thirsty and a little hungry, but I ignored these and other calls of nature for the moment. I felt spurred on my way by the necessity for knowing as much as possible about my surroundings. I found my way to another stairway (or possibly the same one I had climbed before) and again made my way up one flight. Again I found the same sort of arrangement of alcoves (rooms and kitchens, as I thought of them), and now, being utterly exhausted, thought to prepare a cell for myself to gain some sleep. My watch read nearly 5:00, which meant 5:00 A.M. "Earth time." I had every right to be exhausted.

Having relieved myself (in what appeared to be a sink), I hunted for an alcove with only one narrow entrance. There, I discovered a strange carven statue. To look at it made me nervous; to touch it was shocking and repugnant; it made my flesh tingle unpleasantly when I lugged it over to the entrance. I hoped that anyone (or anything) moving it to try to enter would make enough noise to awaken me.

I slept.

V

When I awoke, Shana was there. She stood just outside the door, peering in at me past the statue. I glanced at my watch and saw that I had slept about six hours. My limbs were aching and my back felt sore. But I paid them no mind.

Slowly I rose, watching her. She was as still as that abominable statue. Darkish of skin and slight of build, her features were vaguely Levantine. I could not be absolutely certain, of course, but my later impression was that she may very well be an Assyrian. Perhaps that seems ridiculous, since it makes her several thousand years old, and she appears to be less than thirty. Often I have longed for Bruce and his wide knowledge of obscure languages. Except for Latin, in which I was fluent, and German, French and Spanish, where my knowledge was limited, I was far from being a linguist.

And I made little headway, even after several months, in the effort to learn Shana's own tongue; she did much better at learning English. Her speech was tantalizingly familiar, though, and put me in mind of an old acquaintance of mine who had done a thesis on Gypsies. The language the Gypsies speak among themselves—that was what hers sounded like, a little, and I recalled that my acquaintance had mentioned that some scholars believe the language of the Gypsies is descended from ancient Sanskrit. Her accent, when she attempted to speak English phrases, was quite attractive—she sounded a bit like Zsa Zsa Gabor!

Now, on my first glimpse of her, I saw her as a rather plain, small woman, dressed in some sort of brown smock. She was trying to keep her face expressionless but she was clearly frightened.

"Hello," I said, feeling foolish. And I said other things that I was certain she could not understand, for my first look of her convinced me at once that she could not possibly speak English. Nor could she comprehend Latin, German, French or Spanish—at least, not as I spoke them.

She replied in her own language, haltingly.

Talking to her as I would talk to a frightened puppy, hoping to soothe her with the even sound of my voice, I pushed aside the statue from the entrance and stepped back, inviting her with a gesture to enter my small room. She glanced behind her, fear breaking through the impassiveness on her features, then stepped inside. I noticed she was careful not to touch the statue—an ugly thing with tentacles on its face...

I looked beyond her, out into the corridor, but saw nothing. There was a faint aroma in the air which reminded me of those black sluggish corpses surrounding Bruce's mangled body…but that seemed to permeate the entire place.

I held out my hand to her, palm up, and after a few moments of hesitation she reached out and grasped it for moment, lightly. I smiled. I pointed to myself and spoke my name. She returned the smile, just a little, and pointed to herself: "Shana."

I wondered how I was to proceed from there. In adventure fiction, it seemed, the hero always knew the language, or learned it in a few days, or was an adept at telepathy—or even got an instant education from some magical or super-scientific teaching machine. Not here. In this case, the language barrier was a real barrier, and it was not days but weeks (many of them) before Shana and I could communicate more than the simplest of concepts.

I broke open one of the food containers I carried in my knapsack. I took a bit myself and offered some to Shana. She took it, tasted it, made a face, and handed it back. Well, emergency rations were not exactly a gourmet treat. I suddenly wondered where she lived in this place and where she obtained food. Then she smiled at me again and motioned me to follow her. I did so, but not before replacing the food carton in my knapsack and adjusting it on my shoulders.

Shana led the way back to the set of rooms I had labeled, somewhat facetiously, kitchens and laundry rooms. Evidently I had not been far wrong. Little devices that looked like faucets apparently produced concentrated liquid food; others emitted edible powders. There were not only kitchens but bathrooms, looking not at all like my own at home, and as I found in my subsequent explorations, there were many varieties.

I am etching this very manuscript on these alloy-metal pages by using what must have been intended as a beverage for some outré visitor, and seemed to be a sort of nitric acid cocktail. At first this situation merely amazed me; then I was dumbfounded. The only explanation I could imagine seemed far fetched—that at one time this entire area was devoted to a rather strange collection of guests. And most of them were not at all human. At least, if they could eat and drink some of the concoctions I found in these food dispensers, they could not possibly have been human. But where were they? Why was I (apart from Shana) the only human being around? At least a few of the accustomed visitors must have been human; the food dispensers Shana found for me produced wholesome and even tasty fodder.

Shana herself was an equal mystery. Somehow I had ended up in a cosmic hotel, or way-station; the whereabouts of the other guests, or passengers, was certainly a question I would have to look into. But the existence of a human female in this place was an incredible mystery.

Why should Bruce have been violently attacked and murdered on his appearance into this place, while I seemed to have been presented with a guide and concubine?—it seemed inexplicable. I did not at first realize that she could be something like an Assyrian. But it was clear that she was a very unusual person, to say the least. I could not help wondering if "they" (the sluggish beings?) kept a little supply of females of various races who might be expected to appear in their abode—perhaps in some advanced kind of hibernation or time-stasis…or maybe they kept their chromosome patterns on file and simply grew them in vats when they were needed! Had I been from Mars, would they have arranged for a female Martian to keep me company? Anyway, this sort of treatment—no matter how problematical—had to be an improvement on what Bruce had encountered. Though it didn't stop me from worrying.

The appearance of Shana did solve the two important problems of food and water. I might have lasted a month on the supplies I had brought, but even a month would not have been sufficient to give me the knowledge I required to get back home. She also supplied a third need that I had not planned for: sex. But she was something like the purveyors of the food and water: a little bit mechanical. She was not exactly inexperienced or joyless; she just didn't seem to care much one way or another about it. Indeed, she did not seem to care much about anything at all.

She reminded me not a little of a former mental patient I had once met—after a lobotomy had been performed upon his brain. Sometimes she got on my nerves, and I slipped away from her to explore the immense structure in which I was living.

On one of those forays I had found the observatory. It was more than an observatory, it seemed to me. Although there were devices that could be aimed and seemed to be large telescopes, there were other instruments that I could not comprehend. Some of the things I encountered were simply beyond the knowledge of any twentieth-century scientist—and perhaps beyond the understanding of any human savant, past or present; there was no way to tell.

VI

The medium on which I inscribe these messages is not, of course, paper as we know it—processed wood pulp. It is some kind of very thin, very pliable metal—possibly an alloy of iridium. I am not a metallurgist, so it may not be significant that I have never encountered anything like it before. But I think that my story will be given credence simply because of the means of transmittal—a case of the medium being at least a large part of the message.

The sheets come from a booklet that I found in the library—about which I shall tell you in a moment—and may have other kinds of writing on them than this English script written in black acidic muck.

The muck is, no doubt, coffee or soup or something else culinary to some unimaginably alien creature; it comes from a mechanical spout very similar to the one that provides me with water, only in a different cubicle. As for other writing—the "books" in the library, here, are "written" in many ways: odd alphabets, weird pictographs, queerly indented sheets similar to a kind of inverted braille, sheets consisting of nothing but dots in various patterns, in short, every kind of thing imaginable—including what appear to be perfectly blank pages, such as these upon which I write. Of course, I am aware that there may be a kind of writing here that I cannot detect without equipment—perhaps visible in the infrared or ultra-violet; maybe magnetic in nature (who could "read" a length of recorded magnetic tape, for instance), or radioactive, or simply some bizarre minuscules that need an electron microscope to be deciphered. Now, about the library.

After discovering the observatory, I gave some thought to the nature of this labyrinth. My initial analogy with a university dormitory held up pretty well in light of my discoveries. The presence of the astronomical observatory argued for a scientific orientation... even if science were the only knowledge deemed important to them, there should be a repository of such information—in short, a library. If so, it would be well worth seeking.

After that decision, I began to be much more systematic about my excursions. I had some real paper with me, of course, in my pack; and I started trying to make a general plan of my surroundings, filling in or modifying where necessary as my knowledge expanded.

The obvious way to find it was to learn Shana's language and ask her to show me the way. By this time, actually, we had made fair progress toward this goal, and we could converse with some intelligibility in a kind of bastard patois. But she seemed not to understand me when I asked about books and records. I drew a picture for her of shelves of books, but this did not seem to mean anything to her.

Some human beings, who suffer head injuries or strokes, find themselves in a very tantalizing situation. They can talk and can understand spoken words as well as ever; but they cannot read or write—and an attempt to spell CAT or DOG is mind-blowing; they simply cannot do it. Shana seemed to act this way. She seemed to be unable to comprehend more than the simplest drawing.

By this time I had become inured to my lot. No sign of the slug-beings appeared; I grew careless as time went on—although I did not forget to keep my weapons loaded and easy of access. The danger that had struck down Bruce seemed to have vanished. Yet I believed it still lurked.

Nevertheless, I continued to roam ever more widely until I found the library.

At first I did not recognize the place for what it was—a card filing system. For there were no cards. There were, instead, dozens of devices that reminded me of nothing quite so much as micro-film readers. After a careful examination of one or two of them, I started playing with the buttons and knobs mounted at the base of one of them.

Soon I was learning the system.

I could only describe these devices (in terms familiar to me at that particular time, which I estimate to be early in 1975) as CRT input-output terminals to a gigantic time-sharing computer system.

If the buttons and knobs were pushed and turned in a simple sequence, the face of the tube lit up and a set of characters was displayed for a moment. Then it was displaced downward as another line appeared, and another.

I stared at these for a while, nearly hypnotized by the march of blue-white symbols down the view screen, until a simple fact dawned upon me. Most of the lines were quite different from one another...almost as if they represented entirely different languages.

Of course! If this were a cosmopolitan "university" with students so alien to one another that one "man's" drink was another "man's" ink, then the first step in looking up a book or other reference would have to be the choice of a language.

Watching and counting carefully I encountered over a hundred different kinds of symbols before I recognized anything familiar at all. I was, naturally, hoping for a language that I knew—and if this library was to be of much use to me, the language would almost have to be English or Latin.

(I referred earlier to my knowledge of Latin, which was very helpful in my research for Bruce. My grandfather, with whom I spent quite a lot of time when I was a lad, had been a high-school Latin teacher, and—as a whim, perhaps—had me speaking classical Latin before I was nine years old. Unfortunately, my modern languages are terrible, just good enough to let me squeak through the language examinations for my scientific degrees.)

First I recognized what I thought might be Chinese ideographs. Then I quite definitely saw something vaguely Greek, but very oddly shaped. I did not recognize such scripts as Sanskrit, and was totally unfamiliar with the appearance of such hieroglyphs, but at last I saw a line that made sense, a very elaborate form of early Latin which in effect stated (loosely translated):

"Original Manuscripts and translations in the language of the Republic of Rome."

I poked at several of the buttons and got one that halted the image on the viewer. Then I found what looked very much like a light pencil, clipped to the side of the viewer, and tried touching the Latin phrase with its tip.

Immediately the list was replaced with the first line of a general index. When I came to the line that said "History of Yuggoth," I almost choked. But I retained enough presence of mind to touch the line with the point of the pencil.

What followed were some grinding noises and a thud. The thud came from below the viewer, and on looking beneath the table on which it was mounted, I found a large drawer, which I proceeded to open.

Within it was a thick set of manuscript pages.

I was astounded. Here was the library—but it was nothing like the "library" I had drawn pictures of for Shana. There were no shelves and no books—just a computer bank and an automatic copying device that would make a monkey out of the Xerox Corporation if I could ever master its principles and take it back home with me. (If, I remember thinking, I could first get myself back home.)

Later I found out that this first impression wasn't quite right. There were original manuscripts on shelves and in storage bins, and you could actually get to them if you knew the secret and had the magic code for the computer system. I did find out how to get to some of them, as witness these sheets of metallic paper I am vandalizing. What had come out of the drawer under the computer terminal was a package of something more like plastic—temporary, disposable "paper" as compared with the more permanent "paper" I am writing on.

I am wandering from my main intent, which is to tell you a little of the history of Yuggoth, what the slug-creatures are, what happened to all the inhabitants, and finally what action I might take about all of this (or at least what action I am going to take). But I can't resist one last tidbit that I found on aimlessly hunting through the collection during the first few days after my initial discovery.

There was an alphabetical index, and just for my own amusement I looked up ALHAZRED, ABDUL. But I was not amused. There it was:

ABDUL ALHAZRED: THE NECRONOMICON (original manuscript on sheepskin). Handwritten account by Arab mage dealing with certain aspects of reality and other, false information deduced from faulty memories of various students who returned to earth unfulfilled. Copying this text is forbidden without permission of the head librarian. See cross file: modern languages: Arabic: Mythology: Elder Gods: Cthulhu.

Of course this was all printed out in Latin, and I continue to give fairly free translations. In any case, I don't mind saying that it jolted me.

I looked up "Newton, Sir Isaac," next, but there was no entry. Indeed, there were no English entries in the entire catalog card file. Nor could I find entries for America, the Soviet Union, or Australia.

VII

By now, you have deduced, as I had, that I must actually be in the very city, on the very planet Yuggoth, belonging to certain of Howard Phillips Lovecraft's fictional beings. And there were marvelous points of agreement between what the author wrote and what I was finding. But there were also differences. Where he got his information or ideas I do not know and cannot guess—mostly, like the Necronomicon, they were inaccurate and doubtless included "false information deduced from faulty memories of various students who returned to earth." My reading of the various works of Lovecraft had been quite recent; the stories still stood out clearly in my mind. But they weren't of much help. I didn't know what was reliable and what wasn't. But I shuddered as I recalled certain creatures described in much too much detail in stories such as "The Shadow out of Time" and "At the Mountains of Madness" (not to mention "The Whisperer in Darkness"). When I recalled the slug-things, I wished all of a sudden that I had never read those tales.

There are two major items of immediate interest that I want to relate. One is the situation on Yuggoth as of hundreds of years ago (perhaps thousands). The other is the information regarding the instrumentation located in what I have called the astronomical observatory.

Let's start with the latter.

It wasn't really an observatory—or perhaps I should say, it wasn't only an observatory. It was much more. I shall coin a word for it and call it a transmotation device.

It was computer-operated but hand-programmed, requiring considerable skill in its operation. There were several dozen independent channels of entrance and egress, and they could all be tuned simultaneously to different locations. The equipment connected in some way I cannot understand to receiving and transmitting substations in other places: for example, the Andes. These locations were not only terrestrial, but included many other planets. At one time, this transmotation device, operated by experts, probably carried as much traffic as a small city airport.

But when I found my way there, it was virtually inoperative.

Clearly that isn't entirely true, for Bruce and I had used it, after all. I found that the strange ceremony Bruce had utilized was in essence a kind of sonic code key that operated a solid state "slave" transmitter unit. Even after hundreds (or thousands) of years, it had still functioned.

No, this machinery wasn't entirely inoperative. But most of the channels were turned off, and those that were on had been set in the "receive" mode.

When these facts came to light, I was determined to alter the programming of the system to reverse the effect and send myself to a terrestrial receiver (provided one still existed somewhere). To figure out how to do this took me nearly a year.

In the meantime, other things weighed heavily on my mind. I continued to wonder why everything was in the "receive" mode, or else "off." If the people who had operated this establishment had decided to abandon it, would not at least some of the circuits have been left in the final position of use: namely, transmit? Or was there a reason why they had not been left in this mode?

My imagination continued to picture a very good reason why. If you were escaping through a door, pursued closely by nightmarish monsters, would you leave the door ajar?—or slam it shut!

I kept worrying about the slug creatures. Even when I pushed them from my conscious thoughts, their images stirred around in the depths of my mind. I dreamed about them. Mostly the usual fear-dreams, chase nightmares; but one dream recurred: the dream that in the midst of having sex with Shana I saw her suddenly melt into formless jelly.

Dreams like those were better forgotten; but they put me off Shana just a little. I started to study her more carefully. As far as I could see, she was a real woman, a human woman, and probably (I have said it before) an Assyrian.

I questioned her. She didn't know about airplanes, automobiles, or ocean-going passenger vessels (or even oceans). She had never heard of baseball, football, tennis, or bridge.

She knew about chess, though. That didn't encourage me. Chess is an ancient game, perhaps more ancient than anyone knows.

One result of my nightmares and my waking fears was simply to make me worry more and be less efficient in my studies. Moreover, these feelings compelled me to abandon my analysis of the transmotation system every so often in favor of studying the local situation.

The original book on the history of Yuggoth (my first withdrawal from the library, as it were) was discomforting reading, but I managed to stumble across some other documents that were even more terrifying.

The system computer, of course, translated everything I asked for into Latin. (Thank heaven for my grandfather.)

While reading one of these fearsome records, I was concentrating on the material so hard that a slug-thing could have clouted me over the head without my ever having seen him. One time, a faint slithering noise penetrated my concentration. I looked up. I cannot be certain just what it was that I saw, if anything—a dark image in the darker shadows of the distance corridor—but for a moment I thought it was a shadow like those in my dreams. And I smelled a faint scent of musk, not actually so unpleasant, but not reminiscent of anything comforting. But a sudden bolt of fear surged through me. Trembling, I rose from my seat by the viewer and forced myself to walk over toward the doorway by the outer corridor. I started violently as Shana came walking in.

"Was anyone out there," I demanded of her.

As usual, she didn't seem to understand what I meant.

"No one is ever here," she said.

I had tried, many many times, to ask her about the slug things. She did not seem to understand. I asked if she had been here long; she said she had always been here. I asked if anyone else had ever been here but her and me; she said she couldn't remember.

VIII

It was a university, all right, but the students were as much teachers as students. The beings who lived here (they called themselves only the "Great Race," and used a double circle as a symbol for themselves) were passionate scholars. They wanted, indeed, needed, to know everything there was to know about every place in the universe and every race in the universe. They had a far-flung stellar civilization, and carried on a sort of commerce among themselves, but knowledge was their most precious commodity and this place was one of their largest university centers.

They constructed it on Yuggoth for a number of reasons, I learned. Yuggoth was uninhabited. Therefore they could appropriate it without interference. No other race could resist their advanced technology, but they eschewed warfare. They chose not to conquer other worlds and other cultures—not out of what we might call humanitarian reasons, but because they wished to "avoid disturbance." (This is how their computer translated the phrase into Latin: conversion to English is not the problem. I have no idea what they meant by avoiding disturbance.)

And, I was amazed to learn, there were FIVE other races inhabiting this one stellar system—a marvelous opportunity for in-depth studies of contrasting cultures. The races were not identified and I did not spend the time delving into the library for more information on this subject, but I gathered that there was an intelligent civilization on Saturn, on a moon of Jupiter, and on Venus. I also got the impression that there were TWO intelligent races on earth. (Sometimes I wonder if there are *any!*)

But you can see just how important the library on Yuggoth can be for the intellectual development of the human race. We must learn as much as we can from these archives before we are…prevented…from doing so.

All this time I was spending most of each working "day" trying to learn how to operate the transmoter. And each "evening" before retiring I would read a little more of the history of Yuggoth.

The scholars of the Race had learned in the infancy of their civilization the fundamental secrets of molecular biology, and had bred a species of intelligent creatures from some primitive form of protoplasm found on a distant world eons before. These creatures, whose name is translated by the machine into Latin as the word Ilem, were their slaves. They were golems.

So preoccupied were the Ancient Race with the exploration of other worlds and their studies of other cultures that they required such slaves to perform the menial duties of everyday life. So single-minded was their pursuit of odd facts about distant places that they tended to ignore certain minute changes and odd occurrences that were taking place in their own vicinity. Possibly these changes were universal, common to all the worlds where the Race roamed and settled, but this remains uncertain from the records I have found. Still, what did happen is only too clear: the Ilem evolved.

The evolution of the Ilem took first entirely a mental pathway. Physically they remained the same, but the simple slave mentality created in them by the Ancient Race changed and became distorted into a maniacal lust for revenge and a hatred of authority. Even involved as they were with their pursuit of knowledge, the Race was still far superior from the viewpoint of intelligence. But the Ilem possessed one utterly diabolical physical ability that compensated for their inferior intellectual capacity. They were composed of a flesh that was almost fluid but could be hardened into any form within a certain range of physical size—and they employed that bizarre capability to mimic their masters. They murdered these beings one by one and replaced them with duplicates so that none would grow too soon suspicious.

One scroll that I stumbled upon in the library had been composed by the last remaining survivor, whom I will call Omega. Omega had remained alive only through the expediency of promising to assist the Ilem in conquering all the worlds of their universe. For the Ilem possess certain fundamental intellectual flaws. They are unable to operate many of the sophisticated mechanisms of the Race; in particular, the complex quasi-mathematical coding procedures required for programming the destination of the transmotation device are well beyond their abilities. They cannot even read.

Omega composed the scroll I found indexed under "Yuggoth: Revolt of the Ilem," and in several other places as well, no doubt expecting it to be found later by a member of the Race. He made it clear that the Ilem were traitors, but lacked the ability to operate the Race's complex equipment. He reminded the reader that the Ilem were susceptible to sonic shock waves harmless to the true members of the Race. And he told the tale of the final days of destruction by the Ilem of the last surviving members of the Race.

A few of the survivors had escaped via the transmotation device—presumably to one of the other planets populated by the Race. Omega had remained behind in order to cut off the transmission mechanisms and leave the machinery in a condition such that no member of the Ilem could possibly escape. He had hoped to survive until a rescue party of the Race could return to destroy the usurpers. Obviously he hadn't.

Obviously, too, there had been no rescue party. To me, that meant that all the other worlds of the Race had experienced a similar uprising—or at least, all the ones where knowledge of the Yuggoth facility was widespread. In all likelihood, those of the Race who had escaped Yuggoth had only gone to their doom elsewhere.

As an addendum to his message, Omega listed a set of available corridors both to and from Yuggoth, including the ones located on Earth. There were quite a few. I did not recognize all the place names for the earthly corridors, but one seemed to be in fabled Atlantis, which I did not propose to try, and another was listed as being located in the Plateau of Leng. The Andean one, of course, I did not wish to use for the simple reason that I expected to need it again at some future time, and intended to leave it set for transmission from Earth to Yuggoth. A fourth was deep in the Soviet Union, and seemed more of a "last resort." That left the fifth and final one as the only viable possibility—a location, as well as I could judge, somewhere in Great Britain. This one really astonished me until I recalled two things: the strange knowledge possessed by Sir Isaac Newton concerning the use of what he called "windows;" and the existence of that other "astronomical observatory" of considerable fame (primitive though it might be in many ways), located at Stonehenge.

Doubtless the Ilem, who found Bruce an implacable enemy armed with a weapon capable of inducing fatal sonic breakup of their peculiar form of flesh (impervious, no doubt, to mere bullets), had changed their tactics. They had hoped that when I found out how to operate the transmotation device (if I could), I would leave it in operating condition for them to use. Or worse, they hoped to learn how to use it by observing my own learning processes.

Since it is possible to learn to operate a machine that you don't comprehend, even as complex a device as a transmoter, I cannot say that their incapacity to read or follow complex diagrams would completely rule out their learning to use it. I am sure that I could set up a system, if I so desired, by which they could operate the coding devices. Possibly, had I not found the tell-tale scroll left by Omega, they might have persuaded me to do so. I am not without fear, and physical torture might even now, if sufficiently prolonged, persuade me to do their bidding; who knows what mental tortures they might be capable of.

But of course I have outwitted them. They are, after all, easy enough to outwit—they are not only inferior in mentality to the Great Race but even to us earth-dwelling mammals. Cunning they are, and I give them full marks for that; but they can be fooled.

It took some time. I had to find appropriate components and rig an auxiliary electromechanical contrivance to substitute for the programming system. The other necessary substance I found at hand—the same place where I got the ink to write these words.

I am about to carry out my plans, soon, so I shall be very brief. My explanatory message has purposely been couched in story form for use in a certain limited-edition publication because among you, the readers, are included many of a kindred spirit who will be eager to join me in returning to that planet of marvels, Yuggoth. In a manner of speaking, we shall constitute that rescue party that

Omega had hoped would come, though it will be an army of vengeance rather than rescue.

The editor will acknowledge the fact that this manuscript was written on an alloy strange to terrestrial science. That should be proof enough for you, if not for my scientific colleagues in academia.

Write to the editor. I know him. I know he will agree to act as intermediary. I shall tell him, as soon as I can relocate, where to find me.

Here is what I plan to do in the next few days.

Shana has agreed to come with me; indeed, she seems very eager to leave this place to visit the earth which I have briefly described to her at various times during our acquaintance.

We shall pre-program the transmotation computer, using my auxiliary analog device, giving ourselves just time enough to step to the outward channel leading to that trapezoidal "window" somewhere in the vicinity of Stonehenge.

Immediately thereafter, the programming will be forcibly changed. A food-like substance from one of those alien supper-spouts turned out to be nearly pure nitroglycerine, and I have used it to make a small explosive device—with just enough power to destroy my makeshift programming system without affecting the transmoter itself.

It will be valuable, of course, when we return via that trapezoidal niche in the Andes, to bring not only the usual weapons but some kind of sonic pistol (as described by Omega) that will be fatal to those monstrous Ilem, preferably without harming us.

If you receive this and are reading it, it means that my plans have unfolded successfully. Even as you prepare for your first interview with me, I shall be attacking the problem of the sonic pistol. Its main use is not, of course, solely as a weapon, but also as a testing device—creatures that can mimic members of the Race can certainly mimic human beings. Thus, a device merely annoying to us, but fatal to them, is both a weapon and an infallible tool for weeding out the usurpers.

It would be very nice to have several of the Ilem to try it out on, but that isn't feasible at this time. I'll have to make do with the one

I am bringing along with me.

POSTSCRIPT

In the seventies I was publishing a small press magazine called CHAOS CRAWLINGS devoted to Lovecraftian concepts. That is why Oliver Ward submitted his manuscript to me. But something bizarre happened…

Recently I received a package from the U S Postal Service. During renovation they had discovered a dusty piece of mail lying under a file cabinet in one of their distribution centers. They apologized for the delay in delivering it. When I looked at the packet, I saw that it was postmarked October, 1975. Some delay! Forty years!

What the packet contained you have now read. It was a rather poor xerox copy. I do not have the original, so I do not know if it was inscribed on a metal alloy unknown to human science.

I have searched for Oliver through various sources open to me as a librarian, and I have used the internet, but to no avail. He seems to have dropped off the face of the Earth…apparently during a South American expedition.

Another item worries me…there was a scribbled postmark, to the effect that he had put off his test of the sonic pistol because Shana was now pregnant!

Oliver: if you ever read this, get in touch. I am very disturbed by what you have written, and I need to know for my own peace of mind: is this fiction? Or…?

Walter Quednau, Chief Librarian
Miskatonic University

OTHERS, WHO ARE NOT MEN

I

I had purchased some twelve acres of woodland in the Black Mountains of West Virginia, some eight or ten years ago—on a happy occasion when I had been particularly fortunate in a stock transaction; some Canadian Uranium properties I had obtained for pennies a share had blossomed, and I sold them for dollars before the price could dwindle again, as it subsequently did. The region was utterly wild and unspoiled, save for a dilapidated shack near the foot of the waterfall that bordered my property.

My land, a narrow strip crossed near one end by a nameless stream, was a tiny fraction of privately-owned country sandwiched between two state park areas, and should have been relatively expensive, but was not. I spent an occasional weekend there, fishing and hunting, when I could escape from the constant pressure of business, camping out because the deserted shack was unsuitable as shelter.

When I celebrated my forty-first birthday with a mild heart murmur, my physician warned me that it would be necessary for me to take a lengthy vacation, preferably in a location where I could enjoy mild exercise, breathe unsullied air, and, most important, not be subjected to business worries.

"Hank," he told me, "you must be a fairly wealthy man. You own a thriving business. You're a widower with no family responsibilities. Sell Hartley Enterprises outright, or put it under a good manager for a few months, and take off for that woodland mecca you're always telling me about. Do some physical labor—light labor; don't exert yourself too strenuously, at least not at first. I don't guarantee full recovery, but I'd give odds on it if I were a betting man. What I do guarantee you is that if you go on as you have been, you'll be dead inside of two years."

It's true—I had been working hard. Partly to keep from thinking about Eleanor and Jack, and how they might be alive today, if I had just thought to take—but that is another story, one best forgotten. I had not gone off to the woods in over a year, and I resolved to follow Doc Parry's advice, though I feared solitude and what paths my agitated thoughts might pursue.

I made arrangements through a friend to have a small log hut constructed above the waterfall barely out of sight of the ruined old shack, and spent some time arranging to have my engineering business carried on by a manager. Larry Hanover, whom I chose for the job, had been with me for years, and I looked on him almost as a younger brother. Although not brilliant or imaginative, he was trustworthy. In fact, I have arranged to leave the business to him, if I do not sell it outright, since I have no close relatives, and he loves the work nearly as much as I do.

I arrived early on a chilly evening in March. The cabin, newly completed, was damp and cold. I parked my Ford wagon about two hundred yards downstream, and toted a light bag and some groceries up the gentle knoll to the cabin. When I opened the door, I was panting, despite the very minimal nature of my exertions, and I was disinclined to return to the wagon and fetch my remaining belongings. So I pulled the door to, latched it, and set about starting a fire in the tiny stove. In these times, with chemical starters and fuel-impregnated charcoal, this was relatively simple, and within twenty minutes the chill was gone from the atmosphere within the room. It had had an odd, musty odor that was out of keeping with its newness, but soon I no longer noticed this.

The four hour drive, and the subsequent short walk, had made me tired, so I ate the remainder of my travel lunch, lay down on the bunk, and slept soundly till dawn. In the morning I finished unpacking the station wagon and stowed my belongings away in the cabin.

That first week I did not hunt or fish, but I obtained a modicum of exercise by walking aimlessly about the woods or along the stream with my old, out-of-date Polaroid camera, searching for interesting compositions. Gradually I was recovering my stamina, and although I followed Doc Parry's injunction against too much exercise too soon, I could feel my body growing stronger.

I had brought no reading matter with me, preferring to express my own thoughts, sensations, and speculations—for I had decided to keep a journal.

Each evening after the dinner plate had been washed in the stream, I recorded the trivial happenings of the day. Particularly in view of later events, some of the things I wrote were puerile, others intriguing. I have since destroyed much of that journal as arrant nonsense, but have incorporated some of it into these notes, which detail only the important things and skip the trivia.

II

For the first month I lived a solitary existence, slowly gaining stamina and reveling in the primitive life. I had begun to fish, though I held off trying to do any hunting, contenting myself with a bit of target practice at sparrows. One trip to the village during that time represented my sole contact with the outside world. The villagers are a queer bunch. Although I have come here fairly often for a number of years, and own this land, they still consider me a stranger. During this month they knew I was here (in fact, three of them had been hired to build this cabin), but not even one had dropped by to see how I was doing. For some reason they do not like this part of the territory—they tend to avoid coming around even in my absence—and I had to pay an exorbitant wage (by local standards) to get them to work on the cabin.

Then Bill Fowler stopped by. He was not a villager, only down for the weekend. He owned a stretch of land that began where mine ended.

"Not roughing it any more, I see," he commented as we sat smoking and watching the waterfall.

"I'm down for the whole summer," I said. "Bit of a rest. Been overdoing it."

"Didn't see you here at all last year."

I nodded. "Too busy at the office."

"Funny thing happened here last year," Bill said, relighting the stump of his cigar. "My dog got himself killed."

"How's that?"

"You remember old Silver? Brown and white haired pointer? We'd bagged a few things and I was getting set to head back for camp. We were upstream, down near the edge of your acreage. Silver caught some kind of queer scent and went storming off, barking for all he was worth. I took after him fast, because I'd never seen him act that way before. But I lost him."

"What happened?"

"I heard him give one loud yelp, and then nothing. Hank—that sound put the hairs of my neck on end. I tried to find him and stumbled around for about half an hour, mad as hell, but saw no signs of him. Then I came across that old shack downstream. You know? He was there, just outside the rotten walls, laying on the ground. Dead. Dead as a doornail."

"What killed him, Bill?"

"Damned if I could tell," he said, shaking his head in puzzlement.

"But..." I frowned.

He said with acerbity. "Sure, I'm a physician. I could tell if he was shot or strangled, or mauled by a bear, or even poisoned. Or whatever. But as far as I could see the damned mutt was in perfect shape physically except that he wasn't alive." He paused. "Of course I didn't do an autopsy. I just buried the fella there in the soft ground and chalked it all up as one of those things. But..."

"Yes?"

"Well, nothing. Nothing. Only it was damned queer."

I could see something else was on his mind, but I couldn't persuade him to admit it. I didn't try very hard. What was a dead dog to me, anyway?

As May turned to June, a few other hunters occasionally stopped by for a word or two, and I started doing a bit of hunting myself. One of the others was a fellow I knew pretty well—we had swapped stories over the evening campfire a number of times in the past, and I liked him as a hunting companion. He usually knew when to talk and when to listen. This time he decided to talk.

"Seen Bill Fowler this year?" I nodded.

"Tell you about his dog?"

I nodded.

"Strange. Dog dying like that, not an old dog either. No reason why."

I said, a little worried, "I suppose an excited dog could suffer a heart attack, or something, even a fairly young one."

He shook his head.

"No, there's something queer about it. I'll tell you. I've gotten in with one or two of the local crowd. My wife's mother has cousins hereabouts. They told me some of it. Bill doesn't know the details, but I think he guesses." He lowered his voice. "Silver wasn't the first dog to die there, like that. There have been two others, maybe three, in the past ten years… And still others have disappeared from sight around that area."

"What do you mean? Did they die here by the waterfall?"

"By the shack. That old shack back there. It's why the locals don't care to come around here, I guess, Hank. They say there are hauntings here."

I frowned. "You mean…ghosts?"

"I don't know what I mean, exactly. But you won't catch any of the townspeople near this place after dark. Even the ones who built your cabin—They were gone from here by four o'clock every afternoon."

"Rot," I said, and I meant it.

Afterward, I got to thinking about the situation, however. It was queer enough, certainly, but not so queer as all that. Dogs do die, after all, and in a ten year period it isn't so strange that two or three should die in the same general locale. Especially when that locale includes a broken-down shack, where an animal or two might have made nesting places. That ought to attract dogs, surely. No, there must be something else, as well. Since I was becoming just a wee bit bored, I decided to find out what that something might be. My plan was a simple one…there was a doctor in town, Dr. Jason Rigby, an old fellow who was retired but kept up a local practice. He was originally born in this town, though he had mostly practiced in Henderson (the county seat), thirty miles southwest of here, and I thought he could be approached. I had the perfect excuse to see him.

Next afternoon found me stripped to the waist in Dr. Rigby's office. He probed for a while with stethoscopes and things and took a blood sample. Finally he told me to get dressed, and I sat down as he finished scrawling indecipherable comments on my record card. I waited in silence.

"Course, I don't have any of the new-fangled electronic gadgets down here," he reported, "but I'd say you are in pretty good shape. Some of these modern doctors haven't got the sense of a midwife, but yours seems to have done all right by you."

"Then I'm cured?" I exclaimed incredulously.

"Well on the road to it," he replied. "Stay healthy, live outdoors a lot, do more physical exercise…you might well live to be ninety."

"And if I go back to my business in the city?"

He shrugged. "The strain got you once. It may again. It's your decision." I thought about that for a minute. Then I decided to let it go and make a frontal attack.

"Doctor, you're familiar with the local situation. Is that place of mine really as healthy, or safe, for me as I thought when I came here?"

He stared at me oddly, but did not reply.

"I mean," I stammered, somewhat disconcerted, "I've just been wondering about a couple of things."

"Dogs?" he inquired drily.

"For one thing, dogs," I agreed. "And people, too. It took a lot of persuasion to get some of the local people to build that little cabin of mine. I've spent some time wondering why." I finished almost apologetically. "I have a lot of time on my hands for wondering, these days."

Rigby stared at me with his piercing eyes for so long that I was convinced he would refuse to reply. I fidgeted. Then he asked, "Have you been sleeping soundly?"

I acquiesced, surprised a little. "Very well."

"Rumors—that's all there are, outside of the dogs..." His voice trailed off. "But I do know a little about old Zacharias."

Back when his grandfather was a young man, Rigby told me, old Zacharias had built his shack—the one on my property—where he then lived with his son. The son was even more mysterious than the father, for few people ever caught glimpses of him...those few remarking on his apparent ugliness. He was reputed to be an invalid; at least, one of those who had spotted him outside the cabin remarked that his hands were bandaged and that he appeared to walk with an infirm gait.

Old Zach was very much of a recluse, and rarely entered the town except to obtain a few basic stores such as salt and molasses. Youngsters out hunting might spot his traps occasionally, or even see him fishing, and he would mutter a few words of sullen greeting; but that was all. The son never hunted or fished, presumably because of his infirmity.

Then one evening the thing happened. A toddler, the doctor's own great-aunt Anne, disappeared from the town, and the most diligent search failed to locate her. The doctor did not know how suspicion came to dwell upon old Zach, or even if it was at all justified, but apparently that was what had happened. Six men, armed with rifles and shotguns, went to the shack at sundown of the following day.

Outside the door, just off the trail, legend has it, lay a small sandal, recognizable to Anne's father as having belonged to her. At that, their uneasy and nebulous suspicions confirmed, the men broke into loud curses, and shouted wildly for old Zach and his son to come out and face them. One or two shotguns were fired at the cabin.

Now the doctor's story became indistinct, as though no one had ever really told him the exact details of what had happened. Clearly the men themselves never quite knew. Apparently a wild shriek issued from the cabin, and there was a loud rumbling sound, as though the earth itself were trembling.

Then one wall of the shack collapsed inward with a violent clap, like thunder.

As the doctor told it, the men tried to probe the ruins for the bodies of Zach and his son, or for a sign of the child, Anne; but there were evidently traces of gas about the place that prevented a thorough search. The gas, or whatever it was, was described as having a musty odor, and it produced faintness. Two men were rendered unconscious by its effects, and had to be dragged away from the vicinity by the others. The result of this was a superstitious dread of the region that has persisted even to the present generation.

Dr. Rigby told me his father had a scientific theory regarding the whole affair—he believed that there was an underground pocket of natural gas in the region, which had been breached by the construction of a cellar or storage pit under the house. The shotgun blasts then caused the gas to break loose from its subterranean cavern. This blew up the shack, killing old Zach and his son instantly.

Privately I wondered. The shack still had most of three walls standing, and much of the roof remained intact even after seventy-some years The other wall, as I recalled, had collapsed inward, almost as though some modern Sampson had pulled the entire structure down upon him. Would this have happened if a gas pocket had exploded under the house?

As an afterthought, Rigby told me that the body of little Anne Rigby had been washed ashore the next morning, far downstream in the creek. It was apparently much battered, and it was bruited about that she had been swept over the waterfall; but he said he had the distinct impression that there was something about the corpse that was horribly queer, something his elders would not tell him but would nervously discuss among themselves.

"The gas theory would explain the death of the dogs!" I exclaimed, after Rigby's tale was concluded. "There must still be some gas leaking out there, at least sometimes."

"If you believe the theory, then perhaps so," he responded.

"What other theory can there be?" I queried.

He shook his head. "I don't know." And he refused to discuss the matter further.

III

After a week of contemplation, I decided to take action. I loved hunting, fishing, the outdoor life in general—but I was used to a heavy regime of mental activity, and I was bored doing nothing else. I had a second reason for acting, besides pure curiosity. A practical man, I needed a practical motive. And I remembered in the doctor's tale that the shack was described as smelling musty. That rang a chord—I flipped back through the pages of my original journal to my account of the day I first arrived at the cabin. Yes, I had recorded the fact that my cabin smelled musty, despite its newness, when I first entered it.

Did this mean anything? I thought it might. It could well mean that the gas pocket extended under my cabin as well as under old Zach's; and that could be very dangerous. Furthermore, I came to wonder whether this gas, anesthetic in small dosages as apparently it was, might not be the prime cause of my dreamless, sound sleep. I had never slept so well in my entire life—perhaps in this respect the gas was not dangerous to me; many poisons when taken in small amounts, are beneficial. But I was unhappy, to say the least, at the prospect of continuing to live over a veritable powder keg.

When I determine upon a definite course of action, I make my preparations carefully and methodically. This has been a trait of mine since childhood. My initial step, in this case, was to order some equipment, including an army-surplus gas mask and a scuba diving kit with tanks of compressed oxygen and air. I also purchased two canaries. Despite the advances in technology made by our twentieth century culture, the best contamination-detector for air is still a canary.

Of course, Larry Hanover must have been puzzled about my

instructions, for he acted as my agent in making the purchases, but I am sure he lost no sleep over the matter. As I have mentioned, he is a good fellow but badly equipped when it comes to imagination.

Three days after Labor Day, I was ready. I had noticed that the canaries had little difficulty in adjusting to the living conditions in my cabin. Was it my imagination that they were less active than most such birds? Perhaps. I had never kept canaries before. In any event, the valley was generally windy; the breeze that swept down from the northeast was welcome in the heat of the summer, and my window was constantly open. This might have counteracted the major effects of the gas that I suspected was seeping up through the soft clay soil.

I brought the gas mask and the oxygen tank, which I had equipped with a breathing mask, down to the old shack in my Ford Wagon which I drove right up to the front, for the ground was not too bumpy in this area. It was six o'clock in the morning. No one was around for miles, I was certain. I took the cage in which I had brought one of the canaries and approached the ruined shack, keeping a cautious eye on the bird's demeanor. It was angry at me for disturbing it and a little fearful but it seemed to be perfectly all right physically.

I looked over the ruins. Odd that I had never noticed—there weren't any weeds growing nearby. Well, I hadn't known before that the shack had been deserted for over seventy years. But the wood did not look rotten. I sniffed the air. No musty smell. The bird was quieter now but was still healthy.

I decided to begin my explorations at the wall that was the least ruined. In this wall stood the door, tightly shut. I had taken along a heavy hammer and a chisel, and these proved to be more than sufficient for the task at hand. Two solid blows served to tear loose the crumbling hasp and in another moment I had pried open the door and stood blinking into the dusty interior. Light entered through the many damaged places and I could see fairly well. Just to make certain I did not overlook anything, I lit a Coleman lantern and hung it over the entrance on a peg.

Evidently there had been two rooms in the shack, and this half was not badly damaged at all; the partition was bent awry, and a few timbers from the roof had sagged; that was all. It was the second room, to the rear, that had suffered most of the damage. Still, I was in no hurry to attempt to paw through the worst part of the ruins. A small block and tackle I had rented was lying in the station wagon; I had no intention of clearing up the splintered logs and debris with my hands alone. But before I started that job, I wanted to look over the relatively intact portion of the place thoroughly.

Occasionally I glanced at the canary, whose cage I had put down on a primitive-looking bookshelf, but it seemed perfectly lively. Perhaps in the coolness of the morning, the gas did not seep out, but I would take no chances. I went back out and dragged the oxygen tank into the shack and draped the gas mask around my neck. I could don it in two seconds flat, if I needed to.

The room struck me as being perfectly ordinary—the kind of parlor a hermit of rather primitive means might be expected to have. It had probably never been neat or orderly. In fact, it resembled the inside of my own cabin. There was one difference. I had brought along no reading matter with me; I was never much of a reader, anyway. But this fellow had about five large shelves just jammed with books. I glanced at them curiously, but most of them meant nothing to me.

By a freak of chance, the roof above the bookshelf had remained almost intact, and the books hadn't been weathered irreparably. Not that they were in fine condition; many must have been ancient and faded even before old Zach could ever have purchased them—they were so old. I decided to take some of them back to my cabin with me for study and began to stow them away in the wagon. Once started on the task, I kept at it until I had them all. I decided that would be safer, for some of those books looked valuable and one or two ominous creaking noises had brought home to me the fact that the structure was none too sturdy, and might collapse when I began to clear away the debris in the back room.

At this time, even with concrete evidence before me, I had not the slightest inkling nor premonition of the true situation. I had worked out a scientific theory or one that I thought was scientific, based on Rigby's explanation The only flaw in the gas theory, I had decided, was that an explosion would have blown the wreckage out, whereas the place had obviously collapsed. Once, in college, I had been considering majoring in science, and I'd taken a course or two in chemistry. My recollections, though dim, were that a chemical explosion usually results from the ignition of a mixture of air and an inflammable material because the products of the reaction (normally carbon dioxide and water vapor) are gases at a high temperature, and therefore push outward at a high pressure. This outward push is the explosion. But what if some unknown gas were to produce a solid product (I remembered vaguely that phosphorous pentoxide was such a solid combustion product)? Would this not lead to an *implosion*, not an *explosion*? Surely the result would be that the gas mixture might ignite to produce a solid compound, leaving a partial vacuum behind. Air pressure from outside would collapse the walls. The only difficulty with this theory is that I knew of no gas which would have such properties.

After packing up the books, I decided that I might as well grab everything else in the shack that could be moved. Things like the table, the chairs, and the cot that had lain in one corner of the room I left outside, but there were a few small items that I stowed away in the Ford. They were curiosities. I wondered about them, but they could have been souvenirs of a trip abroad. For example, there were five tiny statuettes of the general sort I have seen for sale in Hawaii and in African shops. Ugly little monsters. One was especially disgusting; the carver must have been a madman, or else he was afflicted by pretty wild nightmares. It had tentacles about its head, and—but there is little point in describing this abomination in these notes; it is, after all, right here on my desk. Odd— once or twice, I have decided to destroy that cursed image, and have actually picked it up with the intention of tossing it over the waterfall. Each time I have changed my mind. Ugly as it may be, it is nevertheless a work of art, one of the most realistic idols I have ever seen, for all that it is a fantastic design.

After cleaning out the accessible part of the shack, I started on the rest. I was glad to get outside again, for I had raised a lot of dust. But there was no sign of gas, and the canary was perfectly all right. I took his cage with me. The job of removing the fallen timbers and logs was not an easy one, even with the use of the block and tackle. But I was not interested in enlisting the aid of the reluctant (and expensive) natives, and the visiting sportsmen had now pretty-much quit these parts. By mid-afternoon, I could see that I would need another half-day to finish, but I persisted until near sundown.

It was with a sudden start of fear that I spotted my canary lying on its side in the cage. Its wings were faintly fluttering.

I reacted by grabbing my gas mask. With fumbling fingers I put it on and tried to breathe. I was trembling. Obviously I had been affected, too, because it must have taken ten or fifteen seconds, not two, for me to adjust the mask upon my face. I felt dizzy, suddenly, and felt myself sink to the ground. I knew the fumes would be stronger there, but I could not help myself.

Gradually I breathed more easily and my head cleared. The gas mask was performing its job. I was thankful—I had never been quite sure it would be effective against an unknown vapor. A soon as I could, I got to my feet and stumbled toward the Ford, carrying my bird cage. I used the small oxygen tank to try to revive the canary, but it was useless—the bird was dead. Shaken, I removed the mask and drove quickly back to my cabin.

Strange to say, this nerve-racking experience did not deter me from my self-appointed task. If anything, it strengthened my resolve. To tell the truth, I had begun to wonder if my elaborate preparations (the gas mask, the canaries, the oxygen, and so forth) were really necessary, or just a game I was playing, or a bit of rather juvenile posturing. Now that the canary and the gas mask had probably saved my life, I felt justified and a little smug.

I found that the after-effects of my experience, a general lassitude only partly attributable to my physical exertions, were erased when I tried breathing pure oxygen. I did this cautiously, for I knew that it was not safe to inhale pure oxygen for long periods of time; but no ill effects occurred.

That night, for the first time in well over five months. my sleep was disturbed. I dreamed incessantly. I do not recall the dreams very vividly, but they seemed to center about figures resembling the statuettes I had rescued from old Zach's hut—particularly the ugly one with tentacles. It seemed to me that I chanted his name, a name that resounded in my brain, a word of great power; but when I woke, the memory faded and vanished. I was drenched in sweat and had fallen out of my cot onto the floor.

I must have hit with a bang, for I would swear that those figurines had moved, changed their positions a little, from where I had placed them. At the time, I shrugged this off as nonsense, but the half-memories of those dreams still disturbed me. When I tried to compose myself for sleep, nothing happened Finally I hunted down the package of capsules Doc Parry had given me to use as a sedative. It was a medicine I had never needed, once I arrived here in this valley. I swallowed two of them and returned to bed. Soon I slept. If I dreamed again I have no recollection of it.

Next day it rained, and I was dog-tired anyway, so I put off finishing the job at the shack and decided to explore my cache of books, instead.

I had made quite a find, I now began to realize. Some of them were perfectly ordinary treatises on scientific subjects—for instance, there was Newton's *Principia*, and an old volume on optics by the German poet-scientist, Goethe. More heavily represented were books on the pseudo-sciences. There were treatises on astrology, on alchemy, on palmistry and phrenology, on Tarot cards, and the like. Most of the books were in English, German or Latin. All were annotated in English in a neat script.

These accounted for perhaps half of my literary treasure trove. The remainder seemed to consist of books on religion or magic or mysticism. I had heard of Albertus Magnus and of the *Tibetan Book of the Dead* and a few others. But I had never encountered such authors as Ibn Fozlan, Cosmas, Jules Bois, and Petrus Cirrelius. And I had never dreamed of the existence of such treatises as Müller's *Beitrag Zur Geschichte des Hesenglaubens ind Hexenprocesses in Siebenburgen,* J. G. Dalyell's *Darker Superstitions of Scotland,* Dom Augustin Calmet's *Traite Sur les Apparitions des Espirits,* Casselius' *De Sacrificiis Porcinis in Cultu Deorum Veterum,* or Colli de Plancy's *Dictionnaire Infernal.*

These represent only a few of the books that I found. Finally, after sorting through this group, I came upon a set of five other books, wrapped carefully in oilcloth. I call them books, but they were really notebooks, filled with the neat hand I had noted earlier in the margins of some of the other volumes, old Zach's no doubt. I read parts of them out of curiosity. They seemed to have been copied from other magical texts or treatises, perhaps ones so rare that old Zach could not buy (or steal) copies, and thus was compelled to make them by hand. But his neat handwriting was as easy to read as a Xerox copy of the original would have been.

And some were prisoned in the farthest stars, others in limitless spaces beyond the Earth. But there are paths between the realms of Earth and those places where they abide. The gates that lead to those ways are closed and locked but keys may be discovered in concealed places. When the stars form the right symbols in the skies, when the proper invocations are recited and the proper sacrifices are made, these gates will swing asunder and those that dwell beyond will enter upon this world. Even when the stars are wrong, men with power can call to them across the vast spaces and they will answer. A likeness, or simulacrum, of the prisoned ones can be used to aid in the conjuration; and such an object can be inhabited temporarily by a multi-dimensional extension of the One-who-is-called.

Men with the power and the knowledge exist, worshipping in secret and waiting until the sky turns round to reveal the proper time.

Others, who are not men, also wait. Some of these others have bred with the sons and daughters of men, giving birth to strange and damned creatures called Iathni. These, in particular, have the power to call upon the imprisoned ones, and, even when the stars are wrong, possess dominion over their messengers. When the Iathni call, the messengers will answer. But their answer means death if the ritual is imperfect or incorrectly voiced.

The others who are not men wait in secret regions beneath the waters of the world and among the snows of the high places and within the sulfurous bowels of the earth.

I was extremely uncomfortable after reading parts of those blasphemous notebooks and as soon as the rain ended, I took a long walk until dark. As I dozed that night, with the help of sleeping pills, I kept thinking of what I had read concerning the sacrifices necessary for calling on the "messengers." It involved the blood and entrails of a child and I could not help feeling quite certain that I knew, now, what there was about the body of little Anne Rigby that was "horribly queer," the subject which the doctor's elders refused to discuss. For in the margin of this notebook, old Zach had written in that clear hand:

Cirrelius implies that a female child under the age of six is ideal here, but that calves or lambs will sometimes do instead. Cannot take a chance—it will have to be the child.

IV

The following morning was overcast but not rainy. After breakfast I felt better, though I had a slight headache from the sleeping tablets. I managed a fairly early start and had finished dragging almost all of the debris from Zach's place by noon. Apparently the gas tended to seep out only in the afternoon. I was not bothered again by any such manifestation, though I kept a careful watch on my second canary. The pickings were slender, compared with the books and curios I had found earlier in the intact portion of the shack. Several rusted pieces of metal, what seemed to be an old notebook but was now a mass of yellow pulp, and another one of the curious statues. And a skeleton. It was a human skeleton, of that I was certain, and since it was about five and a half feet in length, I assumed it was that of old Zach, who must have been caught in the shack when it collapsed. Near the skeleton was a trapdoor.

The door was set into the earth where the far wall of the cabin had been, and consisted of a heavy stone slab with a solid brass handle imbedded therein. The stone slab looked old—really old; but that may have been my imagination. I am no archaeologist. The brass handle was of much more recent origin, though, and was caked with a green film of corrosion. The trapdoor was slightly ajar, as though the explosion or implosion seventy-odd years ago had distorted the opening, preventing the stone slab from fitting properly.

Now I thought I understood the source of the gas. Apparently the trapdoor led to a subterranean passage continuous with the gas pocket; through the partially open trapdoor the gas could slowly escape.

I saw no signs of Zach's son, and could only assume he had been overcome by the gas down in that mysterious vault or tunnel below ground.

I now equipped myself with a flashlight and replacement batteries since the Coleman lantern was probably useless in the atmosphere below. A sudden inspiration took me back to the Ford where in the glove compartment I had cached a stack of political bumper stickers with reflectors. These could serve as trail markers if the subterranean passage turned out to be extensive.

It was difficult for me to get the cart-mounted compressed air tank down to the floor of the tunnel, though it had been easy to open the huge trapdoor using the block and tackle. Once it was down, however, I found the going moderately easy. Pulling the tank along behind me, flashing my light in front, I moved slowly forward on my initial search of the subterranean passageway.

It was no cellar. It was a wide man-made tunnel, perhaps a century old, perhaps older. After I had gone maybe a hundred feet, however, the constitution of the tunnel changed drastically. There were indications of extreme age. Stalactites now studded the ceiling, and queer species of fungi fed upon the crumbling walls and floor. My boots left shallow imprints in the stuff, and they glowed.

When the passageway branched, I chose the right hand path, for the other was smaller and I thought it might be less interesting. I marked it with a reflective sticker. The floor now became relatively smooth as though worn by the passage of many feet over millennia. Now the walls too became less irregular, the cavern gradually took on the aspect of a real tunnel, becoming quite uniformly rectangular, though limestone formations still appeared on the high ceiling.

Suddenly without prior warning, I encountered a barrier. A rock fall had apparently occurred, partly blocking the tunnel. Indeed, I thought initially the blockage had been complete, but on carefully sweeping my flashlight beam across the rubble, I made out a small passageway near one wall. In the shadowy illumination it appeared almost as though the path had been cleared by someone after the rockfall had occurred, but I dismissed this notion as fanciful. This damage must have been made at the same time as the destruction above ground, and after that, who or what could have survived down in this atmosphere of unknown gases?

With some difficulty I managed to drag my equipment through the opening, and in a few minutes I was beyond the barrier. I gasped in utter confusion as I flashed my light around.

I stood at the entrance to a huge cavern, almost an amphitheater. So extensive was it that the beam from my flashlight did not reach the ceiling or the far walls. Scattered about throughout the gigantic room were countless numbers of shadowy figures. Their indistinct outlines made me shudder with cold fear, as the grotesque shapes seemed to be moving toward me.

Then I let my breath out in a heartfelt sigh of relief. My nerves were playing games with me. They had only seemed to move, in the wan beam from the flashlight. They were not alive—they were stone statues of some kind. Slowly, I approached the nearest of them, after fastening a reflective sticker to the wall next to the entrance.

The statue was of a man in a kneeling position. This man, fashioned in the shape and garb of an Indian, carried a bow and a quiver of arrows. The nobility of his perfect masculine form contrasted markedly with the expression on his face, which seemed to be one of joyous yet fearful servility.

He knelt before a second figure that was not human. About

five feet tall, this second idol was sculpted in the form of a squat, rodent-like being which stood upright on its hind legs, the front legs, or arms, being held out toward the man. The "arms" ended not in hands and fingers, but in crab-like claws, one relatively large one and five smaller ones.

Slowly, fear and excitement mounting, I went from statue to statue, studying each for a few moments in the waning light from my torch. There was no doubt of one thing—my batteries would not last much longer. I had purchased them in town and they obviously hadn't been very new. I would have to switch them. I had practiced such a maneuver in the dark some time ago, but now my hands were trembling and a curious chill was creeping down my spine. It was most annoying—I was actually afraid to turn off the light long enough to make the change. Was there a concrete reason for feeling fearful? Had I heard or seen anything down here other than ancient statues? No. It was purely an instinctive reaction, caused, I supposed, by the queerness of the statues.

For the statues were queer—bizarre and unearthly. Some of them were life-size replicas of the tiny statuettes I had found in old Zach's cabin. Others depicted more of the snout-faced, claw-fisted creatures with monstrous unlidded eyes. The rest showed men: Indians, white men, orientals, pygmies, and primitive humans who looked to me amazingly like Neanderthals. Still others were not properly men at all, unless one might call them ape-men.

The men (and ape-men) were always shown in attitudes of supplication or worship, and the objects of this distasteful submission were always the claw-handed ones or the other, more horrible shapes, whose tiny replicas Zach had possessed. One of the scenes shown I could interpret only as a kind of ritual sexual intercourse between one of the male claw-handed creatures and an Indian woman, her face showing a kind of unholy joy; in an adjoining scene the woman was shown bearing a child with the features of a human baby but the hands of a claw-thing. Another scene depicted was apparently a sacrifice, a human child being literally torn to pieces by several of the claw-handed ones who were presenting the bloody flesh respectfully on an altar to the tentacled being, the worst abomination of all. It was disgusting, the more so because each figure was so finely molded as to make one believe it had been sculpted from life! And it is not very hard to imagine how much more the life size figures affected me when even the miniature ones had revolted and depressed me.

At last I took a firm hold on myself and opened the back of my flashlight, dumping the worn-out batteries on the ground, and carefully inserting the new ones. I suddenly realized that I had my eyes closed, and I opened them with a grunt of distaste at my own cowardice. Then I gasped. Somewhere across the huge room was a glow, and the glow appeared to be in motion. With a cracked voice, I foolishly bellowed through my breathing mask: "Who's there? Who is it?"

The glow dimmed and vanished.

With shaking fingers I screwed the back of the flashlight on again. An intense light now flooded my surroundings.

I thought I heard a clicking noise far across the room, but decided that I must have imagined it.

Checking my watch, I realized that I had been underground much longer than I had planned. Quickly I shone the beam of the flashlight on the pressure gauge of the air tank. It was two-thirds empty. Well past time to be getting back.

Now I felt another chill of fear. I could no longer see the entrance through which I had come. I could not even see the walls. I was trapped in the midst of a jungle of obscene statues. Everywhere I turned to look, I saw them. Again my imagination insisted they were moving, coming toward me. For a moment I panicked, then my common sense reasserted itself.

The sacrificial rite scene was the last of those I had studied. I judged that I had come to it slightly from the left of the line between the tentacled monstrosity and the child sacrifice. I retreated along that direction, not encountering a familiar statue, then moved first to my left, then to my right, finally spotting a familiar group. Breathing a sigh of relief, I continued to back away along the line joining these and the previous scene.

Again I heard the clicking sound. It was nearer and it was not imagination. I hurried as much as I could, but twice lost my way. Once I was uncertain of whether I had ever seen one of the groupings before. The clicking sound came again, closer still, and I suddenly had a considerably disturbing thought. I envisioned one of those claw-handed statues opening and closing its claws with a snap! I put the thought from my mind and went on.

Finally, as I flashed my light ahead, I sighted the orange glow which could only have come from my marker; and I hurried forward, panting. When I reached the entrance to my passageway, I laughed aloud in glee. The sound, muffled through my breathing mask, seemed to echo ominously through the cavern.

Click! Click! The nerve-shattering sound seemed to be right at my back. Frantically I pushed my air-tank into the tunnel and along the channel that chance—or someone—or something—had cleared through the fallen boulders.

Once on the other side, I paused and swept the flash back down the tunnel. My heart leapt. I wasn't certain what I saw, but it looked like two eyes—monstrous, huge orbs as big as those of the claw-handers. But my glimpse was transitory—the clicking sound stopped and the eyes, if they were eyes, vanished.

Deep in thought, I made my way back to the end of the tunnel without further incident. I certainly was overjoyed to see the late afternoon sun once more.

V

Next morning I awoke at dawn, having gone to sleep almost immediately after taking a hasty meal and recording my adventures in this journal. I had felt utterly exhausted from exertion and fear.

But in the morning I felt refreshed. In the cheery glow of the dawn sun, my experiences of the previous day seemed absolutely incredible. And my fear of that unearthly clicking sound seemed irrational and laughable. I was keen to go down into that amazing cavern again. This time I intended to take photographs and, if possible, to bring back some other tangible evidence of what I had discovered. I still possessed one full tank of compressed air and I had a box of magnesium flares which would produce the intense light I needed for my somewhat old-fashioned polaroid camera. One of these days I'll have to get one of those newfangled electronic cameras.

Though chuckling at my own cowardice I also decided to bring along a rifle. If something more substantial than phosphorescent fungi or dripping limestone formations lurked in that cavern, a bullet would take good care of it, should it prove hostile.

But how could anything actually live in the foul atmosphere of those caverns?

By tonight I shall have photographic evidence of the most spectacular anthropological find ever made anywhere—a site to make

Easter Island and Stonehenge look like rejects from Disneyland! I'm too weary, though, to speculate on the origins of the grotto or its meaning. Let the experts at Miskatonic U puzzle over it.

VI

Here end the notes left by Hank Hartley, my boss and my friend. About two weeks after the last entry, a passing hunter had discovered Hank's body sprawled in his cabin. The death had been a violent one—gore splattered the floor and walls—and the corpse had been badly mangled and mysteriously *clawed*.

Since Hank had no surviving relatives, the funeral responsibilities devolved upon me. I was his only heir. I at once left the business I'd been managing for him, anxious to find out what had actually happened, and headed for West Virginia. I ran up against a stone wall. The authorities attributed the murder to a (hypothetical) homicidal tramp, and had stamped it unsolved. They seemed to be trying to forget all about it as quickly as possible.

They were not uncooperative in minor ways. They did let me see all the evidence, released Hank's belongings to me, and even let me use the cabin for a while, though they warned me casually that it might be a dangerous place to stay. The Ford station wagon was still parked off the road—its battery had run down and I could not start it. It was still full of a lot of Hank's odd paraphernalia, and apparently it had not been searched. I saw to the thorough cleaning of the cabin (with the aid of a very nervous local woman); then, more or less settled in, I decided to conduct a careful search for any further clues to what had been happening. The journal, parts of which I have already shown you, is one of the first things that I found—under the front seat of the station wagon where Hank had apparently stored it in preparation for a trip to the village.

Unfortunately the journal left even more questions unanswered than before. Had Hank gone insane in his solitude? I found no traces of the strange old books or the demonic carvings or statuettes he had written of. If they had been in the cabin before his death, they had since vanished.

I continued to search the auto but found nothing else of major interest. Then I concentrated on the cabin, hoping that something ignored by the police would prove to be of significance in the light of what I now knew. Shoved under the bunk bed I found the one chilling piece of evidence without which I might even now dismiss the whole affair as a bout of temporary insanity on the part of a sick man. Even now I do not know how completely I believe my own deductions (and Hank had said I was unimaginative!), but that evidence…!

One other place I decided to search carefully was the old shack. I found to my astonishment that it was a total wreck. But Hank's block and tackle arrangement came in handy and I cleared away some of the debris over the rear part of the building. I found the trapdoor, just as Hank had described it, except that it was sunken into the ground. Only after many attempts with the block and tackle did I succeed in wrenching it loose. Below I found nothing but a solid mass of tumbled rock and dirt—the tunnel, if tunnel there had been, was entirely blocked.

Near the trapdoor, under more debris, I made my other significant find—one of the abominable figurines Hank had described It was one of the ugly claw-handed ones, entirely inhuman except that it stood on two legs. I carefully stowed it away with Hank's journal in the back of my car.

In his notes, Hank characterized me as unimaginative and stolid. Perhaps I am, or was. But I am good at one thing at least—as an engineer ought to be—examining evidence and putting it together; erecting a structure of logic. Now here is the evidence that strikes me as undeniable and meaningful:

1. Hank's discovery of the underground passageways leading from the old shack to a marvelous collection of statues or idols.

2. The facts regarding a sort of black magic incantation using the blood and entrails of a murdered child (not necessarily that the magic would actually work)

3. Hank's observation of a presumably claw-handed, snout-faced thing that was able to survive in a noxious atmosphere, but apparently feared his flashlight. Was it trapped below ground until Hank cleared the fallen timbers away from the stone slab?

4. The disappearance of all the books and tiny idols that Hank had found, coincident with his death. (I believed in their existence, now that I had found the one overlooked in the debris of the shack.)

5. The fact that Hank had apparently been *clawed* to death— and not by any animal.

6. The fact that the murderer apparently drank some of Hank's blood and ate his entrails—or at least these were missing; as perhaps was the case with little Anne Rigby long ago.

7. The occurrence of another phenomenon I had uncovered—a minor earthquake that had taken place on approximately the same date as Hank's murder.

If some monstrous creature exists or once existed down there in those subterranean passageways (certainly not old Zach's son by a non-human mother; wouldn't that be absolute nonsense), it might have been able to escape via the trapdoor and to follow Hank to his cabin. That it retrieved the books and idols when it killed Hank seems a foregone conclusion. Did it use Hank's blood and entrails as part of some ghastly calling down ceremony that is beyond any reasonable imagination? Say that the earthquake was a coincidence, a welcome one that buried that abomination forever; or call it an act of God.

Only don't say that I am an unimaginative person. Perhaps I once was; but after the past three days I shall never be one again. Indeed that very first night I began to experience the oddest dreams—I never dreamed before as a rule—dreams of far-off places and odd creatures. And last night I swear I was awakened by a prowler that made an odd, rhythmic clicking sound. Luckily I had installed a solid night latch on the cabin door. I had no weapon with me, and I did not investigate.

A thought occurs to me. Hank mentioned a second passageway in that tunnel. Could it have led to the waterfall? That would account for the little girl's body having been found far down stream, rather than being hidden in the caverns. And if that passageway had been clogged by the first earthquake (that Hank thought to be an implosion), might it not have been opened again by the second one?

Could that creature still be alive and hunting—hunting me, perhaps? Now that *is* imagination!

Nevertheless, I have decided to leave at once. If it wants me (if it is really out there—and I am starting to believe this, despite all common sense) then it will have to trace me all the way back north. Meade will be interested in publishing this information in one of his small press publications. And this manuscript will be safe from marauders in the library at Miskatonic U—they make a specialty of strange manuscripts and books there—and just let that thing even try to find me in the middle of Boston!

At least I'll know it if I see it, for I have its photograph!

Hank must have gone back down below, as he planned. He took his trusty old polaroid camera with him. The camera had been under the bunk bed, as I mentioned before, empty but for the last remnant of a roll of film—whatever photographs he had taken were gone with the books and the idols.

But I was smarter than the creature in this respect at least. If it tossed the empty camera aside, I did not. When the last picture from a roll of type 47 polaroid film has been taken, the negative remains in the camera. And if it is not exposed to light long, it doesn't fade. Furthermore, it may be made permanent by rubbing over it the same solution normally squeegeed over the prints themselves.

The picture had evidently been the last one Hank had had time to snap. Then he must have run from that underground cavern as though all the demons of the dark were after him.

At least one of them really was.

Even on the negative, one could see clearly that the main figure in the photo, limned against a background of weird, misshapen idols, was a living, menacing being.

It was coming toward Hank and it had its peculiar claw-like hands outstretched. It looked a great deal like the claw-handed statue I had found, except for its features.

The worst part, I think, is that its face, though grotesque, is recognizably manlike.

I can't prove it, but I believe it actually was Zach's son.

VII

Miskatonic University Arkham, MA
March 11, 1978

Dear Mr. Meade:

With regard to your recent inquiry, a copy of this curious manuscript was recently removed from our closed stacks under very distressing circumstances—a night custodian was mysteriously *clawed* to death. But of course we make microfilms of all our special materials. A copy of the idol was also taken, though the original remains locked in our special protected vault...together with the original manuscript. We have made inquiries of the man in Boston who delivered these items into our keeping—a Mr. Lawrence Hanover, an engineer—but he seems to have disappeared under mysterious circumstances.

Perhaps in the course of your studies you will be able to elucidate these mysteries.

(SIGNED) Walter Quednau Chief Librarian

Enc.: microfilms of journal of H Hartley; statement of L. Hanover; photograph of claw-handed idol; copy of a negative of a polaroid print.

ESSENTIAL SALTES

ONE: WHAT BOB DID ON HIS SUMMER VACATION AND WHY HE CHANGED HIS MAJOR

This is a true story and was told to me by Bob Corey, a fellow student at the State University.

I hadn't known Bob well, even though we had gone to the same high school. We'd travelled in different circles then, so to speak. But after a year of college, over a few beers at a local bistro (legal in those days in that state), we became pretty friendly.

His two uncles owned a funeral parlor back in our home town. They had promised his widowed mother that he could join them as a partner in the business, which was getting to be more than the two men could handle by themselves. So Bob was doing two years of chemistry as a preliminary to transferring to mortician's school.

This kind of blew my mind, but he was used to that reaction. All his friends seemed to think he was a little bit weird. Actually he was a fairly ordinary looking guy, maybe a little taller than average, with light brown hair and glasses, and not weird at all. He told me that he had no particular problem finding girlfriends…as long as he didn't tell them his proposed major. (He always said it was chemistry.) His grades were mostly B or B+. Just an ordinary good guy whose family was in a somewhat unusual business, at least from most people's standpoint.

But now it wasn't a lie anymore. He hadn't told his folks, yet, but he really was going to change to chemistry. (And he did! He's in chemical engineering, now.)

This decision came as a result of that summer. Of course he had spent that summer working in the family business (whereas I had been working at a Burger King).

He'd helped out a bit in previous summers, of course, but that summer they finally let him operate the crematorium. He hadn't been allowed to touch it, before, but after a year of college he was deemed sufficiently grown-up and responsible to be promoted, as it were, to handling the machinery.

I don't remember all the details, but as I recall, the funeral in question was that of an attractive matron who had died of cancer. The cremation was scheduled for the evening. One of Bob's uncles was supposed to be on hand to keep an eye on things, but a new job had come along, so he had left it all to Bob. It was his first "solo flight," as he put it…and he was a little nervous, but confident.

The coffin, securely fastened on the conveyor, moved gradually along toward the ignition chamber. Bob told me he was sweating a bit as he manipulated the controls that operated the incinerator. But he wasn't really uptight about it.

It went smoothly, at first. The coffin glided into the firing chamber. The door closed. Everything was in readiness. He tested the system. It lit. Slowly he opened the valve and fed fuel into the system. He could hear the roar of the flames inside the chamber. For a moment nothing happened. Then…

…then came the scream. A loud, mournful moaning sound built up to a terrifying shriek. He stared through the viewing window. He told me he had never before known the true meaning of the phrase "His blood ran cold." But he knew it now. The cover had sprung loose from the coffin and the body was sitting up, screaming.

As he stared, transfixed, it fell back and was consumed by the flames.

A short while later, his uncle returned to find Bob in a state of shock. But he just burst out laughing.

Apparently this is quite an ordinary occurrence…uncommon, to be sure, but hardly unique. The intense heat, you see, causes an increase in gas pressure in the corpse's lungs. The moaning noise comes from this hot air, escaping. Sitting up is just another reflex caused by the intense heat. Nothing to worry about. Just a sort of baptism under fire, you might say.

Bob said he just laughed it off.

But after the summer he changed his major to Chemical Engineering.

TWO: WHAT I DID AFTER GRADUATION

Well, Bob went away to engineering school after sophomore year, and I went on to major in English, intending to become a writer and make millions of dollars like Stephen King.

But instead I starved, like H. P. Lovecraft. So I decided that I needed a "day job." But that was the year of the Big Recession. (They called it a Slowdown in the economy, but it was darn near a depression.) There just weren't any jobs for English majors. I considered grad school…but I wanted to write fiction, not do criticism… I wasn't interested in that. So I went back to my home town. My parents had moved to Florida after Dad retired, the year before, and my cousin Jim and his wife were living in our old house. They let me stay in my old room for a very minimum amount of board.

But I still needed some sort of employment while I served my apprenticeship as a writer.

Yes!—you guessed it! I went to work for Bob's uncles. In a small town like ours, it wasn't all that easy for them to find reliable help, even in a recession, and with Bob vouching for me, I got the job.

I suppose I don't have to tell you what kind of fiction I was trying to write, do I—you've guessed that too. I wanted to write horror. And I said to myself, how many horror writers who write scenes in cemeteries at midnight have ever actually spent a night in one themselves? How many ever spent a night in a mausoleum. How many ever…

…worked in a funeral parlor! (I recall vaguely that Seabury Quinn might have done something like that…but anyone else? I doubt it!!)

As you see, I had talked myself into the idea that I was getting local color as well as earning some much-needed cash.

Really, what a boring job it was. In more than a year there were no screams from the coffins, no mysterious noises at midnight, nothing much to break the monotony.

Except…well…there was the time that Ka-Zar, a gorilla at the traveling circus, which passes by once a year or so, died of rabies. We ended up performing the cremation, because the local vet didn't have a big enough furnace to handle something that size. At the time of which I am speaking, his ashes were still kept in one of our standard urns, complete with a carefully typed tag that read *Ka-Zar.*

We were still waiting for the circus proprietor to return and take possession of the *cremains,* or authorize their disposal.

But in fourteen months, this was the one and only thing out of the ordinary.

Until last August.

That's when Old Man Waddely died. Apparently he was only around sixty, but he sure looked old and wrinkled, more like eighty or ninety, the one time I'd gotten a peep at him, a few months earlier.

It was a closed coffin funeral. They say he suffered from some sort of skin disease...his skin was greenish grey and scaly, and he had kind of a fishy odor. The way I understood it later, he had left instructions to be buried—not embalmed—in an underground mausoleum. But his grandson, executor of the estate, had decided to ignore the old man's wishes. In view of the state of the body (which I had not seen), he decided on cremation.

Scuttlebutt had it that the old man was an expert in the occult—maybe even some sort of wizard or male witch. I thought that was pretty silly, of course, in this day and age. Evidently he had possessed a rather fine library of occult books, so naturally he had to be some sort of evil sorcerer. Heck, I had a nice little occult library myself—for reference when writing horror fiction, of course—and I thought it was a perfectly ordinary kind of collection to own.

Really, the beginning of my story isn't all that much different from Bob's.

I had done these cremations several times before, and I happened to be alone when this one was scheduled on a hot evening in August. Both of the uncles were busy that night. Seems as if there was some kind of shoot-out in town, and there were two or three corpses over at the bank—a botched robbery attempt. I have never paid much attention to that because I have had other things to occupy my thoughts.

So... I trundled the coffin onto the conveyor and watched it creep into the ignition chamber. For some reason, Bob's story went through my mind at that point, but I wasn't nervous and I didn't sweat as my hands operated the instruments. In fact, I chuckled to myself. I was just hoping for some kind of excitement, I was so bored.

Well, I got more excitement than I bargained for.

When the fires were up and burning, I suddenly heard a sound over the roar of the flames. It was a low moan, gradually rising in crescendo until it became a shriek.

A tiny shiver started at the base of my spine, working its way upward. I knew of course that this was nothing, nothing at all... just hot air being forced through a dead man's lungs. But I shivered all the same in that hot muggy room.

And then...*words!*

The scream turned into words. I remember them vividly. I can't forget them, in fact...even though most of the words were not in English. What I heard sounded like:

"IA! IA! DAGON! CTHULHU! WGAH'NAGL PHFHTAGN! IA!

IA! SHUB NIGGURATH!"

The chant sounded almost familiar. (It was later, after I delved into my own occult books, that I learned how to spell what I'd heard, and what it may have meant.)

As the chant continued, I stood as still as a stone image.

"PER ADONAI ELOIM, ADONAI JEHOVA, ADONAI SA-BAOTH, METRATON. PER NYAAARLOTHOTEP, PER SHUB NIGGURATH, PER YOG SOTHOTH, PER DAGON, PER CTHULHU CTHULHU CTHULHU..."

That noise! What was that noise!!!?

Gradually, from outside, a moaning sound had grown louder, developing into a stupendous howl like the granddaddy of all tornadoes. Now I felt the entire building sway, as if we were at sea.

Something like a sonic boom, loud as a dozen thunderbolts, shook the building. Amidst the winds and the thunder came sharp little cracks and thuds, as if gigantic hailstones were bombarding the walls and roof.

Astonished, I saw that the lights in the room were growing dim. Even the dull roar of the fiery furnace seemed muted...as if the flames, themselves, hesitated...

But then came a hissing, gurgling sound, and the incantation (if such it was) abruptly ceased. Weakened or not, the flames had done their work.

Outside, the winds subsided, the noise of thunder faded. At last I was able to move. With shaking fingers, I thumbed shut the valves and doused the roaring flames. Then I stumbled to the outside door, lurched against it, fumbled it open.

The sky was clear. Not a cloud showed. The moon was a day or two before full. Gleaming in its light I saw hailstones littering the ground, some as big as golf balls. They were already starting to melt.

Next day the newspaper called it a freak lightning storm. I knew better. I shivered in the suddenly cool night air, and bolted the door. Pretending to be calm, I bent to the familiar task of retrieving the ashes, and dumped them in an urn. With a faint smile I placed it on the shelf next to the other jar of unclaimed ashes. I carefully made out a tag that said *Waddely* and affixed it to the urn.

Then I closed up and went home. There was a quarter bottle of bourbon in my room. I finished it and was able to sleep, though not soundly.

But on waking I could not recall my dreams.

THREE: WHY I NOW LIVE IN TAOS, NEW MEXICO

For the next two days I tried to behave normally. I had reacted to my experience with bravado, and was pretending (even to myself) that nothing out of the ordinary had happened.

On the third day I was planning to work till late evening, so I decided to go out to a restaurant for dinner. I'd accumulated some savings by now (and yes, I'd sold a few stories, but that's another story, indeed), so I could afford it. But mostly I think I just wanted to be among people, and my cousins were out of town on a trip, so the house seemed empty.

Oh, it wasn't a fancy place…just the local Your Host where I could get a beer with my hamburger steak. They weren't busy, this being a Wednesday, and I had a large booth all to myself.

The three customers who subsequently took the booth next to mine were an odd looking bunch, all right. I wondered if they might not have been suffering from the same weird disease that old man Waddely was supposed to have had. I thought that a certain fishy odor wafted its way toward me…an odor that did not emanate from the kitchen. They talked a bit funny, too, slurring their words, almost as if they were foreigners. Certainly I had never seen them before.

I didn't actually mean to overhear them. In fact, I wasn't paying much attention to them at all until I heard one of them refer to Corey's Funeral Parlor. And then one of them mentioned Old Man Waddely. So I listened more carefully. I still couldn't hear them too well, but I got the idea that they were miffed because they had missed the funeral…and they seemed angry about the cremation.

Must be family members, I thought.

Then I heard one of them say something like, "It…no matter to us. We will always be able to…raise…essential saltes."

Now I think I have already mentioned that during the past day or two I had been looking into my occult books. I had found a number of references to Cthulhu and of course to Dagon, and I didn't much like what I found. I already knew the story of what had happened at Innsmouth, of course, and I'd also read something inconclusive about raising dead men from their "essential saltes." (That's how the books spelled it: *saltes*.) Of course, the latter had intrigued me because of my new profession.

After that outburst, unfortunately, they lowered their voices, and I overheard nothing more of consequence.

I then applied myself to my soggy apple pie a la mode, paid my tab, and slipped out of my booth. I don't think they ever noticed me at all.

Need I explain that I was again in a nervous state when I re-entered the funeral home? The corpses laid out for regular burial in our three display rooms didn't bother me in the least, but those strange men and their odd conversation kept nagging at me. I didn't like it.

The books I had read about Innsmouth told of people who had interbred with some kind of sea creatures, and what happened to them after they died…a kind of resurrection in the form of aquatic monsters, so I judged, although the books were not explicit in the matter… And now here were these men who looked vaguely aquatic themselves…and spoke of raising dead men from their essential saltes…

What I did then before I left… I thought I was being foolish, silly…but it did relieve my mind.

And after all nothing had happened that evening So I closed things up and went home to bed.

The next morning I was roused by a phone call. It was one of the uncles.

It seems as if the back door to the crematorium had been broken open. Slimy wet footprints had been found, but seemingly no other damage was done. Nothing seemed to have been taken… except for one item.

Strange! Ah—but you have already guessed it… You are always a step ahead of me, aren't you, sitting there in your armchair, reading about this and sipping a martini or a brandy. Ha! I was living it, and in no mood for quiet introspection.

Yes, you are correct: the urn marked *Waddely* had been stolen. Urn and ashes were gone.

The police had obtained a description from a passer-by. Three odd-looking men had been seen in the vicinity. You can bet they were the same three men I had seen in the restaurant.

The police traced their car, which had been stolen, to a deserted beach. They noticed signs that a small boat had put ashore. The Coast Guard, when notified, sent a helicopter and a patrol boat to search the surrounding area.

Near that point, where the river enters the ocean, there are a few scrubby islands. On one of them, the helicopter personnel noticed a deserted boat. What else they found was not reported in the newspapers. But I contrived to learn more when I talked with one of the Coast Guard men whom I had known pretty well in high school. But that was a little later on.

Another bit of excitement occurred the following week. The circus came back to town. The uncles delegated me to go talk to the proprietor, to remind them that we still had the urn of ashes from Ka-Zar, their gorilla we had cremated.

"What the f— do I want with a bunch of f—king gorilla ashes!" was the approximate comment of the circus proprietor. "You can dump 'em in the f—king garbage for all I care!"

So I did. I dumped the urn marked *Ka-Zar.*

And then I moved to Taos, New Mexico...

...not because it's a well known artists' and writers' colony. Although that's all to the good. No, no. I moved there because it's far away from my home town and far away from the sea. You might say that I suddenly yearned for the desert.

What my old Coast Guard friend had told me (over a few beers while he was off duty) was something like this: when their helicopter landed, he and the pilot had jumped out to look over the boat. Not far away was an odd and fearsome sight.

First, a pool of blood.

Second, in the blood, the footprints, or pawprints, of what seemed to be an ape of some sort, intermingled with man-like prints.

And third...a human arm, found nearby, apparently a man's arm. The site on the stony island was littered with shards of pottery. Among them was a wet and soiled slip of heavy paper, a tag that said *Waddely* in neatly typed capital letters.

But otherwise, the tiny island contained no sign of human life. And they found no apelike creatures either.

Since the beach would be washed clean at high tide, they took numerous photographs, wrapped the arm in oilcloth, and left.

No one-armed man had been found, to match the arm.

The three men were never traced, if they had been there at all. Nor the ape, if any.

You'll admit that the Coast-Guardsman's tale is most unsatisfying. The entire affair remained an impenetrable mystery to the law enforcement officials, and doubtless still does.

But you and I, of course, know the truth.

Yes, I yearned for the desert. Most of all I did not want to be anywhere near that funeral parlor if a one-armed "man," with two companions, should decide to pay a return visit.

You've figured out, by now, what kind of "foolish, silly" thing I did earlier—haven't you?

I'm sure the trio knew well how to call up a dead man, or a dead fish-thing, from his essential saltes. But they must have had one hell of a shock, there on that island, when they tried it.

I imagine that even semi-supernatural quasi-human fish-men would be mighty unhappy, to say the least, when they found themselves suddenly face to face with a newly-restored, and probably very angry, gorilla.

You're exactly right—that was the foolish, silly thing that I had done. I had interchanged the placards on the two urns.

I AM HUMAN

I

My mind sang to the soft strokes of the snare drum. The combo was good, the atmosphere was pleasantly smoky, and the Dortmünder in my mug was foamy and cool. But my fingers twitched nervously. Where was Helen?

Across the table, Pete and Jane seemed to be watching the four couples who were trying to dance on the tiny roped-in dance-floor. It was surrounded by tables and topped by a miniature skylight that was open to the evening. The light level inside was so low that you could actually see one or two of the brighter stars.

Helen had been due at about seven, and it was now nine. I had called her number three times but there was no answer. I saw Pete and Jane look at each other meaningfully as I pushed back my chair and drained my glass. My lips tightened.

"Bill," said Jane, "let me try this time. I'll call Sally, too. Maybe she knows where Helen could have gone."

I stood uncertainly, my chair half-tilted back, as she rose and started toward the ladies' room where it would be quiet, clutching her black purse tightly in her left hand while she rummaged for her cell phone.

"Sit down and have another beer, Bill," said Pete, signaling our waitress. I sat in silence as the brew was poured and the waitress left. Somewhere in my brain, my blood followed the rhythm of the combo, and my thoughts came in silly snatches.

"Where's Helen—boom, ba da—Helen's lost—zwam, ba zam— why, why, why—ba da."

Jane came back and sat down. I raised my eyebrows. She shook her head.

"Bill, old buddy," said Pete in a fatherly tone, "Helen's a big girl now. She's what, twenty-three? She's lived by herself for three years. She doesn't need a keeper. What's really got you so worried anyway?"

Now, that was a good question, Pete, old buddy. What exactly did have me so worried? I took a slow sip of my Dortmünder, watching the gyrating couples on the dance floor (there were six, now), and thought back over the events of the past few days.

Today was Friday, June 16th. On Monday I had made arrangements at the University Accelerator Laboratory to be absent for the rest of the summer. Tuesday morning at 8:30 I bounced into my M.G. Midget, which was laden with baggage, and left Philadelphia. Up the Northeast Extension of the turnpike, up Interstate 81 to Syracuse, then west to Buffalo; with a short stop for lunch, it was about an eight hour trip. I arrived at Pete and Jane's house at 4:45 PM. Pete had left work early, and his crimson TR-4 was glistening in the driveway. I pulled my green Midget up beside the Triumph and clambered out.

I had a pleasant surprise. Helen met me in the entranceway. She offered me a bottle of Schmidt's, which slopped over a bit when I grabbed her and hugged her as hard as I could hug with a bottle of cold beer sticking in my navel.

Jane had originally introduced us. I had been a graduate student in nuclear physics, Helen had been a junior majoring in history. In a school as large as the state university at Buffalo, we might never have met, otherwise. Our professional interests were quite disparate; but in everything else we seemed compatible. We were both shy in crowds, both interested in music and art, both only-children with deceased parents. Everything in my world seemed to shatter and re-form itself with Helen at the focal position.

We had become engaged last July. I had already accepted a job in Philadelphia, research associate at the university accelerator; she had committed herself to teach history at St. Mary's, a preparatory school for girls in Buffalo.

We had seen each other once or twice a month, and had spent the holidays together. Little enough time, we both thought. But now the academic year was over. The wedding was to be on Saturday.

We partied that Tuesday evening until well past midnight, and then I took Helen back to the large, empty house on Ferry Street which had belonged to her parents and where she still lived, alone. For an hour or more we sat side by side in the huge parlor, talking a little nervously, and then we said goodnight.

Wednesday, Helen had a few things to attend to in the morning, so we met for lunch at the Colonial House across from the campus. (How many misty memories associate themselves with that mundane establishment!)

Then we went to the zoo. Odd? We had spent our very first date at the zoo, and had not been back since. Nothing seemed wrong that afternoon; our minds were immersed in reminiscences. We had dinner at Eduardo's—pizza and chianti—and spent the evening first at the movies and subsequently at a cocktail lounge on Delaware Avenue. A satisfying day, simple though it was; wrung from our friends' importunity by our own ruthlessness. We paid, though, on Thursday—visits to relatives, parties with friends and more parties with the bridesmaids and ushers (Pete was to be best man), all packed in together.

Friday afternoon—this afternoon—we had the wedding rehearsal. It went off smoothly. By three o'clock the formal garb was doffed and I suggested we all head back for home base, Pete and Jane's. But Helen demurred. She explained that she had an important meeting, and would see the three of us for dinner at the Sheridan Club at seven. She refused to divulge her errand. I could not understand the expression on her face. She was blushing a little.

"Secrets?" I said rather coolly.

"Probably a whole raft of secret lovers," said Pete.

In the wake of the pleasant-sounding banter, she departed. I put on a smile and we went back to Pete and Jane's for a few drinks. Suddenly I needed them more than ever.

Now it was nine—and Helen was gone. I was badly worried, and I still didn't really comprehend why. Was it age-old instinct, brought to consciousness by a desperate need of which I was totally unconscious? Who can say?

I turned from my reverie to Pete, and spoke in a determined voice.

"I don't understand why, but I'm still worried. Look. You and Jane stay here, in case she does come. I'm going to her place. I'll call you in an hour or so to check with you. Okay?"

"If you think it's necessary."

I rose from the table.

"Nothing could possibly be wrong, Bill," said Jane, reassuringly "She probably just had a flat tire or something."

I said nothing, managed a ghastly grin, and headed for the door.

It closed behind me with a click, abruptly slicing off the wailing rhythm of the combo. In the car, as I made my way through the late evening traffic, I became more and more tense, without realizing why. The girl I loved was in some kind of trouble, or danger, and I had to do something. Only I didn't know what to do, or how to do it. The possibility that I was imagining the whole thing just made matters that much worse.

The house on Ferry Street was dark. I pulled into the narrow driveway, and slipped out onto the wet grass, hunting through my key ring for the front door key that had been mine for nearly a year and a half. I mounted the steps to the porch, tiptoed to the door, and quietly unlocked it and pushed it open. My groping hand found the light switch and I blinked into the flood of illumination until my irises contracted and I could see.

The room was empty. The whole house felt empty. I pushed the door shut behind me and stood staring about. It was just a room, a rather shabby one, but it was populated with poignant memories. I stared at the large, faded couch, regarding it abstractly. It had been the scene of our first kiss, one warm humid autumnal evening. Months later on that same outmoded item of furniture, two inexperienced people had nervously accepted each other's virginity. Yes, I loved Helen. And as these thoughts blazed through my mind, there came to me almost an image, a vision, of sight and sound combined. Helen—crying out in her need for me.

The moment of clairvoyance passed. I suddenly realized I was standing by the door still clutching the knob and drenched in sweat. The worst thing of all was my realization of my own utter helplessness.

But was I really helpless? I shook myself, literally, from my reverie and set about the unlikely task of finding a clue to Helen's whereabouts. There was a telephone in the kitchen. I looked there first, but saw no sign of a notebook or a note. I looked briefly in the study, which was a seething mass of papers, smiled grimly, and decided to leave it for last. I headed for Helen's bedroom, recalling that there was a telephone extension on her night table. It was there that I found the letters. Three letters. They were dated about one year ago, two months ago, and two days ago, respectively.

There is no need to reproduce all three letters here, although they are before me, now, as I write. All were from a man whose name I had never heard before. Ron Elder.

The first was written upon the occasion of our engagement, and although generally incoherent, seemed to be a diatribe against Helen for having been faithless to his pure love, for having (I quote) "played with my poor heart like a football." It was unanswerable, and had apparently remained unanswered. In the second, written two months ago, the melody changed from the plaintive to the protective. Elder was still incoherent, and apparently was still deeply unhappy concerning the loss of his great and one-and-only love. Now, he seemed to feel that Helen was no longer a faithless bitch but a wronged woman. There were several innuendos about me—in one place the term *Don Juan* was indiscriminately tossed around. This letter was just as unanswerable as the first, and apparently Helen had thought so too, for it was roughly crumpled up as though it had been tossed out, then perhaps later retrieved and filed away.

The third letter was a complete reversal of form. It was short, sweet, and to the point. I give it here, verbatim:

R.D. 4 Bucksville, N.Y.
June 14th

Dear Helen,

No doubt you are astonished to hear from me again, and so soon. I am very much ashamed of those other letters I have written to you and I want to apologize. I must have lost my mind, there, for a while, but I feel like a new person now.

I'm writing to tell you that I have just gotten engaged. Remember little Susie? She's grown up now, and she's a grand girl, and I know we are going to be very happy. She knows all about you, and I want very much for the two of you to meet again. I heard you were going to Europe for your honeymoon, so I hoped you might be able to stop and see us before the wedding. I'm living at the farm, now (you remember how to get there, don't you…the old dirt road off the Belldon Creek Drive?), and Sue and I will be here Thursday and Friday.

If you get the chance, please come. Please, please. Bring your fiancé, too, if you want to; but come.

Your friend, Ron

The telephone book was open, on the bed, to the E's. Elder was listed there, all right, with a town address and a phone number at which I guessed there would be no answer. I was right—I tried calling it and got a recorded message; the number had been discontinued.

It looked very much as though Helen had gone to Elder's farm, though I was puzzled to understand why. I had some vague ideas about what might have followed, melodramatic ideas that you can probably guess at. How could I have begun to imagine the ghastly truth? But my surmises, wrong though they were, spurred me to action. I picked up the telephone and called Pete's cell phone. Pete was a local sports-car-club officer, and knew the countryside around Buffalo intimately. After an interminable time, Pete answered.

"Helen's not home," I said.

"She hasn't shown up here either," Pete said.

"I think she may have gone to visit someone who lives in a place called Bucksville. I never heard of it. Off a road called the Belldon Creek Drive. Know it?"

"Are you still at Helen's place?"

I told him yes. He then proceeded to draw me a verbal map. I jotted down every instruction, using the back of Elder's last letter. I refused his offer of further assistance, but told him to expect to hear from me within a few hours.

After turning out the lights and locking the door behind me, I got into the Midget and rummaged about for my local map. By the map-light I tried to draw out my route according to Pete's instructions; but some of the roads he told me about weren't even on the map. So I put it away for future reference and unlocked the glove compartment. I drew out the .32 caliber automatic that I have always carried on long trips, since being held up once, six years ago. I made sure it was loaded, then slipped it into my jacket pocket. It was not too conspicuous. After that, I started the engine and swung the little car out on to Ferry Street.

You might think it incredible that within thirty miles of a large eastern city like Buffalo there could be wilderness, deserted hills, forest lands, fields choked with ragged weeds. Perhaps in the shadows that sprang from the yellow beams of my headlamps, the wildness and loneliness of the terrain were exaggerated. I got lost three times, and there were six or seven other instances when I thought I was lost. The blacktop roads became narrower and narrower, and more and more winding. My fuel gauge began to get uncomfortably low. I had not thought to stop and fill the tank. And my normally-mild hay fever was beginning to make its presence felt.

Finally, well past eleven o'clock, I made it to Bucksville. The town was hardly more than an accident, several people having chosen to build near one another. It boasted one gasoline station which looked deserted, though there was a light on. I stopped near the pumps, and a man came out. He seemed about sixty and was dressed in an old but serviceable army coat. He approached the car.

"Fill it, please," I said, and he proceeded to do so.

"At first I wasn't sure you were open," I said.

"Just starting to close up," was the response.

When I paid him, I said, "Afraid I'm a little bit lost. Are we anywhere near Belldon Creek Drive?"

"Got about a mile to go, yet," he grunted. Then he added, "I could use a lift to the creek myself."

When he had finished locking up, he got in the car and I drove off. After a while, he pointed out a shack dimly visible off to the side of the road, and asked me to stop. I pulled up in front of it. He said:

"The creek road's a couple hundred feet farther on down. Y'can't miss it."

He started to get out. I said, "The Elder Place. You know it? It's a farm, I guess."

He finished clambering out, then leaned back into the car and said, in a different tone, "Yeah, I know it. Left, and down th' creek a mite. Dirt road, to the left. What you want to go there for? I wouldn't if I was you."

"I've got to go there," I replied. "What's wrong there? Do you know Ron Elder?"

He grunted. "Ronny's folks died two, three months back. Ronny's a funny one." He paused. "Funnier than ever, since a few days ago. Since the meter fell."

"What do you mean? Meter? You mean meteor?"

"Yeah, like the whole world was on fire. Landed somewheres near the Elder place. Sky was bright, like daylight. An' smoke? We thought there'd be a big fire, sure. But there weren't."

"How do you mean, Ronny's funnier than ever?"

The old man spat. "Sheriff went out next mornin' to check. Don't usually get along too good, him an' me. But he tol' Slim, at the general store, and Slim tol' me. Ronny wouldn't let him in, an' ordered him off the property. He allus was queer, that Ronny, but he ain't never done nothin' like that before. You know anythin' about meters, mister? Might be that meter, it'd be pure gold, or suthin'? Might be that's how come you're down here, eh?"

"Rot!" I said. "Meteors are usually rock or nickel-iron, not gold or precious metals. It's impossible. Complete rot. But thanks for the directions."

He nodded, grunted, spat, and slammed the door. I put the car in gear and moved forward, looking for the creek road. It crossed just in front of a single lane bridge. I turned left, as the old man had told me to, and drove slowly ahead, looking for the dirt road. Twice I thought I saw it, but I was mistaken each time; then I finally spotted it ahead. A sign by the road said, ELDER FARM— PRIVATE PROPERTY.

I turned down the road, switching off my headlights, and drove forward in the faint glow from the cloud-covered moon.

After a while I saw a gate, and nearly ran into Helen's VW, when I tried to avoid smashing into the fence. I switched off the ignition and in one quick movement tumbled out of the Midget and onto the road where I crouched, listening and staring about.

Far ahead, beyond the fenced meadow, was a house with two or three lighted windows. Helen's car was deserted, its engine cold. There was no one around. A faint odor of scorched earth pervaded the atmosphere, a smell so subtle that at first I could not place it.

Satisfied that I was unobserved, I vaulted the fence and, still crouching, proceeded slowly toward the farmhouse. I had never been in combat, but I had stalked deer and bear, and now went as quietly and carefully as I could. I got to the farm house without incident and cautiously peered into one of the windows.

Immediately I felt like a fool—the prize ass of the age. Bill Gall, superhero. Bah! Helen and a young fellow, presumably this Ronny Elder, were seated in two of the chairs in an unpretentious living room. Ostensibly they were simply conversing quietly. Disgusted with myself, I half-turned to flee, but something stopped me. Cursing myself for a fool under my breath, I strode to the door and knocked loudly. For a moment there was silence—then came the muffled sound of footsteps and the door was unlocked and swung open.

Ronny was a blond fellow with rather long hair and a minute mustache. He was slight of build and perhaps four or five inches below my six-feet two. He studied me with a queer, measuring stare, like a housewife looking over a steak at the meat market.

"Sorry to disturb you, but I've come to talk to Helen," I said, gruffly.

"Come in," he replied with a high-voiced laugh. "Come right in, Mr. Bill Gall."

He stepped backward, and I followed.

Then the oddest feeling I had ever experienced washed over me. It was fear. Not ordinary fear—stark, raving, mad, unthinking fear. It halted me in my tracks for a terrible instant. Then I mastered myself and strode shakily on past Elder, toward the door to the room where I had seen Helen.

From behind me came the sound of a metallic click. I started to turn, but I never finished the action. A black cloud suddenly enveloped me. The last thing I remember is the floor coming slowly up to meet me. Then nothing.

II

I lay on a hard surface, face up. Noise reached me—clicking sounds, the hum of a dynamo. Odors, too—the scent of ozone, tart and oily, and another scent: something unknown but frightening! I let my eyelids quiver open, just slightly. The room was dimly lit, and the wall in front of me was bare and metallic, studded with buttons like a huge control panel.

I knew I was no longer in the farmhouse. But where was I?

Cautiously I tried to move, and discovered that I was manacled to the table on which I sprawled. Apparently my slight movements were audible, for a panel slid open behind me, and a voice said, "Awake, Gall?"

I fought down panic and said, somewhat unsteadily, "What's this all about. Elder? Is that you? What is this?"

"Soon, now, you will learn everything. More than you wish." Elder walked around in front of me, and stood looking down at me.

"Where's Helen? What have you done with her, you bastard?" He was unruffled.

"Helen is driving your car around to the back of the house where it cannot be seen from the road. Already she has telephoned your friends that she was delayed by an automobile accident, nothing serious. No one will come in search of you this night."

I grasped the words, but the meanings eluded me. Was he saying that Helen—*Helen*—was helping him to do…to do…

"Just what in hell are you trying to do?" I asked, desperately. My thoughts whirled.

"I shall explain briefly. Why not? I am not really Ron Elder. Helen is not Helen. Their personalities have been destroyed, as yours shall be, and have been replaced by ours."

This sounded like absolute gibberish to me. The old man had sure hit the nail on the head when he told me Ronny was "funny."

"We are Yoth-Sugoth, a race as old as the universe. Our minds are as far in advance of yours as yours are beyond the minds of vermin. Our native world is a planet of Aldebaran. You are in the main laboratory aboard the small space-time vessel which has carried three of our race to this world. Do you understand these concepts?"

I remained silent.

"Our purpose is simple. Regrettably our sun is about to become a supernova. Our world will be destroyed. Because we are not adaptable, biologically, to other worlds, our civilization is doomed. But we ourselves shall survive. Through eons of study we have learned how to project the soul, or ego, of one person into the body of another. The exchange can be performed individually with the assistance of the machinery in this laboratory. Then our minds, once in the bodies of humans, will serve as the three prime foci through which (with the aid of the receptors in this vessel), the minds of all the individuals of our race can migrate through space-time to human bodies."

The man was mad. Hopelessly mad. Yet, as he spoke, waves of utter fear ripped over me, lapping at my frantic soul. *My soul knew!*

"We are, of course nothing at all in appearance or biological structure like humans. But in all intelligent life, there is one similarity, one common constituent. That is the mind, or as you often say, the *psyche*, the *soul*. It is the greatest achievement of our race—to be able to transfer the mind of one individual to the body of another. And we have developed and perfected the technique just in time to save ourselves from annihilation." He paused for emphasis. "Now you shall meet the last of our group of three, whose mind will be transferred into your own human form."

So saying, the madman turned and threw open a sliding panel that I had not previously observed. Then he stepped back, waiting deferentially.

God. Oh, God! If that man was mad, then what was I? Mad?—both of us were mad. How else but as a madman could I gaze upon that nightmarish creature without losing consciousness?

Describe it? Describe the hydra; or Medusa. Know what song the Sirens sang, or catch a falling star. Nonetheless—picture a giant amoeba, colored colossally grey and covering two or three square yards of floor, with a height commensurate. But not a fleshy amoeba, not entirely—a creature of some solidity, surely, but also with a wispiness about it as if it did not entirely conform to the laws of our physical universe. It *wavered.*

I vomited. The remnants of half-digested Dortmünder and bread spilled down my shirt front and dripped from my chin. My stomach heaved again and again, disgust being my chief reaction, even beyond sheer horror.

But finally the icy needle of stark fear penetrated to the nethermost pit of my being. The thing *spoke.* Between the extraneous sibilances, the whispered clicks, the whistlings, as if the sounds emanated from a defective organ pipe, I could discern words in my own tongue. *English words, from that mouthless monstrosity!*

"The creature knowss it'ss ffate, now. Iss all in readinessss?"

"It is, oh Captain," spoke Elder. He followed the slugly abomination to a position behind me. By squirming and tugging on my manacles, I could just glimpse a table similar to mine. The creature was *flowing* up onto it.

Elder made a few adjustments, then came to stand before me again.

"My own conversion was so difficult. I think the host mind was strange, even for one of your kind. It required nearly a day before I could think coherently. With Helen, the exchange was much smoother. Already, after two or three hours, she is in full control of herself. I had anticipated that my letter would bring both you and her together, but it has worked out much better this way. Within a few hours, our invasion of your entire human race will become an accomplished fact."

It seemed as though, having begun the lengthy explanation, he could not stop. Or was he telling himself the story? The new mind addressing the old brain? Or had the alien mind taken on, with possession of the new body, some of its human qualities? Was he seeking my admiration of his cleverness? No matter. In any case, I no longer doubted his tale. I shuddered at the noise of restlessness from the table behind me.

Elder went on without a pause.

"Unfortunately we have had to carry out our program without proper preparation. But who, save perhaps the elder gods, could have predicted such a disaster? We shall have to learn may things about life as humans—the most urgent problems will be reproduction of our own kind, and the extension of our individual life spans. Of course the children of our sexual unions will be entirely human; but continued use of the mind-exchange technique will enable us to maintain our existence indefinitely until those goals are achieved."

At this, my mind finally bore loose from its moorings of sanity. I strained with the strength of a madman at the fastenings which held me. I am no weakling under any circumstances, and these creatures had not quite understood how much power the muscles of a strong, desperate man could generate. My right wrist came free with a loud snap.

They had not noticed my gun. As the startled Elder, or pseudo-elder, stared at me comically in disbelief, I drew it and shot him. He sprawled on the floor. The bullet had plowed through the fleshy part of his forearm and on into the wall behind him. The lights flickered.

But I was not paying any further attention to him. I had turned and without hesitation was firing again and again into the shapeless shape of the monster behind me.

It shuddered and shrieked as each of the five bullets struck it. Unlike an amoeba, that wavery form contained vital organs of some kind, and I knew instinctively that I had dealt it a mortal blow.

Suddenly Elder flung himself at me from behind. I was hampered by my tied feet and left wrist, but I managed at last to overpower him, for he was a physical weakling compared with me, and the bullet wound had taken toll of his strength. I had boxed and wrestled a bit in college days, and my muscles were still in good shape. I clipped him hard on the nape of the neck, and let him drop unconscious to the floor.

I groped for my penknife and started sawing at the plastic or leather straps that held my left wrist. Then a noise came at the door. I looked up. It was Helen: pointing something at me. Something vaguely like a weapon.

I said, "Helen…" but I knew it was not really Helen, there in the doorway. If I had had a cartridge left in my gun, would I have shot her? Could I? I doubt it. I doubt it.

I heard that familiar metallic click! Again that black mist enveloped me.

Again I sank into endless night.

III

My second awakening was groggy; my mind was slow. I seemed to hear Helen, speaking from infinity.

"Hurry, Ron. Those bullets hurt Baa-nk-rwee'un badly. He's dying."

"I have it almost repaired now, Helen," said the other monster.

Experimentally I attempted to move. But I was fastened so tightly now that I could scarcely breathe.

Helen spied my abortive motion and spoke.

"Farewell, human. Yours was a noble struggle and your body shall be a fit abode for the noblest of the Yoth-Sugoth, my Earth husband-to-be."

"At last!" cried Elder, and depressed an invisible stud. Blasphemous machinery whirred.

I was in two bodies at the same time.

One mind, my own, was resisting the inevitable intrusion; the other was inviting and welcoming. And the other mind was stronger.

This is my most vivid memory of that event.

I crouched at the tip of the present and viewed the panorama of a past that telescoped through over five hundred thousand years, years of stark horror. Five hundred millennia on the world of the Yoth-Sugoth; amongst the weird laboratories that spawned strange, artificial living plasmae that crawled obscenely into the sunlight and died, raging Years, centuries without end, amidst the queer basalt structures of the huge city on that aeon-old planet, structures without form or plan. Structures without doors, without windows. And the great sun, the awesome sun the tinted sun that beat upon the rooftops of basalt and marble and strange violet stone. I was budded, by a great one, and grew and budded in turn three creatures like me; and sought and understood secrets of universes beyond my own. For I was Baa-nk-rwee'un, even as he was I.

My glimpses of that out-world culture were sufficiently horrifying to stun my senses, but far worse were the insidious half-formed fears that lurked about the edges and crevices of the creature's brain. These beings had existed for a length of time impossible to imagine, their race was in its infancy before our earth was cool enough to support its liquid oceans, and they possessed powers and knowledge of a universe that to me were indescribably terrifying. Their knowledge seemed to have few bounds on future or past, and it ranged far and wide through the known galaxies. And in that knowledge lurked the concepts, almost legendary, of the strange elder gods of the universe, grotesque and fearsome extradimensions, and a queer unfathomed terror of certain unaccountable creatures known only by bizarre appellations which I have since forgotten, although one of these may be sounded, in Earthly tones, as "Azza-tot" or "Ashtoth."

All this occurred in, I believe, a quantum of time, a mere moment that seemed ageless only because in some queer fashion it was not within the universe of time but *outside* it.

Then, trapped in the mortally wounded body of that monster, I died.

IV

After an eternity of dreaming, I was awakened by screams. The room in which I found myself was dim and unfamiliar and the screams issued from a figure convulsed by terror, a figure who lay next to me in a wide, soft bed. Automatically, I gathered her into my arms, and soothed her fears, while my own fears mounted swiftly.

It was Helen.

"Helen," I whispered, holding her close. "It's all right. What's wrong?" Yet, while I mouthed assurances, my own mind was racing madly. Where were we? Who were we? Gradually details filtered into my mind, from my memory—or someone's. Details of things I was sure, even then, I had never really done But I must have done them.

We were married. We were on our honeymoon in France. I recalled the wedding ceremony, didn't I?

Helen whimpered. I flicked on a lamp by the bedside and stared about. "We're in a hotel, Helen. On our honeymoon."

Inwardly I quailed. But her fright forced courage into my own breast. "Could it have been a dream? Could it? Bill, was it a dream?

A nightmare?"

I knew what she meant. I knew.

"I doubt it," I said. "But if it was a nightmare, it's over, now."

We did not stay in Paris. We could not. We caught the first available flight home. We were so distraught that we did not notice anything peculiar about the outside world, about people. We went about in a daze.

Pete and Jane were astonished to see us, after only two weeks, when we stopped over in Buffalo to recover my car and to arrange for the sale of Helen's old house. They seemed perfectly normal, outwardly, kidding us about the usual things and bringing out photographs of the wedding. But every now and again I saw a flicker of something in their eyes. Was it memory?

No one could understand why we had come back so soon. But we never tried to explain. We shrugged off questions, and hurried home to the small house where I had been living in suburban Philadelphia. I burned up a lot of rubber getting us there. Neither of us was in a mood for anything but solitude.

But that was not the end. It was not over. It was the beginning…the beginning of the dreams.

Because Helen is more sensitive and artistic than I am, her dreams were clearer and more detailed than mine. They resembled mine, but were more distinct. Most of the dreams, hers and mine, centered about bizarre landscapes and a grotesque metropolis, large as a world. It was sculptured of marble and basalt and a stone that looked like ebony, without structure as structure is pictured by our Euclidean architects. Nowhere in the city did we perceive doors. Only rarely did we see it in daylight; our visions were nearly always of a shadowy monstrosity, dimly lit by the stars, and the stars themselves were strangely disoriented and unfamiliar. When dreams did come during daylight, we saw a blazing tinted orb of a sun, which seemed ten times as huge as our own, yet an oddly familiar sight; its queer radiation thrilled my being, in those dreams, and at the same time induced a faint feeling of ultimate horror.

Once Helen woke shrieking from a dream of bizarre elder gods, gods who antedated even that antique city, and cried out those startling syllables that sounded like Ath-toth and, once, Kshsulu. Recently Helen has been doing library research on pre-historical mythologies, and she thinks she has found what might be reference to such beings in a tattered and rotting manuscript that shall here be nameless; even worse, there is some mention of them in a more recent volume, the rare *Darker Superstitions of Scotland,* written by Dalyell in 1834. Why such references should exist here on Earth I cannot guess.

There is one odd thing that makes me certain our experience was real. Helen and I went to the library to look at the newspapers for the period starting on Saturday, June 17th. And there were none! There was a hiatus in all newspaper publishing for three days. Suddenly, on the twentieth, publication resumed, with no comment about the lag. Business as usual during alterations, I wondered? Or total recovery.

We developed Machievellian subterfuges to question our friends and acquaintances about that three day period. "Say, Joe, I tried to call the accelerator lab the Saturday after I went on leave, but could not get an answer. What was up?"

"Don't tell me anybody took a day off around this think-factory?"

"Huh? What day? Hell I don't remember."

My notes are voluminous but I shall record only one other interesting detail about those three missing days. One evening I happened to encounter a psychiatrist affiliated with a nearby insane asylum. We were at a cocktail party, and I managed to steer the conversation around to strange dreams and hallucinations, giving a watered-down version of some of Helen's and mine. He was quite interested, since he actually remembered that some of the inmates of the asylum had had a few especially restive nights in mid-June, and even now some still had oddly similar delusions of immense, phantasmagorical cities, inhabited by strange, blob-like creatures of fantastic mental capability. One of the inmates had even insisted he *was* such a creature, Raass-hovanth of Yoth-somewhere, the doctor told me, with a slight laugh. Shock treatment took good care of that delusion, though, he added. After another martini or two, he confided that the dreams of the patients were so queer that for a while even he himself had started to dream about antique races and aeon-old worlds, and some fearsome entity called Klulu. He had resorted to a heavy dosage of soporifics, for a week, till the dreams ceased to intrude upon his slumber.

Helen has reached a conclusion that I shall share with you, though I must, regretfully, disagree with some of her views.

She believes that our experience (only half-remembered) was

real. That when and if we decide to return to Ron Elder's farm, we can locate and examine the spaceship, or space-time ship. She thinks it is still there, although we have been unable to locate Ronny.

Helen thinks the attempt failed. She thinks that even the mind-transference to the three of us with the aid of the machine, was incomplete. She thinks that the overall attempt at migration failed. One factor, perhaps significant, is that the star Aldebaran has not yet given evidence of becoming a nova. Of course the ship travelled through space-*time*, and when it started we cannot even guess.

In Helen's view, the only effect of their attempt at mental invasion was a momentary meshing of minds between the inhabitants of earth and those of Yoth-Sugoth, which has resulted in recurrent dreams in the case of the most sensitive individuals, and perhaps even in a few successful transferences, as in the case of the maniac.

I am afraid that she is wrong, however. I have another explanation that I hesitate to contemplate for long—one too mind-shattering to discuss with Helen.

I saw and heard Ronny and Helen after their exposure to the mind-transference. I cannot believe it failed. I think, instead, it was entirely successful, not only with the three of us but with everybody…even *you*. And I do not see why or how our human egos could still survive. No, I believe they perished when that ancient sun exploded into a supernova.

But what is ego? Mind? Soul? What can happen when the ego, the personality of one individual is replaced by that of another, totally foreign one? The aliens believed that the memories of the invader would dominate, while those of the host faded gradually from consciousness.

But the Yoth-Sugoth had no long-term experience with their process, except among themselves. Because of the onset of the terrible sun-instability that had doomed their civilization, they dared not make long-range studies with us. They had to act, and act quickly.

Do you begin to perceive why this is repugnant to me? I can hardly bear even to put it down on paper. I shall try very very strongly to believe in Helen's explanation. I must believe it. I shall, I will believe, that I am William Gall, human being, born on earth and in the full prime of existence. I refuse to believe that I am really a creature from that loathsome planet of Aldebaran who has inexplicably, together with all his fellows, lost all memory of that world save in dreams, and is unknowingly trapped for a lifetime in the mortal identity of his earthly host.

I am not Yoth-Sugoth! I am Bill Gall! I am human! I am human!

WORMS

As I closed the door to the computer terminal room, the girl's laughter still rang in my ears. I knew my face had turned a bright red color, and my heart was pounding. I hadn't expected a reaction like hers to a perfectly ordinary question.

What was so comical about asking a Braun University librarian to help me dig up information about Miskatonic University? Why had she burst out giggling?

"Next thing you know," she'd said, without troubling to stifle her derision, "you will be wanting to see our copy of the *Necronomicon!*"

"Not at all," I had managed (I thought) a cool reply. "I have a Xerox copy of that at home."

That really started her off. Laughing even harder, she called another one of the librarians over to share the joke. Meantime, I retired (in some confusion) to the computer room.

No one else was there. It was vacation; no students were using the library facilities. Well, it was still quite early in the morning. I hadn't been able to sleep very well that night, so I had arrived just as they were opening up.

The place hadn't changed all that much in the three years since I'd been there as a student.

I accessed the library computer and it routinely indicated the date and the time. When I asked it to print out data on Mistakonic University, it didn't laugh at me. It just did nothing at all.

After thinking it over for a few minutes, I had it list all the universities and colleges in the United States. It obediently printed them out, alphabetically, but without any sign of the Miskatonic. Then I tried a geographical listing. But there did not seem to be a Miskatonic City, Town, Village, County, etc.

Not one to give up easily, I continued hunting around for a while, but was unable to find any references remotely resembling the name. I even searched the file on defunct universities and colleges. Miskatonic U didn't exist, and evidently it never had…according to the computer anyway.

But…my friend Stan Morozowski had gone there. He had been a graduate student. He had told me a lot about the place. He had worked for Dr. Wilmarth there…

On a hunch, I tried the town of Arkham, only to find that it, too, was nonexistent.

Unable to comprehend what was happening, I keyed in a request for the *Necronomicon*. Even in those early days of the internet, they had already made all books in the English language available to the widespread inter-library computer system. It would check the master list, find the most convenient source, and display whatever you requested (nowadays that's routine, of course).

It didn't take long to find a reference to the *Necronomicon*, but I didn't like what I found. The computer stated that the *Necronomicon* of Abdul Alhazred was nothing but a fiction…invented by some obscure New England writer I had only vaguely heard of. There was no such book.

No wonder they had laughed at me even harder when I claimed to have a Xerox copy of this book back at my place!

Only…I did have one. Which I'd gotten from Stan. Who had gotten it from Wilmarth. Who was a professor at Miskatonic. Which didn't exist.

I switched tactics and asked for "Who's Who." The computer obligingly printed out the W's for me, and there were several Wilmarths. None of them seemed right, though. There was no "Wingate Laban Wilmarth," nor any listing for Miskatonic.

Using the terminal as a microcomputer, I wrote a quick program in PASCAL to trace every telephone directory in New England for the names *Miskatonic* and *Wilmarth*. It would take a while, since this information was not in the computer's own data banks. It would have to access a large number of other computers to gain the information I needed. The sort itself was trivial but the rest of it was a much slower process (a lot different from today!).

So—I had some time to think.

I had come to the University Library because my own computer was useless at this juncture, either for computations or as a terminal for accessing national computer centers. It was the very newest Apple model, the Golden Delicious, but the core had a worm in it.

The core as you may know contains the memory, but maybe you don't remember what a worm is (we tend to use the term *virus*, these days). It's a concealed program, somehow infiltrated into the system, and primed to destroy it by making annoying modifications to the operating system software. I must have picked it up along with some programs I had copied (illegally) from a friend's floppy. I did a lot of such swapping back and forth. The worm had affected a large number of my own programs, too, and using a new operating system hadn't solved matters; evidently the worm was widespread and had already infiltrated the new system also.

I didn't think that Alhazred had this in mind when he wrote about the soul of the devil-bought that instructs the "very worm that gnaws," but—dammit—someone somewhere had instructed the worm that was gnawing away inside my Apple. And I was perfectly willing to sell the son of a hacker who did it to Shub-Niggurath, if he wasn't already "devil-bought."

Anyway, I had lots of time to think about things while the library computer accessed and sorted through the entire population from thousands of individual telephone books and other directories in every town in the area, searching for *Miskatonic* and *Wilmarth*.

This had all started (for me, anyway) with Stanley Morozowski.

Stan was a good deal older than I was. He'd spent some time traveling the world before settling down to study of archaeology, anthropology, mythology, and a number of other *-ologies*. Originally from Warsaw, he'd settled in this country after both his parents had died in an accident.

He had smuggled out copies of three books that had been in his family for generations. One was an excerpt from the *Necronomicon* that had been translated into Polish by some unnamed ancestor. Another was a copy of the original Von Junst book about "unspeakable" cults. The third was a book by Nicholas Copernicus, whose heliocentric theory of the solar system had helped to revolutionize astronomy in the age of Galileo and Kepler. But this book by Copernicus wasn't on the subject of astronomy at all, having to do with some bizarre study of Polish mythology. Its title, translated loosely, was *Prehuman Mythologies of Rural Poland.*

As far as I had gathered, possession of this latter book was the key which permitted Stan to enter Miskatonic University as a graduate student, even though his undergraduate degree from the

U of Warsaw had never been completed. Those savants at Miskatonic had never seen it before, if indeed they had ever known of the book's existence.

Afterward, when I had become well acquainted with him, Stan had visited Braun to utilize the more extensive computer facilities here. Evidently for some unknown reason the Miskatonic computers were not tied in with the rest of the net…which I now realized with some excitement explained not only why he had come here to work on his studies, but also explained why this computer network did not seem to have any data on Miskatonic.

But the real question was this: could I discover anything at all to explain what I had found in Stan's apartment the previous night: the strange pool of ichor, the queer note in Stan's nearly-illegible handwriting—what could he have meant by the silly phrase, "Beware the asterisks."

But he had warned me several times—in case of his disappearance—to get the news to Wilmarth, and that was exactly what I was trying to do!

Too bad he hadn't told me how to do it.

I was jerked from my reverie by the soft buzzing of the printer. I had instructed the computer to print out any useful results, and it seemed to be doing just that. I watched the printout as the machine fed it into the receptacle. Yes, there were some names and addresses here—including a Professor Wilmarth, who lived on a street called Miskatonic Lane, but it hadn't yet printed out the name of the town, when…

Suddenly, as I watched, the printer emitted a funny chattering sound and ground to a halt. The last few lines it printed out were gibberish—a bunch of asterisks. I looked at the display on the color monitor. It was flashing in a random way, displaying more asterisks. I recognized the symptoms. And then it hit me: "Beware the asterisks!" Stan's cryptic note!

It was the worm. My worm—the same one. The worm had somehow reached the library computer. Perhaps someone, somewhere, had fed in a program containing that very worm, just at the instant when I was getting some useful information. Or maybe my queries had initiated a hidden instruction which had suddenly activated the worm.

And the worm had destroyed the operating system, shutting down at least this library computer, if not all computers tied to it.

I ripped off the printout, stuffed it in my pocket, and left, trying to look casual.

I suspected that the giggling librarians might try to blame me for this breakdown—and in a sense they wouldn't be wrong, if my queries had activated the worm.

At least I had one address to track down—if I could figure out what town it was in.

I drove to Salem, where I stopped at a little hole-in-the-wall travel agency. When I explained what I was looking for, nobody laughed. But they did point out that something had closed down all their computer facilities.

I turned to leave, then turned back. Did they have any old-fashioned types of references?—like maps for example? They did.

I had tried Salem because I now recalled, vaguely, that the town of Arkham was supposed to be another name (maybe an old Indian name?) for Salem. I was wrong about that, but right to think I might get some help there. Some of their maps were quite old and I was able to find the Miskatonic River at last. Armed with a Xerox copy of the appropriate map, I headed north and west, getting lost several times because the map was so out of date, and finally found the tiny stream I was hunting for.

I drove for miles along a winding road that occasionally crossed over a low bridge to the other side, then later crossed back again. But I didn't come across anything like a university campus. The only thing I could find that even vaguely resembled such a campus was the Shrewsbury Foundation. Something about the name rang a faint bell at the back of my mind.

When I was about ready to give up, I decided to try the Foundation. Maybe they could at least give me a pointer or two, since they were familiar with the territory.

And there it was—Miskatonic University—in disguise.

"An underground University?" I blurted out, astonished.

The little old man with the white beard coughed.

"There was too much publicity. First, that Lovecraft character—how he found out about us I cannot imagine. And Derleth. He wasn't quite so inquisitive. But then came that fellow, Lumley, the Brit...and the other one, Campbell. We had to do something about it, especially when the Commonwealth of Massachusetts wanted to take us over and run Miskatonic as a local state university campus."

I laughed. "I suppose those bureaucrats would've been pretty surprised at some of your records…and some of your rare books would've shocked them, too!"

"That would have been the case, I fear. But it became impractical to keep running an undergraduate college here, so we simply turned it into a foundation, the Shrewsbury Foundation. We give scholarships to appropriate students at other colleges, we maintain an independent library, and our position as a foundation permits us to maintain our privacy.

I nodded.

"And our privacy is essential. But evidently we have gone too far, making it impossible not only for our enemies to find us, but also our friends."

I started to explain in an incoherent manner why I had tried to find them. When I mentioned the worm and the asterisks that were showing up in all the computers, his reaction startled me.

"My God, it's come at last!" he shouted. "They are trying again!"

"They?"

"But we are ready for them."

It turned out that their own computers had not recently been tied into the net, so they had not known about the worm that had shut down all the computers in the Northeast…or maybe in the entire world. But they were not without recourse.

"Dull scavengers wax crafty," he muttered, picking up his telephone. "Hello, Jonathan? It's happening, happening already. Evidently it's the asterisk system, though I don't quite know… Get our system tied into the national computer network.

"My God!" The voice on the other end was shrill and I couldn't help hearing it through his telephone. "I'll get busy immediately, Dr. Wilmarth."

"Now," said Wilmarth to me, "go back and tell me everything—including why you were hunting for us in the first place."

"Is that what got the worm going?" I asked. "All those computers tied together for my library research?"

"Probably. Or the nature of your research. A little ahead of their schedule, I presume. But they will have extended their influence by now—probably world wide. Go on."

"Yes, of course, sir." I explained about my friend Stan; how I had found him gone, with a puddle of strange black slime left in the center of his apartment; and a note to me, cryptically telling me to get help from Professor Wilmarth of Miskatonic. He had evidently been playing around with something just a little too tricky for him.

"As above, so below," said the note. "And as below, so above. Beware the asterisks. Beware the messenger of Nyarlathotep."

"Too bad about Morozowski," the professor said. "I'm afraid it's too late to help him. But there is the rest of the world to worry about now."

He flipped on the small computer terminal in his office, and I saw it: a whole screen full of flying asterisks.

Now I saw the meaning of Stan's bizarre warning: *Beware the asterisks.* Or did I? Hell, no!

"What's happening—the asterisks…"

Professor Wilmarth explained.

"An old occult concept: *as above, so below.* Basically it means, for instance, that the pattern of the stars in the sky (above) determines the pattern of existence here on the earth (below). It is an obvious basis for the belief in astrology."

"But—"

"The reverse: *as below, so above?* Yes, that seems puzzling until you understand the key. It reverses the whole process of cause and effect. It is, of course, a kind of imitative magic. Or science, perhaps. With the strength of Cthulhu's Cousins behind the manifestation, however—a strength of will undiminished by their aeon-old imprisonment… I admit that I am afraid."

I certainly didn't understand more than a fraction of this explanation, and I said so!

"The clue is simple. What is another name for an asterisk?"

"Why…a star," I replied slowly.

I hesitated, then exclaimed: "A star! A star! Oh my god!" I recalled a comment Stan had made numerous times. "When the stars are right…" I said it aloud.

Professor Wilmarth nodded, pleased, as if an idiot student, after a semester of straight D grades, had finally said something meaningful.

"When the stars are right, the time of imprisonment will end, and Cthulhu's Cousins will be able to escape their prisons and will come to take possession of earth. To them we are even less than worms, we humans. Those who die will be the lucky ones—if it happens."

Common sense (or what I thought was common sense) reasserted itself.

"Come on, Professor Wilmarth. Surely you don't believe…" I hesitated. "…just what is it that you do believe…?" I finished lamely.

"There are many computers in existence, all over the world, in this advanced age. Even in places like Africa, Australia, Antarctica. Enough of them will be turned on, and infiltrated by the worm, to display these asterisks—or stars."

"You mean—"

"The stars will be right."

I couldn't believe it. "The asterisks on the computer displays will somehow…somehow move the stars in the heavens to the right positions?" I burst out incredulously. "You can't believe that!"

"You don't understand," he replied. "Of course the stars in the heavens will remain unchanged. But…" He held up a palm to stop my next outburst, and went on calmly:

"But the asterisk-stars will be right. And it doesn't matter. Cthulhu's Cousins are not imprisoned by steel bars or cement or the pressure of oceans. They are imprisoned by psychological bars, conditioned to remain in their prisons safely as long as the stars are wrong." He laughed, mirthlessly.

"It really doesn't matter," he went on, "if the stars are celestial suns a thousand light years away, or if they are another kind of star. As below, so above."

A shock went through me, and I seemed to hear that message reverberating through me: *Beware the asterisks!*

"But it's not too late," added the professor.

I pointed wordlessly to the computer terminal. The asterisks were shining brightly, moving around the screen like greenish fireflies.

"These have been programmed in by one of their human dupes…but neither he nor they actually know the true configuration of the stars that is required for their release. See the asterisks moving around? The computers are randomly changing their coordinates, searching for the correct pattern. We have computed that it could take as long as ten hours to find it."

He continued pointing at the screen.

"Unless they are lucky, and get it right a lot sooner, we should be able to accomplish something…"

"What can we do?"

"Watch!"

I watched. The greenish asterisks kept moving around randomly, seeking a pattern that would destroy us all. What did he mean? Then—I saw something different.

Gradually, beginning as a faint greenish blob, *it* appeared, *its* outlines growing stronger. At first I thought it was something of theirs. It looked batrachian, like a spawn of the sea-things.

It was basically a head—just a head, with five appendages like arms radiating from it. Then the head's mouth opened, showing teeth, like shark's teeth. I shuddered.

"Keep watching."

"But what in all the hells…"

"It's a star-stone. A star-stone, with a head, and teeth, as you see."

As I watched, the mouth opened, the star-stone darted forward. *Gulp!* An asterisk disappeared. *Gulp! Gulp!* Two asterisks gone! *Gulp! Gulp! Gulp!* Three!

I burst out laughing. "Ours," I yelled incoherently, "It's ours." Wilmarth nodded, smiling for the first time since I had met him.

I kept on laughing. "Not an octopus! A starfish with teeth!" I laughed some more. I started crying, I was laughing so hard. "A star-stone Pac-Man!!!!!" Gulp! Gulp! Gulp!

The asterisks were disappearing. The star-eating star-stone expanded till it covered the entire screen, then abruptly disappeared. Not an asterisk remained.

Suddenly an ordinary print-out appeared. I realized that whatever program had been in operation at the instant the computers had failed was now resuming, was working again. The worm was gone.

"Oh, not gone," said the professor in response to my comment. "The worm is still in there, but it's currently inactive." He chuckled. "You see, we inserted a program of our own, into the world's computers, for just such an eventuality as this. Call it a virus. It counteracted the worm, but the worm program is still there in all the computers of the world. It cannot be removed, any more than the virus can."

Well, that's about it, the whole crazy story, except for one other point of interest. It turns out that while all this was going on, every lunatic asylum in the world was disturbed by a peculiar phenomenon—even the catatonics took part. The inmates began chanting a mysterious long-winded incredible incantation supposedly nonsensical but actually (I soon learned) in the language of the Old Ones. Evidently the asterisks themselves were not sufficient to open the gates of the Old Ones' prisons, but were to be augmented by this magical (or perhaps scientific) ritual. When the Star-Stone Pac-Man did its stuff, the chanting died away.

And it wasn't only inmates of asylums that did the chanting. Sensitives everywhere were affected and there were soon many more candidates for the funny-farms after it was all over, including several well-known horror writers.

About poor old Stan: nothing could be done. Seems he was on the track of what the evil plan actually was, the specific details, and they got him. But his message started me off on the trail to Miskatonic and my searches caused the computer systems to be infiltrated prematurely. Had they waited longer, they might have improved their worm sufficiently to overcome the virus and we wouldn't be here any more. But Stan's message changed all that and led to our victory. For the moment.

But the battle continues. I've enlisted in Stan's place and am now officially a graduate student of Miskatonic U. Wonder what that cute librarian at Braun University would say if I showed her my I.D. Yes, though concealed as a Foundation, the grounds of Miskatonic University still harbor a degree program, but there's only one major: MS.

Which stands for Mythos Studies.

FALLOUT

I awoke suddenly, but the cobwebs of sleep still clogged my brain. I must have been taking a nap, I thought fuzzily…but why was I so exhausted? I opened my eyes and gasped.

I was clinging to the wide silver branches of a gigantic tree, the trunk of which must have been ten feet in diameter. I sat in a crotch formed by one branch several feet thick. My hands clutched at smaller branches growing at each side of the one I was balanced on. My legs were half-twined about the large branch. My left side was pressed uncomfortably against the trunk.

The dim light all about me was silver-grey, as if it were bright moonlight filtered through a haze too thick to see through. Above me I could see nothing but the white haze, and below me was a similar curtain of silver. All I could see anywhere, besides the haze, was the tree, a huge section of trunk that faded all too quickly into the mists above and below. Its color, too, was silver, and its bark was smooth and slimy.

Tiny leaves and buds, like needles, sprouted randomly from the twigs.

On all sides of me, too, was the impenetrable fog. In one or two directions there seemed to be faint vertical shadows, as though other trees like mine might be growing skyward just at the edge of my vision.

I was gasping for breath—and my back, my arms, my legs—how they ached! My hands, too, were painful, and I could see clearly enough in the dim illumination that they were covered with lacerations and blisters. Somehow, before falling asleep—or while dreaming—I must have climbed a long way, whether up or down I could not tell.

Yet my memory had not failed me in other ways. I knew my name—Will Yance—and I remembered clearly that I was a mathematics instructor at JWU in Providence. I knew what year it was. I knew that I planned to wed an attractive redhead named Arlyn as soon as the exam period was over. And we were in process of moving into a nice apartment on Barnes Street. I recalled all these details without any particular effort, just the way that anyone can always remember pertinent facts about himself and his life.

Only I could not understand how I had come to be where I was.

I remembered last night. My memories had nothing of tree climbing in them. I looked down at myself. I was dressed in the same clothing that I recalled donning that evening for the informal math department party that was an end-of-the-year tradition at JWU. Dark blue shirt, grey pants, light weight black shoes. They were all in sad condition—the shirt was ripped in many places and stained with blood from the wounds on my palms. The shoes were badly scuffed, and the pants too were torn in many places. But they were indisputably the same clothes I remembered putting on last evening. What could have happened?

Had I drunk too much at the party? Had someone slipped a few drops of LSD in my beer? I thought about it. I did not feel as though I were under the influence of any drug, let alone ethanol. I merely felt bone-weary; although I must have slept for at least some of the night, I was not refreshed.

No, I did not remember drinking too much. It's happened to me once or twice in my life, of course, but last night I only had a few mugs of beer. I even remembered leaving the party with Lyn, dropping her off at her home, and getting back to the apartment. We'd been in the process of moving into this comfortable old place, and most of my belongings were scattered around in cardboard cartons—I recall thinking that Lyn and I could get most of them unpacked over the weekend.

I even remember going to bed.

And that's all.

Bed. I looked around again. Was I asleep in bed? Was this a dream? I felt the ache in my body, the rawness of my hands. Much as I would have liked to believe I was sleeping and dreaming, I could not. This was too real. Weird, grotesque, absurd, yes…but real by any common test of reality.

The compulsion to climb gripped me. I felt it was urgent to start moving. There was no uncertainty about which way to go: I knew that I had to climb upward, and fast. Even as I searched my own mind for some reason for such a belief, my limbs were operating. I was already climbing.

Luckily not all the branches were a foot in diameter. They came in all sizes, including many small ones for me to use almost like the rungs of a ladder. Not that it was so simple—sometimes I had to jump for a high branch and pull myself across an intervening place where no other branches sprouted. Other times, there were no problems at all. I climbed as slowly and deliberately as I could, trying to rationalize or at least assert dominance over that inner compulsion to climb.

The bottom portion of the tree trunk disappeared into the clouds below.

From the clouds above more of the trunk re-emerged. The pale glow all around me neither waxed nor waned.

I climbed. And climbed.

Before starting up the tree I had checked my watch, a self-winding calendar watch that Lyn had given me as a birthday present not long before. I even wore it to bed! It had read 8:30 A.M. Now it read a little past 9:30—I felt as if I had been climbing forever, while only an hour had passed by my watch. I was very tired and very thirsty and very very hungry, and I stopped for a brief respite. I knew I could not last out the day, but the urge to climb mounted until it became unbearable. I did not rest long.

Once I dared to consider climbing down instead of up—surely there was a bottom to this tree, somewhere down there? Should I not be moving downward, rather than upward? However, at these thoughts my body shivered with horror. It was not mere horror of the unknown—it was horror of something unknown only to my conscious self, but somehow maddeningly familiar to the rest of my being. I trembled with the desire to climb upward even faster.

Somewhere, either far below me or deep within my memory, I seemed to hear cries or yelps of anger and rage, almost like the baying of supernatural hounds…

Like a figure on a vertical treadmill, I climbed, never seeming to make progress.

The pain in my palms! The hunger! The thirst! This was no dream.

I continued upward like an automaton. The void in my consciousness did not fill… I had no concept of what I was laboring to escape—but the urge remained powerful, supplanting all conscious endeavor, overcoming utter weariness of body, all hopelessness of mind.

At last something changed.

Above me, almost still hidden in the churning mists, the tree trunk seemed to have reached an end.

Unbelieving, I found the energy to climb faster. Once, reckless and trembling, I lost my hold on a small twig, for my hands were slippery with my own blood. But with a tremendous effort, I managed to grasp another and steady myself upright for the few moments necessary to gain a sounder foothold. For a time I was too frightened to move, and I just hung there, panting, clinging to the branches and pressing my body against that bulky tree trunk as though it were my mother's breast. Then the uncanny urge to climb returned in full force and, though I was a little more cautious, I had to go on.

As I rose ever upward, I continued to rivet my gaze upon the top of the tree trunk. Now I saw clearly that it did end.

When I reached the edge of the top, I saw it more clearly and was amazed—the top of this giant tree seemed to have been severed cleanly, much like a blade of grass slashed off by a lawnmower.

There were no more handholds up this high. I laughed and cried and mouthed prayers and curses as I climbed. Upward, spoke the inner voice—*upward.*

Like a mountaineer surging over the final cliff toward the ultimate peak that was his goal, I hurled myself over the rim of the tree and fell moaning and gasping to lie on the smooth, sticky surface. Then I blacked out from the effort.

After a short time I regained my senses and stared about me with awe. The trunk had been severed horizontally. Sap, fresh sap, had oozed out through the open wounds near the rim of the tree, though the interior section was dry and hard. It seemed to me that the tree had been cut as recently as yesterday—if time meant anything at all in this world of moon-mist. Shaking, I rose to my feet. I could stand on that five foot diameter treetop without giddiness. I peered about me, but could see nothing but the fog.

Yet I could still hear (almost in my mind's ear) the baying of hounds.

Now I took note of something that I had not seen before. Above me, the fog had grown immeasurably thicker. I raised my hand above my head; even at a distance of a foot the seeing was poor.

Suppose, I said to myself, there is something above me. Another tree trunk, perhaps, or some sort of support. Or even the rest of my tree, just hanging there overhead. Whatever might be there, one thing was sure: I could not see it, and I could not tell what might be there.

Suppose, I said to myself, there is something above. I would have to jump. Jump blindly up into the fog, to try to reach whatever might lie up there, try to pull myself up. If I missed, I might be off-balance—might tumble off the tree to a horrible death at the faraway surface.

Suppose, I said to myself, there is something above me, something above me, something above me... I caught myself with a start of fear. Why was I having such thoughts? What had put it into my head to leap off this incredible tree trunk, this five-foot table in the sky? I could rest here, ease my aches for a while. But I shuddered. I knew what was happening to me. It was the influence of that deep urge that said: *go higher.* It still boomed within me. I would have to climb higher, higher, higher...only there was nothing to climb.

"I can't climb any higher!" I shrieked the words at the top of my lungs, and at the same time I started to hear those sounds of pursuit, those barking, groaning, roaring, growlings below me. I must have gone mad from the strain. Perhaps I fancied that the urge *within* me came instead from *outside* me—that I could speak to it like an entity, reason with it, threaten it, cajole it. "I can't do it!" I screamed again.

"Will!"

Was that a voice? Did I truly hear someone call my name? "Will! Where are you? Will, is that you?"

Was that the voice of Arlyn, my fiancee? I could barely tell. It was so faint, so very faint, compared with the sounds of my pursuers. Her voice seemed to emanate from another space, echoing hollowly through unknown barriers.

From below me, too, I heard other sounds...a scraping of skin or claw on wood. The rustle of the needle-thin leaves. Yes, it was true: someone or something was climbing the tree after me.

The urge within me reached a sudden peak of frenzy, I did not want to see what manner of creature was following my spoor up that accursed tree trunk. I dared not look. I had to climb, or jump, or do something.

I screamed unknowable words in my frustration. I tried to

jump. Many were the leaps upward I made, arms outstretched, fingers clutching at fog. But I felt nothing up there but emptiness.

"Will!" The voice came again. I fancied it came from above. I jumped again and heard the voice again, louder, as I rose in the air, touched nothingness, and fell again. It seemed to be coming not directly from above, but off toward one side of the tree.

Then came another sound from behind me, a sound that drove me to insanity for a brief moment.

It was my name, again, "Will!"—but bellowed from below me, this time, and not in Arlyn's sweet voice but in a hoarse abomination of a growl, a sound with hunger in it, an indescribable sound.

I dared not even glimpse the thing that climbed over the edge of the trunk. Instead I raced to the edge of the tree trunk, opposite, and leaped up as far as I could…

…without conscious intent I was leaping to my death to escape that thing that had pursued me so far. But by an unimaginable stroke of luck (or I would not be here to tell you of these matters), my leap of frenzy and despair was made in just the right place. Something indeed was up there—up there in the almost impenetrable clouds—something solid. My fingers grabbed and held. I pulled my whole body upward with a surge of energy I never could have managed even in perfect health and freshly rested. It was the last energy that comes to a man in the most dire extremity of his existence.

My eyes were closed. Something scraped roughly against my shoe. I hung on grimly, pulling myself higher. I heard a scream, then, and two hands clutched at my arms and pulled. There was a thump, as my body fell a scant two feet to the floor.

I opened my eyes. I was lying on the floor of my almost empty bedroom, next to the same old bed in which I had slept for years.

Arlyn was bending over me, her face wide both with terror and curiosity and saying, "Will, what happened, Will, what happened?" over and over again.

I just looked at her for a while, and squeezed her hand.

"You were there, your arms were coming up out of the bed—right up out of the bed. I saw the watch I gave you," she muttered. "But there's no hole in the bed, no hole… No opening at all."

"Yes there is," I said…even though I could see none. And I thought of the thing on the tree top, the thing that had climbed after me to the top and touched my heel at the last minute. And I won-

dered whether it could make the same kind of leap I had made…
and in a burst of energy I was on my feet.

Protesting, questioning, Lyn watched as I moved that damned
bed over to the other side of the room…several feet farther over in
a direction that I knew, without knowing how, to be the right one.

Would that be enough?

We waited for a while, but nothing happened.

Arlyn quieted down slightly, and I told her the gist of my adventure.

"And—and that thing is down there somewhere waiting to
come up here?" she asked fearfully.

"No," I said. "It can't be. It must have been a dream after all,
the whole thing."

She laughed a little hysterically. "You came up out of the bed.
Right up through the floor, it must have been. Up out of nothing!
And look at you. A dream? A dream, was it? Look at you!"

Slowly I peered at my bloody hands, my torn clothes, felt the
ache of hunger and ultimate exertion.

I nodded.

"I need food and I need sleep. You can bandage my hands."

She looked toward the bedroom.

I said, "No. Not here. I'm never setting foot in this apartment
again. And neither are you."

I quickly rummaged around in my meager clothing supply and
found a shirt and pair of trousers and changed. I looked pretty sad,
still, but not like an accident victim.

"We aren't taking that bed with us, either!" said Arlyn sharply.
I did not argue.

Well, that's all. No grand climax, no explanation to satisfy my
readers. Just a bare recital of what happened to me one time when
I tried moving into a new apartment.

Of course there are possible explanations—plural. Lots of
them. Here: take your pick…

Joe Filly, a guy I used to know, has a quaint theory of life—
he claims that all of us are really telepathic cabbages growing on
some planet like Mars, and merely dreaming collectively about
earthly existence. Humanity is just a thing we have created in one
of our weirder nightmares. On that theory anything whatsoever
can happen to us at any time, because life is just a dream anyway.

Dr. Bob Birney, a philosopher I know (he also has a degree in mathematical physics), occasionally speaks of space-time continua, parallel universes, nine-dimensional strings, and worm-holes between dimensions. It sounds impressive, but doesn't prove anything. In the end, it's no better than Joe's crazy idea, though the mathematics behind it seems solid, at least to me, albeit quite a bit beyond my comprehension.

My father-in-law is a psychiatrist. He's heard the story, too (of course we pretended it was a dream). He talks of sperm swimming up long channels, and lemmings swimming the ocean, and trees as phallic symbols, and on and on. Well, the human mind is mighty peculiar, and can do strange things—no one could argue against that.

Then there's my friend Hal Morris, who heard the story and muttered soothing things about the stars being right (or was it wrong?), and talked a little about some things he called the *Crawling Chaos* and *the Hounds of Tindalos.*

Anyway, the emotional impact of what happened has worn off to some extent—it had to, if I were ever to live a reasonably normal existence again. And nothing else like it has happened, at least not in the time that has passed since then…at least, not to me… except that on some occasions, if I have had a few glasses of wine, I begin to think that I can discern the faint baying of hounds.

Arlyn and I discuss it regularly—we can explain away most things if we try hard enough, but not one: not the fact that Arlyn saw my hands come up through the bed. Not behind it, *through* it. And there was no opening there. And Arlyn wasn't asleep or dreaming! She helped pull me up through an exit that was not there. Or anyway there was no passageway that anyone in our world could comprehend.

One or two further remarks, and I'll quit. First of all, the sticky stuff on my clothing and hands and the many needle-leaves in my clothing: sap from a tree, leaves from a tree. I had it looked at by the head of the JWU biology department…asked him what kind of tree would exude such sap. He was very excited, examined it very carefully and was unable to identify it. He talked about white chlorophyll, and insisted on knowing where it came from; but on hearing a portion of my story, he refused to believe it. Thinks I was playing some kind of weird prank on him. He isn't speaking to me any longer.

All I think is this. I was tired. I fell asleep on the bed without even taking off my clothes. And then I literally fell out of this world to somewhere else. And I ran from something I saw but have repressed from conscious memory. Or something I encountered that had no meaning in terms of my own experience.

Use one of Hal's terms, Azathoth, for it if you like. At least it's a word, a name, and that's better than nothing at all to use as a referent.

My old friend, George Wetzel, talked about *Cthulhu's Cousins.*

Anyway I fell in. And I got lucky. I came back.

I have wondered many times since that night who else might be living in that apartment now, and whether some day he, too, will fall asleep in the wrong place at the wrong time—(maybe only while the stars are wrong, Hal)—and fall out of our world.

Almost certainly he won't be as lucky as I was. He'll never make it back. I'd like to go warn him, but how can I?

Would you believe this story if I came and told it to you?

I hope so. Because, my friend, if you have recently moved into a large, spacious apartment, *you may be living where I was living.* And in that case, I *am* telling you. I am telling you that I don't like the way your furniture is arranged, and if you are wise, you will move out of there right now.

Move out—or fall out.

THE VAULT OF KARNUNNA

Mad thoughts whirled in Hubbik Tombola's mind as he stared from his high window down at the battlefield. There, in a monstrous maelstrom of flesh, thousands of horses and men danced and died.

He raised his head as his adjutant hurried into the room.

"Your honor; permission to speak?"

Tombola, the Emperor, nodded brusquely.

"A contingent of Balzikkers has broken through at the west gate, sire. Three battalions of the city guard have been sent against them, but that has weakened the defenses here on the eastern wall." His voice trailed off in a husky cough. Tombola could see the swell of the bandage which covered his left side; he had been wounded only yesterday in a brief skirmish outside the gate.

"What of the Third Army?" Tombola snarled. "Is there any word of their approach?"

"Another messenger arrived just before I left the field. He managed to speak before he died of his wounds. We understood him to say that the Third Army is engaged in battle at the city of Balzzun with an army dispatched by the Troikarch of Zebendu."

Tombola felt the red blood seeping into his face, turning his complexion almost purple. He had himself placed the Troikarch on his shaky throne. So this was how a traitor repaid a debt of honor. *Well,* he muttered to himself, *all is not yet lost... In the end, all traitors shall die.*

"Xixxim," he spoke after a painful moment of indecision. "Take full command of the battle. Do your utmost to stem the tide as long as possible. That moment has arrived—that moment I once swore would never come to pass."

"Yes, sire," replied Xixxim. He bowed deeply in spite of the wound that pained him. As the emperor's confidant and faithful follower for many years, he knew precisely what Hubbik Tombola meant, and further explanations were totally unnecessary.

Tombola, King of Posidon and Emperor of the Far North East, rose abruptly and strode to the side of his golden throne. Toward the rear, on the left side, just under the weighty arm of the impressive throne, was a small keyhole. Tombola withdrew a silver chain from about his neck, a chain that he always wore next to his bare skin. A key, golden and delicate, dangled at the end of the chain. No man of the king's realm had seen that key in over twenty years; only the women of the harem, during intercourse with the great ruler, had seen and wondered at it. One vixen, originally a slave girl from the barren north, tall and husky and flaxen-haired, had essayed to steal it; but she had failed and expired in a manner best left unspecified.

For the first time in twenty years, the king put his golden key into the keyhole shaped for it; and carefully withdrew from the little vault, built into the throne, an odd medallion.

The medallion was a queer contrast to the golden key and the silver chain. It was roughly fashioned of iron and hung from a necklace of hand-forged, crudely-rounded iron links. The runes upon both front and back were indecipherable, though he had been told that they referred to Karnunna, sometimes called the Horned God.

Clutching the iron amulet loosely in his right hand, the king turned toward the wall of his chamber, where, by pressing in a certain sequence upon certain ostensibly ornamental carvings, he succeeded in causing an ancient panel to creak half-heartedly open. Creeping within the corridor revealed by the half-open panel, he slid it protestingly shut behind him, and waited for his eyes to accustom themselves to the semi-darkness. He then began to sidle to his left.

Small shafts of illumination seeped into the hidden corridor through ornate openings high on the walls, invisible from without. He went about thirty feet in one direction and then started down a very narrow stairway. The way down was interminable, and he could not keep from remembering the one other time he had made this journey.

At that other time, twenty years before, he had not been the mighty Hubbik Tombola, emperor of the realm, but only frightened, scrawny teen-aged Hub Tombola, eighteenth prince in line for the throne. Such princes as he generally ended up on the rubbish heap, as well he knew; for upon succession of the eldest son of the ruler, it was common practice for the other siblings to meet a quick, safe demise.

However, this had not been an ordinary succession. The first sons of the emperor were twins, each deeming himself more fit to rule in the place of their father. Each possessed a retinue of supporters, and the death of the old ruler had given rise to a gigantic, six-month-long civil war that had culminated in a pitched battle for the capital city of Posidon. Some of the brothers had chosen sides, hoping to circumvent their ritual deaths upon the succession of the twin they chose, by proving their loyalty to his cause.

Young Hub Tombola, however, had been scorned by both sides as a weak, pimply-faced nonentity, and he would soon have been executed if Xixxim had not led him secretly out of the palace into the streets of the city.

There, after days spent scrabbling for food amidst the insurrection, he had encountered his uncle, Bartomik Tombola. The fact that an uncle existed at all was startling in itself, because of the usual custom of imperial fratricide; equally startling was the fact that this ancient uncle was a mage. The mage explained plausibly that his own survival, in fact, was due to his expertise in wizardry; how else could one escape the king's executioners.

"My mother," he told the frightened Hub Tombola, after spiriting him to a small house away from the crowds, "was a seeress. She was a chosen one of the Goddess Phthathnee. She detested the king, who had kidnapped her from faraway Quoraine, and placed her in his harem. And she detested me, fruit of that union she abhorred. But at the last, she taught me most of her secrets in hopes that I might ultimately revenge her upon the king."

"And have you done so?" Hub asked, quivering.

"Kings are strong. Even wizards must bow when kings pass by."

"Then you have no true power against kings…"

There followed a few moments of silence.

Then his uncle Bartomik laughed merrily. "Ho," he cried, "would the little princelet, then, wish to become a king of this land?" He laughed again, uproariously, then paused. "Why not? Better than those dogs and jackals that disturb the peace of the city.

He drew close and began, now, to whisper.

"There exists an amulet, strange and powerful, which belonged to the first of our line of kings. My mother told me much about it.

It is located deep in the bowels of the palace, where it has rested for perhaps centuries, untouched. My mother wanted me to fetch it and use it to carry out her revenge—for it seems that a man only, not a woman, would be able to utilize the power of this strange object.

"But she had revealed more about it than is good to know. I was satisfied with my knowledge of wizardry. I would not touch it."

When Hub Tombola continued to insist upon more information, his uncle gradually and carefully outlined what he wished the youth to know. He described the entrance to the corridors internal in the palace; how to open the sliding panel that led from the throne room; and what twists and turns to take in the dark tunnels beneath the palace, so as to reach the room where the amulet was hidden…the vault of Karnunna.

No warning did he give, concerning the use of the amulet, save to mention that no overwhelming danger existed the first time it was used, while there might be considerable peril in using it ever again.

As Hubbik Tombola, Emperor of the North East, continued down the winding passageway, occasionally taking one turn or the other in accordance with the twenty-year-old instructions from his uncle Bartomik, he continued to remember wryly that first and only other time he had passed along these ways.

Then, his step had not been confident. Then, his heart did not beat slowly and disdainfully.

He had nearly been caught in the throne-room, in the act of opening the panel, and only at the last minute had he escaped the watchful guard by scampering over to the throne itself and concealing his scrawny body behind it. It had seemed ages before the guard decided to leave the room once more; further ages before he regained the courage to return to the panel and finally wrench it open. It had squeaked then, too, when he had forced it wide enough open in order to slip inside.

And that long, clumsy passageway—he knew his uncle Bartomik had not told him everything, and he feared there might be a terrifying guardian within to protect that amulet. So his progress down the lengthy deserted corridors beneath the palace was accompanied by fear and terror of an intensity which a young person, raised in a safe and civilized community, could hardly begin to understand. Still, death waited hungrily for him outside, so he steeled himself and went onward, not quite sure whether he was demonstrating a courage of the highest order or simply a greater fear of going back than going forward.

Finally he saw it—the amulet, resting in its crystal case in front of the statue of a strange, dark god—a god with tusks and horns and sharp claws and odd tentacles, unlike any deity he had ever seen.

Hub bowed deeply before that image, as Bartomik had instructed him to do, and took the amulet into his hand. Then he carefully used a knife blade to open a small wound in the ball of his left thumb. He slowly squeezed out two drops of his blood onto the two sides of the amulet.

After placing the amulet around his neck, letting it hang loosely from the crude iron chain, he spoke the words of ritual that he had memorized.

Swiftly a great pain tore through his body—and he fainted. But before he lost consciousness entirely, he saw the figure of the Horned God slowly begin to stir, flexing its muscles as though it had been severely cramped for a long long time.

Suddenly he was again conscious and seeing clearly—almost as though he were truly awake for the first time in his life.

It took several moments of confusion to realize that he was not in his own body but that his identity, or ego, or ka, seemed to be in possession of the grotesque and terrifying shape of the Horned God—and the name, Karnunna, came to him like a cry from the throats of a thousand dead men.

"I am now the Horned God without a name," he thought dismally, if irrationally. "I am Karnunna." Then he started to realize that he was not, after all, completely in control of this bizarre new body—for it moved freely without his own volition, through the tunnels and into the throne room, where it encountered its first victim.

The suspicious guard, who had entered before when the boy cowered behind the throne, was making another thorough search of the room. He had evidently heard the squeal of the panel, and returned to discover its meaning. Now he remained on guard in the midst of the throne room.

The desires of Hub Tombola and the Horned God were ideally matched: the god reached for the startled guard, who was too astonished to move a muscle, and slashed him to death with tusks and horn.

Then the form of the Horned God moved outward, where the embattled armies of the twin sons of the Emperor fought in the streets of the city.

A gigantic voice came from its throat, not at all in the intonations of young Hub, and the words it spoke were "Cease to fight, and obey the rule of the true emperor—Hubbick Tombola."

No one laughed at this silly statement; everyone was too terrified. And they had reason for terror. For the shape of Karnunna, the Horned God, loomed over them, and proved to be immune to the hazards of all known weapons, from sword and spear and arrow to the curses of wizards. Even the super-weapon of kings, a kind of Greek Fire, merely burned itself out upon his body without having any effect whatsoever upon his actions.

For eight days and nights, the figure of the horned god passed about the city, destroying the enemies of Hubbik Tombola. It began with his brothers, the twins; continued through the rest of his family, and ended with the soldiers of the armies that still battled in the name of the dead claimants.

In its body the mind of Hubbik Tombola continued to live, and slowly, slowly, slowly he came to control the actions of this potent entity. After a time, it was he whose conscious desires directed the arm of the god as it grasped and twisted the neck of an enemy. After a time, it was his mind that formulated the words spoken by the monstrous and vast voice that issued from the throat of Karnunna.

"Lay down your arms and offer fealty to your new emperor, Hubbick Tombola," he would cry; and many times over he would succeed in obtaining recruits to his banner.

After a week of bloodshed and terror, a large faction in the city and a larger faction in the army supported Hub Tombola. Soon, all the populace supported him…for he was the last remaining kin to the deceased Emperor.

Even Bartomik Tombola, known as Rureval Bartomik to his neighbors—he had no friends—had succumbed to the strength of the Horned God. Hubbik Tombola was absolutely determined to leave NO relatives at all to plague him; the error of his father had taught him caution. And he intended that no one alive should know the whereabouts of that secret cavern beneath the palace, or the meaning of the iron amulet.

When the city had quieted and order had been restored, he returned in the form of the god to the subterranean crypt where the body of Hub Tombola lay in a coma, hardly breathing, on the cold floor—and, indeed, had so lain for over eight days. He cried out at the sight of himself, but resolutely carried out his plan. As his uncle had taught him, he intoned the words *utha uthgago* in a fierce bawling voice, and fainted from the sudden pain which struck him.

Hours later, waking in his own body, weary and weak from its long coma, Hubbik Tombola had crept querulously back to the throne room, medallion in hand, to receive the crown of King of Posidon and Emperor of the Far North West.

He was fearful of what his appearance would bring; of whether the legions who had sworn their fealty to the Horned God would carry out their oaths now that he, weak and powerless, stood before them. But he encountered no difficulty. Eight days of terror had convinced the entire empire to kneel to his rule; peace and a return to trade and prosperity was all anyone desired.

So came Hubbik Tombola to power.

He was now remembering more than just the accession to the throne; he was remembering how, as he grew in strength and wisdom, his rule prospered, and he became a good emperor, with concern for his people and love for his vast domain.

In the harem, he had discovered the delights of sexual congress, not only with the loveliest of girls and women, but also with boys, with animals, and with Tsneea, those man-like delicate creatures that live in the far southland, which some say were once shipwrecked upon this world in the course of travels from far stars to far stars.

In the field, he discovered the delights of war. From a scrawny youth he developed into a muscular and lithe warrior, who learned to manipulate the weapons of war nearly as well as his finest soldiers, and who also learned to manipulate the armies of war better than his most knowledgeable generals.

In the classroom, he discovered the wonders of knowledge, both in fields such as science and engineering, and in the humanities. He even became conversant with the scripts of long-dead nations and civilizations, and the time came when he was able to reach into his mind and pluck from it the form of the inscriptions on that amulet and compare them with the hieroglyphs of many an ancient land. But he never learned of any foreign land in which such a tongue was known.

Now, Hubbik Tombola, King of Posidon and Emperor of the Far North East, shivered a little, as he entered the vast room where the monstrous Karnunna sat brooding. He shivered a bit more as he saw that the tusks and the horns of the idol displayed a brown patina of ancient blood. He shivered not with the raw fear of that youth who had once dared this sanctum rather than face death on the streets of the city, but with the adult perception of a man in the prime of life, who knows that this is a mystery beyond all mysteries known to the sages of his world.

Needless to say he had never dared seek information amongst the votaries of the Goddess Phthathnee. Better, he'd quipped to himself, let sleeping goddesses lie.

Now, as before, he placed the medallion around his neck and went through the ritual. And, as before, he felt the sharp pain of separation of body and soul, and (despite his resolve to withstand it) lost consciousness for an instant.

Sooner than before, he became aware of himself in the body of the god—and sooner than before he knew himself to be in total command of that invincible body.

He laughed aloud, and the sound made the very walls of the cavern shudder; a few cracks appeared at the sides of the tunnel. His only thought was to reach the surface, to succor his faithful armies, to destroy the hated Balzikkers and also pay his respects to that disloyal vassal, the Troikarch of Zebendu.

His appearance was greeted with cries of awe from the enemy and with cheers from the populace. The younger people of his nation had heard upon numerous occasions the tales of their elders without much belief. But even they knew, at once, that here was the secret weapon of their emperor, his ghastly, ghostly, godlike ally—and now, this time, the strength of that supernatural being was to be directed outward, rather than against dwellers in the city. There was not a person in the entire army of Posidon who did not feel somewhat like a miniature godling himself—invincible and unconquerable, as each followed this indomitable leader into battle.

The slaughter was indescribable. Initially, the Horned God began to crush those enemies who had penetrated into the city itself until once again the loyal defenders were in charge of the walls. Then the god loped out beyond the walls and rushed fiercely toward the foe where they stood massed upon the plains.

Within hours the siege was lifted, the leaders of the invading army were dead, and the vanquished foe itself, demoralized, was straggling as fast as possible away from the city and the kingdom.

Already, then, Karnunna had left to succor the allies of Hubbik Tombola at the capitol city of Balzikku; but that proved unnecessary. The gallant Third Army had been victorious. Pausing only to give instructions to the cheering survivors of that decimated unit, he hastened toward the city of Zebendu, to mete out vengeance upon the Troikarch.

Only three days were required to return the entire realm to a state of peace. Reparations had been demanded and received from the Empire of Balzikku, and Hubbik Tombola knew it would be a very long time before another invading army was dispatched into his realm from that land.

Again he returned to that chamber in the earth's bowels; again he went through the ritual, pronouncing the mighty phrase *utha uthgago,* again felt a mighty tearing at his soul and (despite his innermost resolve) again fainted.

But this time he regained consciousness to find himself still occupying the body of the Horned God. Bewildered at first, he realized gradually that he was immobile, trapped in the solid form of the idol, and entirely helpless to do aught but see straight before him. He could not even gain a glimpse of his own fleshly form upon the floor.

Then a sight that horrified him came slowly swimming into his area of vision. It was his own mortal body...still relatively young and vigorous, watching him, and casually dangling the medallion from his left hand.

He wanted to speak, to question what was happening, but no sound at all stirred the air in that deep cave.

Still, the other apparently understood well his feelings, for he spoke briefly.

"Perhaps," he smiled, "you were warned not to use this amulet more than once. Now you know why. I made the same error, long ago. I have lain here, going mad, for hundreds of years. I have been particularly anxious for the past twenty years, wondering if the time would ever come when you would again require the help of the Horned God, Karnunna." He smiled again, faintly, and before he turned to depart, spoke once more:

"Now at last I shall regain my rightful place as Emperor…for I was the first of your line!"

The panel closed behind him. Darkness descended.

THE GREAT HERO

The voices of the men in the tavern held a kind of frantic note, and they were more boisterous than ever, and possibly more drunken, upon that seventh evening before *Adventum.*

In other years, the tavern and indeed the entire Street of Merchants would have been festooned gaily with silver ribbons and jeweled banners; and the noise of the crowds in the midst of the great holiday fortnight would have been a joyous and carefree sound, pleasant to the ear and uplifting to the spirit. Even a runt of a thief, such as Joad Ul Riccim (for that was my name) could discover good cheer and merry laughter, and, mayhap, a buxom and willing wanton with whom to dawdle through a warm and lusty night.

But in this, the seventeenth year of the Cockatoo, a certain barbarian warrior named Iximantoc had cast a damper upon the annual celebration of the Ever-Rising Spirit. Iximantoc and his hellions from the rocky plains beyond the high mountains had invaded our soft land, and in the space of five weeks they had already taken and razed to the ground three of the principal cities of the realm of Quoraine. And at this very time, rumor had it, he was marching for our own capitol city of Quifilan, and was expected to arrive, with his army of several thousand strong, outside the city walls before the dawn of another day.

Though he had lost many of his men in his previous battle, Iximantoc had won his greatest victory there. Not only had he destroyed one of the finest of the armies of Quoraine, but (so the voices in the streets had whispered) one of his knights had transfixed and obliterated that celebrated hero of our land—the great Cavellaron Ul Tocco.

I had never laid eyes on this great hero, save for one time, nine years earlier—when I was but a lad of fourteen, thieving in the crowds that watched the triumphant procession of the king's army, as it returned from a successful battle in the west. A giant of a man was this Cavellaron, who went almost naked into battle when compared with his fellows who swathed themselves from head to toe in flexible armor coating woven from pliant steel. Cavellaron wore only the ancient breek-and-chest armor such as our ancestors had used five centuries before.

It was, indeed, whispered in the dark corridors of Quifilan that Cavellaron himself had lived in those ancient days. I had had one version of this story some years ago from a magician's apprentice, a raggedy fellow named Awauk Ul Montan, who told me in guarded tones, as we sat and quaffed rice-ale in the tavern of Wiccinan, of the truth of the matter.

This truth, as he knew it, involved the wizardry of an entire contingent of the king's mages—his own master being one of that company—and it included long rituals and fasts ending in human sacrifice, all to one end: the preservation of Cavellaron as a lusty youth in all his strength and cleverness. For the hero was not merely large, muscular, and lithe; but clever, and a battle strategist of the first water.

Without Cavellaron in our armies, our city appeared to be doomed.

And it was this awareness that lent a frantic overtone to the voices of the crowd that attempted to drown their knowledge of doom in drink and in joy.

Since the barbarian Iximantoc made no distinction between killing hero or slave, noble or thief, I had myself joined the city guard and was wearing the sword and dirk of the king. One's armor, however, must be purchased out of one's private funds. I had few private funds, since I had spent the proceeds of many successful robberies on the beauteous but fickle Usynna Ut Sanu, dancer in the Place of the Tides.

Now, I sat disconsolately in the low tavern of Wiccinan quaffing rice-ale, the most primitive of brews, and fingering my dwindling hoard of cash. That I still had any at all was due to the generosity of even this lowborn clientele, who had recognized me as one of the defenders of the city walls, and purchased the majority of my drinks.

Finishing my fourth mug of rice-ale, I made as if to signal to fat Ghonanna, the waitress and whore who served this tavern, when suddenly my attention was seized and held by a loud voice bawling:

"Riccim! Joad Ul Riccim, by the devils of Quoraine!"

My own name, bandied about in the midst of this trash?—I stared furiously across the heads of the sodden masses—to behold, strangely altered after five years, a familiar countenance.

"Montan!" I screamed back across the din of the crowd; but subsided when he put a hand to his lips in a sign to hold my tongue. Magicians, even more than thieves, are strangely averse to hearing their names, especially their true-born names, blared out in the midst of a public place. And I had known Awauk Ul Montan, son of a slave woman, as was I, long before we were old enough to smack each other with wooden swords in childish emulation of the soldiers of Quoraine. On occasion, I am told, we had suckled on the same pair of breasts.

But upon being taken into the clan of mages, he had in essence disappeared from the community that I frequented. If I had not known him from boyhood on, there would have been small chance of recognizing that ragged waif of fourteen or fifteen in this tall thin rangy fellow garbed in the imposing black and silver lace of a First Apprentice Wizard.

"Here you are at last," quoth this fellow, seating himself next to me upon the rough, scarred bench. Those around us automatically inched away, as one tends to do from a wizard, and he smiled grimly.

"Have you been seeking me?" I asked, as Montan easily caught the attention of the slut and his fine cool voice filtered through the cries of the low-born, ordering Sphinix brandy. She brought to him an entire litre of the cool violet tincture of the Western Pear; and he poured me a glass, and then himself, and toasted my health.

I swallowed it gratefully; it was good to get the taste of the rice-ale out of my mouth. He refilled my glass and I looked at him appraisingly.

"I observe," I said, "that your efforts during the nine years past have been crowned with no small success."

He smiled saturninely. "Yours, as well, have on occasion made tongues wag and hearts leap," he replied courteously. "Indeed, I was astonished to find you absent from the *Placo di Tides* and the side of the fair Ut Sanu. I am doubly astonished to see you wearing the sword and dirk of Quifilan."

I shrugged. One had had two choices: to run from Quifilan as fast as a Kha-mel could carry you; or to stay and defend her. Not owning a Kha-mel made the choice easier.

"Had I recked with the death of Cavellaron, I might even have risked stealing a Kha-mel from the herds of the guards."

He laughed, a delighted, normal laugh, much like the old ragged Montan that I remembered so well. "So that is why you have joined the city guards," he said. "Well, it is too late to run now. We must both stay and fight it out."

"Why is it," I brooded, sipping mournfully at my Sphinix, "that swords always turn out to be more powerful than spells? Even though the old saying has it otherwise."

"The wand is mightier than the rapier? One can guess, at least among what manner of folk that saying originated."

I knew he wanted something of me. A wizard of the first class would never seek out one such as I in a low tavern like Wiccinan's merely to renew an old friendship, certainly. We had aways been wary of each other. Now was a time to be doubly wary, I felt.

Well, if he wanted something, he would have to initiate the bargaining; I was willing to sit and wait and drink his Sphinix brandy.

"Are you in excellent health?" was his first question after a pregnant pause. I alleged that I was. I suffered from neither pox nor the leaping sickness; nor suffered I from the potions of the self-proclaimed physicians which could kill a healthy man sooner than a poniard, and I leave it to your own imagination what they could accomplish when prescribed for one who is ill.

"Are you a true patriot?" was the next query; and I was ready for that one. "No less true than thou, old brother and mighty wizard."

He frowned. He gazed penetratingly at me, but officers of the peace-squad had often gazed at me in just that way, and with no better results. He finally nodded to himself, and smiled what was meant to be a winning and friendly smile. I shuddered within but did not exhibit any outward emotion.

"The king has need of such as you, tonight," he spoke. "It will mean more silver and gold, and precious gems, than you could steal in a lifetime. Especially in a short lifetime," he added, and in the instant I saw that he was armed with a Ffyve.

A Ffyve is perhaps an animal, or perhaps something less or more, which is to be found in a wild state many thousands of miles north of our own shores. It is extremely poisonous, but in its native habitat it is not more dangerous than any ordinary poisonous snake, for it is lethargic. Under the control of a magician, however, it is swift and silent, and can be hurled like a miniature dart to kill painfully and quickly.

"I've rarely seen Ffyves," I commented coolly, drinking the last of my current glass of brandy. "Interesting looking creatures. So small, yet so deadly. Well—had I not wished to serve the king, I would not have joined the guard."

"Very good. Then follow me, and be wary."

Had Montan been an ordinary man—or even a Hero—I could have slipped from behind him in the crowds, and effectively disappeared into the dingy alleys and corridors of this part of the city, which I knew well, surely better than Montan did; for such things change in a span of even a few years. But I dared not try such a maneuver in this case; and the Sphinix brandy had worked its usual low-level kind of magic upon my brain—I felt both brave and curious. Entirely sober, I would merely have felt curious; I am neither brave nor cowardly, only sensible.

I followed my magician friend through a maze of streets until I saw that he was leading me, by a circuitous route, to the temple of Bel-Mazzadon, a major deity of a minor religious sect of whom much was bruited about and little known for certain. Adherents of the god Bel-Mazzadon were said to eschew both drinks and sexual pleasure of all kinds, which makes it unlikely that our paths would ever cross.

The night was dark; clouds mantled the sky and blotted out the light of the moon and stars. Possibly Iximantoc and his hordes would put off attacking our city tomorrow; it was known that he liked his astrologers to sift omens and predict a victorious outcome before he attacked in earnest. Or possibly they had already made their predictions on the previous night. There was no way of knowing for certain.

When Montan beckoned to me, I saw that he had opened a tiny oddly-shaped door at the rear of the temple building, a door I had occasionally passed and wondered about. It had no handle or keyhole, and I had supposed, in my folly, that it could be opened only from within. But there seemed to be no one within to have opened it, although the blackness outside was only slightly more impenetrable than the greyness within.

I hesitated—then fell, dizzily, across the threshold, cursing myself for a fool.

I had been on the alert for wizardry or simple physical treachery. But Montan had done something even more elementary. He had doped the brandy.

* * * *

My view of the inside of the Temple of Bel-Mazzadon was perhaps the best in the house. Yet I would gladly have exchanged places with even the eldest of the elderly priests who clustered about below me. I was fastened securely within the metallic grip of the idol of Bel-Mazzadon, and several of the lesser priests were scurrying about me, attaching oddly shaped amulets to various parts of my body.

I was entirely naked. The amulets pierced my skin; their backs were multiply fanged; but I felt little pain, presumably because I was still partially under the effects of the drug Montan had given me. A weird pulsating light filled the interior of the temple; it shifted colors slowly, bathing the scene first in blood red, then in squeamish ochre, then in a succession of rainbow colors, ending in a blueish purple glow that looked like an entrance to the caves of Hel.

I could not cry out; my vocal cords seemed frozen; and then another wave of fear went through my body as I realized that I could not move at all. It is one thing to be tied to an idol; another, to be unable to resist. Even where resistance is hopeless, its possibility helps lift the spirits.

The rest seems, now, like a dream; but it was reality, to that I can attest. They tortured me. The torture had a certain intellectual appeal. They had made me insensitive to small hurts, by drugging me, so they had to resort to bizarre means to excite the pain centers of my body and brain. I saw and felt them stretching my limbs into grotesque shapes, I saw and felt them washing my body in acids that seemed to burn like fiery lava. With gigantic needles they injected me with fluids intended to seek out and stimulate every cell of my body; and that was the ultimate in pain.

Near the end, I fathomed the true purpose of that drug with which they had numbed my body. It was to keep my brain alive and true until the end; to keep me entirely cognizant of every indignity and every painful operation performed upon my sad flesh.

I couldn't help wondering *why:* even in the final minutes when at last I defeated them and swam down into the dregs of darkness where I curled up and lay, shuddering at the depths of human depravity.

My last wish was that I had had a clean death in the fight against Iximantoc. Barbarian and murderer of babes though he was, he did not torture men with the cleverness of those priests of a degenerate god. He was a warrior.

* * * *

"He is a warrior!"

I turned my head and stared down at the speaker. I was hard put to recall his name. Yes…Montan. Awauk Ul Montan. I looked at him warily, for I never trusted these priests, these magicians, these toadies to gods out of Hel's lowest dungeons.

"I know him," I replied in a booming, confident tone. For some reason I was surprised to hear the sound of my own voice; but why should I be? It hadn't changed.

"You have been ill; but now you are well once more," intoned the priest. Fool! I knew that; could I not feel the power surging up the muscles of my arms; the lithe quickness in my legs; the sureness of my stride.

"He is a warrior, and I shall seek him out and challenge him." He will accept the challenge, perhaps, I thought. Although he had defeated me the last time…my thoughts tailed off. I could not recall the fight, yet I was certain he had defeated me. I continued to be pensive, ignoring the last minute rallying cries of my comrades, ignoring even the cheers of the populace thronging the walls and high places, as they saw that I was not dead.

I leapt aboard my charger, the white horse Dolyeyee, one of the few war horses in this city large enough to carry my bulk, and cantered out to do battle with the barbarians. They had not attacked today, and were holding back to make preparations for a siege. Since they evidently felt this day was unlucky for them, we on our part felt the opposite. Unlucky for them meant lucky for us.

We galloped toward them in attack formation. That was when total recall struck me.

The last words of the magician Awauk Ul Montan burned in my brain. "Joad, my friend," he had said, "you think I have done you a great wrong; and perhaps I have. Yet this is an opportunity for which many would yield their souls. For five hundred years, we of this temple have kept alive the legendary hero of our people, not by the sort of magic that is talked about in the streets and in the alleys of the slums, but by another kind of wizardry. The original hero died centuries ago; but the great god Bal-Mazzadon, to whom he was a lay acolyte, has provided substitutes. Through the ages have men come to us and been flayed, willingly, into the image of the hero. He who was to come tonight was killed in a street battle; and so I have chosen you in his stead. Such men must have courage enough to fill the breast of a hero, and sense enough to conduct themselves as a hero should. You were my choice and you shall fill me with pride."

Awauk Ul Montan, I thought to myself as I rode, I shall fill your belly with my sword.

"Your lifetime will be short," the mage had said, "but for perhaps fifteen years—if you survive your battles—you, scrawny Joad Ul Riccim, will be the largest, strongest, bravest, most ferocious and cleverest warrior of the ages."

Cursing him, I rode into battle to face Iximantoc—I, the great hero, Cavellaron Ul Tocco, Cavellaron the Undying. The populace that lined the walls, and each soldier of the army, and even the staff of generals cheered and gestured in their adulation. And great waves of superstitious fear smote the opposing army, as one whom they had seen killed rose again as powerful as before; and you could watch them cringe in the face of our charge.

Victory was inevitable and glorious.

IN THE TEMPLE OF PHTHATHNEE

Too befuddled to know what to do, I meekly allowed the two large females to clutch me by the arms, frog-walk me to the doorway, and toss me feet-first into the gutter.

The smaller of the two, hardly a finger less than six feet tall, weighed perhaps 180 pounds. The other looked at least six feet or more, and she probably topped the scale at 240 pounds stripped. And she must have been quite a sight, stripped; one I did not hanker for seeing.

When I landed in the muck, I twisted my ankle badly. I cursed. In all my travels throughout Quoraine and the lands to the north, I had never before encountered female bouncers. They were incompetent. A pair of men would have thrown me out on the seat of my pants, and at worst I would have struck my head and suffered for a day or two from double vision.

But what use is a swordsman with a fractured ankle? I retched, producing a half-pint of filthy rice-ale, which spiced the already nauseating collection of garbage in which I sprawled. Then I explored my left leg with anxious fingers. Perhaps the bone was not truly broken; but it hurt, and I could not walk. So I crawled out of the gutter onto the pebbled walkway and sat glaring fiercely at the closed doors of the Tavern of Swords.

Had I been Zeukadon, whose eyes can pierce stone, thunderbolts would have razed the structure to the ground. But I was only Juddik Ul Mathorn, itinerant swordsman, poet, and musician, and all that happened was that my eyes started to water, and I had to blink furiously to retain my clarity of vision.

Suddenly, so suddenly that she might have been formed on the instant from the air itself, a third female appeared. This one, however, was more pleasing to the eye; about two fingers short of five feet, with hair braided in the manner of a child, soft silky blonde hair of the sort that the brawny Vuikoings possess. But she was no child, for the dark tunic that entirely covered her figure yet bulged most pleasingly at breast and hip.

I could not help yielding her my most gallant smile of approval and admiration. She, on her part, looked surprised, but stopped and examined me carefully.

"I wish that I could rise in order that I might bow down again before one so lovely as thou, princess of the dusk," I intoned in the traditional, but rather archaic, courtly dialect. "Juddik Ul Mathorn at thy service."

She laughed delightedly, taking it for a jest, as it was meant, and said, more mundanely, "Are you badly injured?" I explained my plight.

She nodded.

"Could you walk if you were not so badly…hurt?" she asked, then—intimating, of course, that I might be sodden with brandy or another of the more nefarious concoctions for which the Tavern of Swords is justly famous.

Indignantly I claimed to be sober; and the claim was not far from the truth, since pain and upchucking had combined to clear my head.

"Then," said the delicious creature in the courtly manner, "come thou with me, and I shall offer thee tidbits of grape and pomegranate and bowls of Sphinix wine."

And she actually bent to assist me in rising.

Though small and slender (save where breast and hip swelled enticingly), she was not without a certain wiry strength. With some effort, she succeeded in aiding me to rise and stand, tottering, on my one good leg.

I looked doubtfully at the wench. "How far do you propose that we travel?" I asked. The stench of the gutter clung to my clothing, and some of its juices now stained her own garment. But she ignored this entirely, and allowed me to put my left arm about her shoulders so that my damaged leg need not support more than a small fraction of my weight.

"Not far, brave warrior," she replied. She hid a slight smile by turning away to survey the street, and I was not certain whether she intended sarcasm or merely spoke simple truth. It seemed unlikely that this young girl of the streets had heard the name of Juddik Ul Mathorn, but I had been rather active in repelling bandits two weeks earlier when the Prince of Quelinon had been picnicking at his summer palace on the Brein…and my name might not be entirely unknown to a young woman, who daydreamed of valiant heroes and warrior-princes...

I allowed her to help me and we made our way slowly along the Street of the Grapes, turning next down the Street of Merchants and then, another block later, the Alley of Serpents.

I enjoyed the touch of her body solidly upon mine, but made no effort to take advantage of the situation, for several reasons. The most obvious reason was the fact that she might resist my advances in the simplest way—by letting go her support of me, thereby toppling me once more into a gutter. To be cast twice of an evening into the gutters of Quelinon, and by women, was too monstrous a possibility to provoke. Secondly, I allowed myself to imagine that she might already be favorably disposed toward me—or why else had she come to my aid, when a typical harlot of the streets might well have tried to rob me as I lay there puking. Thirdly, I kept envisioning those tidbits and that brandy she had promised (for Sphinix wine is not wine at all, but a delicious brandy concocted from the juices of the Western Pear, a hybrid fruit incorporating the finest characteristics of both the plum and the ordinary, or garden-variety, pear).

I decided, as we walked, that my ankle was not actually broken. The pain had subsided to an extent, and I was able to bear more of my weight upon my left leg as we went. True, this might result in prolonged agony on the next day; yet I found it prudent to try to walk normally, for we passed at a late hour along streets rarely patrolled by the King's Guardians. It would not do for anyone to suppose that I was other than a healthy swordsman strolling with his arm rather amorously about his harlot. Helpless men do not long survive in those back alleys of Quelinon. Once or twice I let my right hand rest lightly upon the hilt of my sword, but we were not molested.

When my guide turned toward a small, dingy building, partially isolated from its neighbors by tall wooden fence posts, my curiosity was aroused. "Is this not the temple of Phthathnee?" I asked in a low voice.

"It is," came the musical response. "Do you fear the virgin goddess, then?"

"Nay," I replied carefully. "Though she may not entirely approve of one such as I." I winced as we made our way up a flight of stone steps, for it became harder for her to continue supporting my weight in a stable manner. "But I must admit…" and I hesitated, but went on boldly… "that I might have been more pleased if you had been an acolyte of the goddess Shebaree."

Phthathnee, as you know, is a virgin goddess (the means by which she birthed the twins Zelphon and Zelphaz being a part of the inner mysteries of the order). Shebaree, on the other hand, is the goddess of harlots and also of the spring. At many vernal festivals I had enjoyed worshipping together with Shebaree's votaries, who dress to emulate her and copulate with every man who so desires. The sect of Phthathnee, on the other hand, was very small and relatively mysterious; I suspected, but did not truly know, that her priestesses were as virginal as she.

The girl seemed flustered at first…then smiled as if I had complimented her (which was true). She said, "Yes, you must not meet many young women who so nicely fit into your arms."

That was a sweet, but not altogether laudatory, reference to my stature. I am less than five feet and a hand tall.

Now, many men and many women have chuckled at my lack of full height; yet I am twenty nine years of age, and have managed to survive successfully in a world filled with danger. Although I am relatively short, I have killed many taller men, for I am faster on my feet and I am deceptively strong. My sword is actually more of a rapier, although it has a cutting edge as well. I designed it myself, and the famous smith Zanzinan forged it personally in my presence, so pleased was he to hear my celebrated (but then brand new) epic concerning Zanzinan and the maidens of Malinori.

Unfortunately, my fighting style demands above all entirely healthy arms and legs, so the troublesome accident to my ankle was more debilitating to me than it might have been to some brawnier hero who could sit upon a stone and swing a nine-foot broadsword round his head all day long.

Without a weapon, I am not an insignificant opponent either, for I have studied the methods of unarmed combat perfected by the natives of Xanxhi—a large country of men of small stature and yellow-tinged skin color, which is located so far to the northwest that in Quoraine it is not even whispered of in legend. In the cities to the east of the empire of Quoraine, one or two bulky wrestlers had found to their astonishment that their solid muscles and their simple art were of no use against my tactics. In one case, when a rogue pilfered my sword while I slept in the fields, I even managed to disarm him before giving him a lesson in elementary Khu Xana-hi, which left him alive but (unfortunately for him) with a broken neck bone. I never learned if he survived; probably not.

On occasions I have attempted to explain, as I have done for you, what my abilities and talents really are; but most people simply laugh, if they are rude, or else avert their gaze and change the subject, if they are polite. So I have become accustomed to ignoring the sly remarks of others, as long as they can be ignored with honor, letting my deeds speak for themselves. Yet do I tell you these things, that you shall know me for who and what I am.

At the top of the steps she helped me to lean my weight against a pillar, and went for succor, tripping with light feet and a broad smile into the interior of the temple.

The two women who came to assist me were much older and more staid in manner than my sweet nymph, although they were not uncomely. They helped me to a small room deep within the temple, where I was given a pallet to lie upon and await the promised tidbits and Sphinix brandy.

"Serannia will return soon," they promised.

At least now I had finally learned her name!

Unfortunately I was exhausted; if my priestess did come to me that night, I did not know it, lout that I was. In three minutes I was sound asleep, and (if the spiteful jests of various companions may be credited) snoring ferociously.

In the morning my ankle felt better. The priestesses had provided me with a solid, heavy walking stick, that I might hobble about if I should wish. I also received a change of clothing and a bath. The bath was not as luxurious as a king might be accustomed to, but was considerably better than a cold plunge in a stream, which was more nearly my own custom.

They had also dressed my ankle with a bundle of leaves and herbs which I presumed to have restorative powers; and truly the pain was only annoying if I tried to put excessive weight upon it.

At times, during that afternoon, it seemed to me that my experience of the previous night must have been a dream; that my desirable young priestess (Serannia) was but an invention of my own mind. Yet, I reminded myself, here I was, still in the temple of Phthathnee, being clothed and fed and ministered to by her own priestesses.

Being compelled to remain at rest because of a weak ankle is anathema to one as normally active as I; yet I made the best of it, composing in my mind a series of poems praising the beauty and grace of Serannia, and not neglecting from prudence to devise one poem, though slightly inferior, celebrating the goddess Phthathnee. For goddesses are ever women foremost and deities second; and goddesses have been known to be jealous of mere mortals on certain occasions.

I was dozing lightly on my pallet, after the cerebral strain of versifying, when I heard a light clinking sound, and awoke. A swift glance about my narrow cell indicated no one; the room was dimly lit, but my eyes were well accustomed to the low level of illumination. And yet—and yet, the tiny table only two feet from my pallet was no longer bare, but was laden with dishes of fruit and nut-bread.

I blinked my eyes and stirred myself into a sitting position, wincing at the twinge in my ankle; I had momentarily forgotten my injury. Yet that small pain reminded me that this was no dream, no vision. And then I beheld a sight to make me gasp aloud—a bowl of Sphinix brandy being delicately borne across the room and gently placed on the table immediately before me. I could see the decanter and the two small glasses as clearly as I could discern the fruit; but by what agency they appeared I could not imagine.

I gasped as the bowl, seemingly of its own volition, rose and dipped and poured out two glasses of Sphinix wine…one of which then seemed to offer itself almost into my very fingers. Not knowing whether to grasp it or shrink away in mortal terror, I hesitated; then, mostly because I needed that drink very badly at this instant, I clutched at the glass. There was a fleet touch of—fingers?—brushing mine; and then the fiery brandy was warming my throat and searching out my innards.

The action was repeated again, and yet again. I grew lightheaded, for I had not eaten since the previous noon. I stared as hard as I could to try to determine what manner of creature shared my room with me; but it was perfectly invisible.

"Can you still not see me!" The speaker was exasperated; yet the tone was familiar, and I realized after a moment that my companion spoke with the voice of Serannia. She gave a cry of annoyance, and there came a noise that might be associated with the sound of a small female stamping her foot in petty anger…and then another full glass came toward my lips once more—overshot my trembling hand—and smashed right into my nose.

My nose was an especially tender organ, as a natural outcome of the altercation of the previous evening. The sharp blow brought tears to my eyes; and I blinked, involuntarily, several times rapidly.

And the figure of Serannia swam into focus, fluttered a bit, and then clarified.

"Serannia!" I cried, foolishly. "It *is* you!"

The expression of anger on her face melted into a smile that made me forgive her at once for bruising my nose and splashing just a tittle of brandy upon my collar. Her hair was undone and floated, golden, like an aura behind her. She was clad in quite a fetching costume. Although it was more sedate than the garments worn by tavern bawds, it did reveal the delicate swelling above the two perfect mounds that were her breasts, and the slits in her gown provided glimpses of smooth creamy thighs that set my blood boiling and made my breath come faster.

"So you can see me now, man," was her comment after a moment's silent inspection.

"More of you than I was able to see last night, though not as much as I—" I did not finish the speech, for I recalled where I was and to whom I spoke. Still, she completed it to herself, mentally, and then gradually smiled.

Offering me a slice of nut bread lavishly o'erspread with cow's butter and tartberry jam, she sat down provocatively close to me on the pallet and took a slice herself. She made no sound when I daringly put my right arm around her waist, holding the bread in my left hand and munching delicately.

She hesitated. "You are truly Juddik Ul Mathorn?" she asked.

"I am he," I replied, squeezing her thigh very gently and with only the very slightest tinge of carnal intent. She removed my hand, replacing it upon her waist, and held it there with her own.

"He who fought for the Prince of Quelinon that day on the Brein?"

"I am he," I replied once more.

"Oft times story and song embellish the deeds of an ordinary man," she muttered doubtfully.

"Particularly when the man himself composes and sings them." I smiled agreeably.

"Then you are he—warrior, poet, and minstrel, so I am told."

"Did you know me yesterday, then? Did you seek me out?"

She shook her head. "I sought you, or one like you; but I did not know you then. Still, knowledge, when desired, is not difficult to attain, if one is an acolyte of the goddess."

I was disappointed, slightly. "So you are indeed a priestess of the Virgin Goddess," I muttered. "And therefore…"

She laughed, a golden sound. "…and therefore, a virgin myself," she finished my thought aloud.

"Ah, but there are mysteries," I muttered, thinking of the twin sons of the Virgin Goddess Phthathnee. She pressed my hand.

Dinner was most pleasant, even though I did not seriously expect it to end in quite the same manner as a meal with a votary of Shebaree. Yet before my delightful rescuer left, she allowed me a long and stimulating kiss, and did not flinch when I caressed the voluptuous nipples that threatened to pierce the front of her gold and silver-hued garment. When I would have held her longer, she twisted away with a laugh, breathless with the same joy that I felt, and ran off.

Some time afterward, as I consoled myself with the final glass of Sphinix brandy, the two older priestesses came and stood silently over me.

"The High Priestess of Phthathnee will now receive you," announced one of them rather coldly. I got up clumsily. Using my walking stick as well as I could after imbibing nearly a flask of brandy, I followed them slowly through a complicated set of passageways. I could not help thinking that I should have treated Serannia less lustily—not that the lass had objected—but clearly, spies had been set to watch us.

The high priestess was ancient—she looked at least ninety, maybe older. She was seated in a chair laced with spun gold. She wore a white robe, the symbol of virginity and also of the moon. She was roughly the same height as Serannia, and I thought I detected a family resemblance. Being a virgin, she could not have birthed a direct line leading to Serannia—could she? But my golden nymph could easily have been her great-niece. Now I was truly beginning to worry again.

She spoke. "Juddik Ul Mathorn," she queried in a high, parched tone, "would you be of assistance to us and to the goddess Phthathnee?"

"If I can be," I spoke, showing no hint of my foreboding. "As you have assisted me, so would I return good for good."

"Well spoken," was the rejoinder. "What do you think of Se-rannia?" There was no expression in that lined face, but I thought I detected just the hint of a twinkle in the eyes.

I breathed deeply. "I love her," I said simply.

This seemed to take her aback; the truth often does, when one's questioner is anticipating lies or slight evasions. I used to work the same trick upon my own mother when I was a lad—not all the truth, of course, but enough to lend credence to whatever else I might say.

"And yet," she finally said, smiling, "you have never actually seen her."

I gaped at her and my thoughts tumbled back to that moment when the invisible servitor poured my brandy. Would you believe I had temporarily forgotten about that outré performance, so ob-sessed was I with Serannia's own sweet person?

"Have you ever heard the expression, *walking the air?*" the high priestess then asked.

"Yes," I said after a moment's pause for thought. Air-walkers, I knew, were said to be earth-bound spirits, loosed from the bodies of adepts to walk the sky, or the earth, or wherever they wished to walk. No dungeon could hold them in or keep them out. Thus it was, I had heard, that the marvelous poet Brinacian obtained from the two Walled-In-Princes of Patheron the particulars of their sad lot. After he composed an epic containing such precise information concerning their plight, the usurper King, Bathrion the Bold, had had all three assassinated within the year.

She went on. "Only a very few adepts can air-walk; it requires infinite patience and infinite pains, and a peculiar inborn ability. This is a talent at present shared only by myself and Serannia— only the two of us among this entire temple of thirty-eight priest-esses of Phthathnee."

I faced her down and spoke with passion: "Do not try to tell me that Serannia was air-walking—first, no man can see an air-walker, except he be another air-walker himself; second," I hesitated, and my eyes fell from hers... "second, I know what women-flesh feels like when I hold it in my arms!"

I was expecting a sermon. Instead, the high priestess laughed.

"You are a most intriguing man," she said. "You have not lied to me yet, and we have been conversing for at least five minutes!"

"Why is it," I gave her a sidelong look, "that priests and priestesses of the noblest and most praiseworthy of deities ofttimes display the most cynical of views?"

She did not accept the bait; although there were few priests, priestesses, or mages, among those whom I have met, who could resist a metaphorical or metaphysical discussion, especially when it relates either to the habits of their kind or the deficiencies of the common man.

"You," she said bluntly, "bear the power to see an air-walker. It was in hopes of finding such a person that dear Serannia walked the streets of Quelinon last evening, as she has done for the entire seven days since the defection of the Priestess Saunaura Ut Naisa. On occasion, certain sensitive non-adepts can detect an air-walker, and we desperately needed someone with that ability. We have begged your aid, and you have pledged."

I nodded, too surprised and confused to question her further at that instant.

"There seems to be a flaw in your ability, however," she pointed out, "in that you appear to be capable of this mysterious astral vision only when moderately intoxicated. Serannia had to feed you several cups of Sphinix wine before you could see her."

"Then," I gasped, "she was air-walking all that time! But she was solid flesh." I flushed and added quickly "—otherwise, she could not have helped me to the temple last night; or even poured me a glass of brandy."

The high priestess then provided me with a brief description of the basic qualities of air-walkers. It was a state in which the adept could move from room to room and place to place, even through walls, by an effort of will. However, Serannia had had to open the door to my cell in order to enter, since she could not will the brandy and glasses through the wall along with her. Thus, if air-walkers bore a sword or dagger, planning an assassination, they would have to enter rooms by natural means; and they were likewise susceptible to wounds themselves when attempting to wield such weapons.

A thought struck me. "Clothing," I said, thinking of Serannia, and wondering how she could walk through walls in that dress, while, indeed, thinking of her walking through walls without it.

The priestess nodded. "The air-walker does not wear additional clothing, but appears in the same costume that the body of the adept actually wears during the procedure. An interesting fact, but one which need not concern you now—the ancient adept, Andersol Ul Pinia, wrote at length upon the phenomenon. Provided that the clothing contains no metallic element, the form of the air-walker is precisely the same as the physical appearance of the adept, at least in the case of the very young adept."

"And if I should strike an air-walker with my fist or with my sword—say, even, a fatal sword-thrust—would the adept take injury from this deed?"

"The air-walker is impervious to small hurts; but death in such a form is yet death. The mortal body of the adept ceases to live upon the instant that the air-walker is injured fatally."

She paused for a moment.

"But come. Enough of explanation and philosophy. You will aid us?" Once again I affirmed my willingness to be of service.

"You may name your reward if we are successful in our purpose." She hesitated. "…Gold? Jewels? We have much in the way of earthly riches."

I looked at the old crone steadfastly.

"Naturally I could use some funds, enough earthly riches to care for my more earthly requirements, such as food and shelter. But you surely know the reward I would truly claim, if it were indeed possible."

"Ah?" Something appeared to strike her as humorous. "You would, then, bed our Serannia?"

I nodded solemnly.

"Would you even wed the wench, then," she asked slyly, peering at me sideways, "if that were possible?"

I shook my head. "How can a man such as I marry? Women love homes, children, and husbands contentedly sitting by the hearth; minstrels and poets make poor husbands."

"Unbelievable." I thought I heard her mutter in a very low voice: "Ten minutes and not yet a lie. What a marvelous man!" But I was not certain I really heard her say that; it may have been but the silky rustle of her voluminous robes as she shifted position in her chair.

* * * *

I sat on a hassock outside the Door of Minor Votaries. I had sat there for an entire night, the previous one, without incident; and now it was nearly the middle of the second night. I yawned. I had not seen Serannia since my interview with the High Priestess, and I longed for the touch of her. I must have been truly besotted, for even the brush of her fingers against mine would have been most welcome.

There were two doors to the Chamber of Worship. The Door of Minor Votaries let into a kind of dressing room (from what little I could gather) behind the left side of the altar of Phthathnee. Beyond the Chamber of Worship was the Door of Major Votaries, which also opened onto a smaller room, and then onto the right side of the altar.

Stationed at these two entrances into the Sacred Chamber—which could be reached in no other manner—were Serannia (so I was told) and I. We were the guardians, on watch for two intruding air-walkers: the renegade priestess Saunaura Ut Naisa and a former priest of the Dawn Flame, Pinthr Ul Jorsca by name.

It seemed these two had been a major force behind that recent coup attempt on the Prince of Quelinon…when I had fought in his defense at the Brein.

Now this lawless pair intended to steal the sacred bauble used by the High Priestess in the Ultimate Ceremony of Phthathnee, a two-day ritual that was performed once every twelve-day by the priestesses, and which assisted them in maintaining their virtues and powers over nature. Not only would such a theft have unpredictable repercussions on the plane of the gods, but it would lead to serious consequences for mortals—particularly the Prince—since it would give the renegade priest and priestess an unimaginable fountainhead of power. Such power were best not used for ill; and how else would such a pair seek to employ it?

Thus had I been convinced of the extreme importance of my watch…although it was the thought of my reward that kept me ready for their onslaught.

Nearby sat three hefty women armed with swords and bucklers—not as brawny as the bouncers who had flung me from the Tavern of Swords and caused my injury; but very competent-looking. Since I could yet but hobble painfully on my unsound ankle, they were there to assist me. I was to be their eyes, and thus render the invisible visible; Serannia, with three other female guardians, performed the same service at the other portal; and presumably the High Priestess was now conducting the second half of the two-day Ultimate Service of Phthathnee. Even through two closed doors I fancied I could detect the chant of the priestesses as they intoned the ritual in unison.

Needless to say, I was rather drunk…

…and that is why I did not react swiftly when the sword swooped down out of nothingness to gash the throat of one of the women. A dagger followed it, spraying the blood of a second guard over the floor. The third woman was holding her sword on guard, backing away and peering helplessly at the unseen.

For my part—I gaped, took a swig of brandy, and gaped once more—but saw nothing. In my befuddlement I slid off my hassock with the intention of joining the fray, and put my full weight on my ankle.

Next instant I sprawled on the floor, smashing my tender nose and loosening a tooth or two. The pain of my nose and my ankle cleared my head a little. Blinking away the tears, I rolled to a sitting position—

—and saw them! A youngish woman with dark hair dressed in a nondescript close-fitting tunic, and armed with a dagger; and a short, stocky man with rumpled brown hair, who grasped a bloodied sword in his left hand. He was garbed in the accouterments of a priest: long flowing robes and a scarlet turban.

Limping, I moved toward the uneven battle that raged in the corner. The man was biding his time until he could slide his sword through the guard's defensive pattern without danger to himself.

I had the presence of mind to pretend that I was going to her defense, rather than aiming to attack her assailant. Only at the last minute did I turn toward him, and with a swift motion thrust him through the chest.

I was thinking, then, that a visible man is just as invisible to an invisible man as an invisible man is to a visible man if the invisible man thinks the visible man cannot see him, only in this case he could…as you see, my thoughts were admittedly incoherent. The slight relaxation of tension that followed my successful dispatch of the swordsman had reopened the gate, so to speak; I was smashed again. I could almost swear the whole thing was a drunken hallucination, as the man's body slowly vanished—except for the sight of the two bodies of the woman guards on the floor.

Finally in my stupor I recalled the priestess, and looked around; but she had opened the door to the next room and slipped inside, leaving it ajar. I lurched after her, yelling to the surviving guard to sound an alarm.

Men were not actually forbidden the inner chamber, but male guests at the Ultimate Ceremony were seldom invited—unless of course His Royal Highness should express a desire to be present. Thus, when I burst open the door to the Chamber of Worship, I was met with a glare of horrified eyes from the sea of virgins within.

The woman I followed had made an error. She should have dressed in the same garb as the others—then I would not have identified her so easily—but I picked her out at once. She was silently, invisibly stealing upon the Second High Priestess who was performing the ceremony at the center of the dais.

Abruptly the other door burst open and the running figure of Serannia appeared. She took in the scene at once and quickly leapt forward, snatching the sacred amulet from the Second High Priestess, just as the interloper was about to grab it herself.

"Kill her!" she cried to me, and I hobbled forward, sword in hand, to confront the intruder.

"But—how can you see me!?!" shrieked the thief. It was not an unreasonable question. As far as she knew, her companion had murdered us all, without being detected by my gaze. But it was the wrong time and place for questions and answers.

At the last minute, I found myself unable to slash her with my blade, and instead brought my walking stick down upon her head. She had essayed to levitate, and was actually a foot above the altar when I reached up and struck her with the cudgel. Her limp form dropped like a leaf, drifting gradually toward the floor, at last coming to rest at Serannia's feet.

Serannia ripped the dagger from her hand and stabbed her once in the heart. Blood squirted from the wound—then both blood and body vanished from our sight like dissipating fog.

"Now we are safe!" she cried. "The traitress is dead."

I nodded soberly. The cold-blooded murder did not faze me, though I myself had not wished to kill a woman, even an evil woman, in that manner. Here indeed was a mistress with determination and courage to do that which she must—and soon, if the high priestess had not lied, she would be mine.

* * * *

When the knock sounded on the door to my small room, I sat up on the pallet and called to her to enter. I was certain it would be Serannia; but it was not. It was, instead, the High Priestess. The aged crone moved over to the pallet and sat down next to me.

"You performed well," she spoke, "although it was as a seeing-eye that you were to serve, and not as a gory defender of the faith."

I told her the truth—I had figured out by now that it was not the brandy alone which caused me to see the air-walkers, but the tears that welled up in my eyes in involuntary response to pain. I touched my bruised nose, now swollen to half again its normal size, and the High Priestess emitted an involuntary giggle—an incongruous sound for one of her station and maturity to produce.

"Now you wish to claim your reward," she said quietly.

I nodded in assent.

"I have a surprise for you, Juddik Ul Mathorn. I have never told you my name. I am Serannia Ut Rasa."

I grunted. "Do you then seek to fob me off with a simple twisting of names? A kind of pun? You knew as well as I the precise Serannia whom I meant when we spoke the other day."

"You do not find me as appetizing?" She laughed in her cracked voice. I could not help feeling a twinge of sadness at what the years had done to one who had once doubtless been as beautiful as my own Serannia...and what they would, likewise, inevitably do in the future to Serannia herself. And to me, of course.

But she went on, sternly: "It is no trick. You did not see me present in the chamber at the evening ceremony. The Second High Priestess conducted it. That is because I, Serannia, guarded the second door. It was I, Serannia, who plunged the dagger into the heart of that accursed traitress!"

I shook my head in bewilderment.

She ran her hands over her shriveled figure. "This mortal husk has withered like a dried fruit after the passing of autumn; but the creature within—the essence of me, the spirit, which is manifested as an air-walker: that spirit never ages beyond a certain point. Air-walkers, like souls, are ever youthful."

I know truth when I hear it. I laughed. I enjoy a good jest, even if it happens to be on myself—though naturally I enjoy it even better if someone else is the butt.

"Very well," I said. "I was promised Serannia for a mistress, and now I have her." I forced a grin. "As you said, in speaking of your mortal husk—there is a certain amount of withering. However," I added impishly, "I recall a certain Benjm Ul Farkln, a close friend of mine in years bygone, who always recommended older women as being best of all to lie with. He was contemptuous of my predilection for youngish girls; he claimed that an old woman was like an old wine, and that once I had experienced the delights of love with such a mistress I would never again want aught to do with merely nubile girls."

She stared at me quizzically.

"However," I went on, sliding my arm about her shoulders, "I hope you will not be offended if I suggest that it will be more romantic to dim the candlelight."

"Wait!" she said. "We shall eat and drink first, like civilized lovers," and she cackled leeringly at me.

"I am as putty in your hands," I said.

When she had gone to arrange for food and drink, I remained sitting for a long time—considering whether to make a mad dash for the street, or whether Benjm Ul Farkln might have known more than I gave him credit for…and whether I might profitably take his advice at least this one time.

As I sat, pondering, there suddenly came a giggle, and a sharp blow struck my poor swollen nose and brought tears to my eyes for the second time that night. Serannia—my young Serannia—my young nude Serannia—stood before me laughing.

I beckoned to her and she danced into my arms.

It was considerably later, as we finally began to enjoy our repast, that a stray thought entered my mind. While not a theologian by any means, I realized that I had gained considerable insight into the innermost mystery of the cult of Phthathnee—namely, the means by which a virgin goddess might have conceived and borne twin sons.

MEMORY

"It happened somewhere around here, Jill," I said, peering about.

The landscape was arid, strewn with boulders…like an artist's conception of the moon. Bleak!—to describe it in one word. Yet the history books say, and I knew, that this territory was lush and fruitful thousands of years ago.

Gillian Miles followed me patiently over the edge of a small rocky hill and down to a hollow where a few scrubby trees tried to find nourishment but were barely managing.

Gillian is nobody's idea of a Hollywood starlet. She isn't quite scrawny, but the word voluptuous doesn't fit her either. Lithe she is, though. And her mousy brown hair had gotten lighter from exposure to a good deal of sunlight…almost blonde. I contemplated her for a moment… I've never been exactly a Casanova type, but I had been attracted to Gillian ever since I had met her. She had different ideas though. She was an archaeologist, and a very very serious young woman. And she believed I was a liar.

I thought about how we had met, back in Dayton, Ohio. I had served a term, as guest lecturer, in the graduate school of the University. It was one of those periods, you may recall, when the economy wasn't doing so well. My small but adequate income had become small but inadequate. So I augmented it by accepting an offer of long standing from Bill Muldoon to come and give his graduate students the benefit of my lifetime of experience in the field work he was trying to prepare them for. (Not that forty is a lifetime… I plan to be around quite a while, yet…maybe another fifty years or so, if I don't encounter another one of those…but I am getting ahead of my story.)

I usually keep my mouth firmly buttoned when it comes to the more outré experiences of my life… Indeed, my reputation (such as it is) owes quite a lot to a certain talent of mine that, if made public, would cause noses and eyebrows to rise and my reputation, in their view, to fall. But I was getting a bit bored with my job, and there was plenty of Jack Daniels at Gillian's little party one fateful evening, and I said more than enough to whet her interest.

The upshot of it all was that Jill in effect blackmailed me into giving her proof of what I had long known to be true.

"I don't see anything at all," she said ominously. Then she laughed. "It's a good place to camp, anyway."

I was a little dubious, but we had a large supply of water, and of course there was no threat of rain, no chance of being bothered by animals (even snakes shunned this region). And we were both exhausted by our first full day in the wild.

We went back to the pack horse, unwrapped our plastic tents, and dug out our sleeping bags. The tents were for modesty; Gillian had insisted on them. The bags were intended for one occupant apiece. I envisioned a lonely night.

I knew there would be dreams here, so close to this place. So I took a good dose of sleeping powder. Then I made a half-hearted pass at my traveling companion, who warded it off with automatic ease, as expected. Finally I curled up in my tent and sleeping bag. Weariness, plus the sleeping medicine, put me under at once.

My last waking thought…wondering how well Jill would sleep. Surely even someone who seemed as stoic and insensitive as she did would still have to feel something here. Something… then I must have fallen into a sound sleep.

I never heard Jill screaming. I was too soundly under. I didn't stir at all until she came tottering into my tent and threw herself bodily upon me in my sleeping bag. Then I grunted and came blearily awake. It was still evening.

I had been right. She had had the dream—vividly.

"It was no dream." She seemed very positive.

I kept my arms around her where I had automatically put them when first coming out of my stupor. But I made no effort to do anything but hold her. She was one step away from hysteria.

"It was more than a dream, more than reliving a memory." She paused to consider. "It was like being there—Like having my soul shifted from here to there, for a while. I've never had a dream like that."

I was more than a little startled. She had seemed so insensitive, so stubborn about refusing to believe in my occasional power of clairvoyance, that I had never expected to get this sort of reaction from her. This place produced dreams, certainly, no doubt about that. The natives of this region never came near here if they could avoid it; they certainly would never have spent the night here.

"You say you don't believe in such things, Jill," I said. "But you must nonetheless have a certain sensitivity to past events, much as I do." I paused for a moment for thought. "I didn't expect any such reaction from my young and attractive little skeptic."

She was crying. She raised her head and put her cheek near mine.

"Of course I've always known I had it," she said, almost matter-of-factly. "But I never wanted it. It isn't a good thing."

I did not quite know what to say.

"I denied it because I didn't want it. And I denied you too, though I wanted you." She giggled nervously. She tightened her arms about me. "I guess I'm a fool, but if you still want me, you can…well, here I am."

She was a bit excited. Well, she'd recover her poise in the morning. And if she didn't…the morning was time enough for the other thing.

"I want you," I said slowly, "but not here, like this. And let's stop talking like a grade B soap opera. Tell me about your dream… or vision."

She let go of me and sat cross-legged on the ground. I lit a cigarette and passed one to her. Her eyes were glistening while I lit the smokes. She was laughing and crying at the same time.

Well, it had hit me hard, too, that time nearly twenty years earlier.

"Let me tell you again what I saw," I said to her, seeing that she was reluctant to speak. "See if my story matches yours."

I could remember it as though it had just happened—as though I had come crying in the night to her, rather than the other way around.

I was twenty, then—five years younger than Jill was right now. In those days, travel was a little harder in this area than it is today; but my father was a world-famous explorer, and many doors opened for him that for most others would have been slammed tightly shut. It was my summer vacation, between my junior and senior years of college…and the first time I ever had accompanied him on a trip. My mother was recently deceased; she had never wanted me to go along; and since it saved trouble all around, I hadn't ever gone before.

We'd decided to camp out here among the rocks that covered an ancient graveyard of history, mostly because we wanted to spend several days in preliminary explorations, but also because the locals had advised against it. I was young; perhaps my father had never really grown up himself; so we both looked upon it as a lark.

I had observed in myself a slight talent for psychometry—I had never followed it up because my mother forbade it. She was so vehement about it that I rarely tried it. Just having an old object in my hands brought me delicate visions, wisps of thought, from another age—previous owners of the object formed as faces in my mind's eye. Once I found a lost little boy by holding his old pair of glasses in my hand, closing my eyes, and seeing—somehow—that he was in the woods, near a stream, sitting beside a sapling and nursing a broken ankle. My description helped them find him. It was a ten day wonder in the town. My mother tanned me good for it, too.

Now I was surrounded by ancient things—engulfed in the distant past. The very ground under me was made of the dust of long-dead peoples; the very rocks had existed for untold centuries; the air I breathed seemed loaded with ancient aromas and the scents of forgotten ages. There was no doubt in my mind that I would experience visions. But what visions!

Nagging thoughts had edged into my mind all day; occasionally a streak of color seemed to pass before my eyes, till I blinked it away. The influences were there, but I resisted them. Until I slept.

My dream was real. I knew it then, and always afterward I knew.

I walked in a garden. All around me were trees like willows whose branches arched gracefully through the sky to drop at last near earth. Intertwined among the trees were vines with red and purple berries. The berries were poisonous; I knew that and did not try to pluck them. In the center of the garden, where riotous blooms of an unrecognizable species covered the earth among the tree trunks, was a fountain. I bent over and drank. The water was ice cold; it emerged from a deep underground river.

"Danay," said a girl's voice. I knew the voice, and I knew the name she used. Danay. I was called Danay. (A voice in my deepest interior whispered into the dream *Your name is Danny, Danny Long.* Vaguely I recognized the coincidence even as I ignored it.)

I turned to smile at my sister, Mora. She was tall and thin, dressed in a garment of white that was badly stained with purple juice. She carried a leather pouch and held it up to me.

"I have finished."

I took it from her, looked inside. A dark ichor, distilled from the poisonous berries, gurgled sluggishly. I nodded.

"Well done," I said.

"Danay, I beg of you—"

I shook my head.

"Please. Do not follow Chaila into the caverns. She is doomed; you cannot save her. Do not go."

"You know that I intend to go. You made this for me. So you know." I held up the leather pouch. "And I will go. Now." She hung her head.

"Now…you go," I told her. "What you have done for me is a godless act and you must change your clothes and sacrifice a lamb to the Mother."

She acquiesced, leaving without a further word.

I strode from the Garden of the Mother, carefully guarding the pouch of poisonous ichor, and went to the edge of the forest where I had left my horse. I had only a knife, but the horse carried my provisions and my bow and pouch of arrows. He was small, hardly taller than my head, and well trained; he obeyed me like a hunting dog. But I had no dog, not now. I had sent Squirrel with Chaila.

I laughed, wryly. Squirrel was a name he had been given as a puppy. He had tried to play with the squirrels, and tried to put their nuts in his mouth as he had seen them do. He should have been called Lion; such were his courage and his size. He had killed a full-grown wildcat once, single-handedly, though he had been badly mauled. So I'd had some hope of protection for Chaila. I myself could not go with her. I was the chief's son. It would not have been permitted. Three men, loyal to my father, would have thrown me to the ground, had I tried. I was tall, well muscled, an experienced hunter, and an able fighter. But they are huge, quick men, and I would have had no chance against them. Nor had I a weapon, then, not even my knife. Ordinary weapons were not permitted at the Ceremony.

But when I sent my dog to join Chaila, as she started into the cavern—my wonderful ugly scarred Squirrel!—they were confused, undecided. They finally did nothing. And for a while, knowing my Squirrel and the courage of my young Chaila, I had hope.

But through the ensuing day hope dwindled. Now my heart and my soul were filled with hatred.

Gillian, that time in Dayton, after her party had broken up, had sat listening to my story, and at this juncture she had laughed heartily.

"Danny—Danay!" she gurgled. "And Chaila—sounds a little like Gillian, doesn't it? Why don't you admit that you are putting me on!"

Somewhat drunkenly, I denied it. I strove by the force of my words to convince her. And I think she was taken aback. At last she said:

"Those caverns. What was in them?"

Even in my intoxication, I shuddered at the memory.

"At the time, I didn't know, truly," I said. "All we ever knew was that an evil folk dwelled within; once upon a time, they had forayed out of the caverns periodically and murdered and eaten our people. In a gigantic battle, we drove them back into the caverns. But we were essentially a defeated tribe after that. And a truce was arranged, somehow. They to stay within the caverns, we to dwell without.

On every new moon a sacrifice was sent into the caves, sent to the ones who loved to eat human flesh. It had all happened, ages before, and the custom was a long-established one. Usually we sent slaves or prisoners from other tribes into those caverns. Forced them in, if necessary. But on occasion, it was one of our own people."

Gillian's voice was mocking.

"Surely, the beloved chief's son…" she began, suggestively.

"Chaila, your namesake, was the daughter of a slave. You see?"

All afternoon I dipped my arrowheads into the poison that my sister, my only true friend left in this world, had prepared. My spear, too, I covered over with that sticky substance, and my long bronze knife.

Suddenly I saw a slight shadow and whirled around. My father appeared behind me, a sword in his hand.

I stood, holding the knife.

He said, "I know what you plan to do."

"You cannot stop me," I replied.

"I can stop you—now. But…you would go tomorrow—or the

next day."

I nodded, waiting. "Take this with you."

He tossed me the sword, underhanded, and I caught it in mid air, gasping as its weight nearly overbalanced me This was a ceremonial weapon, used only in battle and in certain rites pertaining to war. It was the only weapon of its kind, and my great-grandfather had taken it from the corpse of a strange warrior, a little man of dark skin and darker hair, who wore odd clothing. He had wielded it in battle against a forest bear, and though he died from his wounds, he had killed the bear.

My great-grandfather had scooped the bear's heart out with his knife, then scooped out the man's heart, and ate them both raw. The strength of the bear, the courage of the man. He was not yet, at that time, full chief of the tribe, but with this strength and this courage added to his own, and the might of the strange weapon that bleeds brown if not kept from the moisture of the rainy season, he attained that goal.

This was the blade my father had tossed me so casually...without further comment. The enormity of the gift gave me pause. Before I could find the words to thank him, he was gone.

I picked up my gear, thrust the sword into my pack, and led my horse along the trail toward the caverns. The trail was narrow but not overgrown. It was, after all, used every new moon.

Dusk fell. The guardians of the cave, two giant warriors delegated to prevent anyone from entering or leaving, were sound asleep.

Mora, my sister, had drugged their wine. I felt no pang at putting them out of action by such an underhanded scheme. Never in recent memory had the cave dwellers attempted to come out; and only once had a man—crazed with grief because his wife had been forced to tread that path on the previous morning—attempted to enter. He had been killed by the guards. That incident had given me warning; I might be killed too, but not before my enemies had felt the searing poison of my arrows.

I had not dipped the sword into the poison. It was in itself a thing of power.

On reaching the cave, I donned a belt, with the sword strapped in it, around my waist, and tied the quiver of poisoned arrows on my back. In my one hand I carried my spear and bow, and in the other I held a torch made of long-burning pitch. With my flint, I lit it. Then I gave the outside world one final glance before entering the dark cave.

The cave was cool and damp, becoming cooler and damper as I walked along.

The ground was packed hard, though it seemed to be mud rather than stone, and at the sides of the irregular corridor were little mounds of bones, cracked open for marrow by sharp teeth and cast aside. I found myself on the watch for a sight of Chaila's bones there in the dusty corners. I did not find them. But, after walking for a time, I did find something else nearly as bad: the corpse of Squirrel. He was covered with blood and fearfully mangled; someone, or something, had eaten his entrails. Perhaps, I thought, there were rats in the caves, although I heard nothing.

Not much farther along, I came upon the first sign of life. It was apparently a guard, serving the same kind of purpose that the two warriors by the cave mouth had done. Only, like them, he was asleep. I say "he" because at the time, the guard looked human. It was shadowy ahead, anyway, in the flickering light of the torch. He had the vague form of a man.

Quietly I notched an arrow and carefully aimed, coming close, placing the torch on the ground, where it sputtered but threw off enough light to see by.

Eerie shadows leapt and danced about me as I fired the arrow into the guard's throat. Then the torch went out.

Cautiously I picked it up. The figure on the ground ahead of me was writhing; I could hear it. And low moans were coming from that broken neck, gashed terribly by my arrow, as the fiery poison completed the job the sharp missile had begun.

With the torch extinguished, I realized for the first time that there was a natural light in the cavern. It was very dim, and of a greenish hue; but in a few moments, as my eyes adjusted, I could see well enough.

Upon examining the creature I had murdered, I wished that I couldn't see quite so well. It was no man. It was vaguely manlike, but its arms were like tentacles (I thought of them as wormlike), and its body was fleshy, with no skeletal structure even remotely resembling my own. It writhed like a dying snake. I realized that it *was* a snake, a humanoid snake. My hands trembled at the realization that I fought something other than a man. But then I took courage at the fact that after all, I had emerged victoriously from my first encounter. Cautiously, I groped my way forward through the cavern. It widened, then it narrowed till I could scarcely slip through, then it widened again. Finally, deep in the mountain, it widened out even more, into a natural amphitheater as large as the village of my people.

The entire area was vacant, except for a region far across the spacious room. There were perhaps fifty of them, fifty parodies of man, lounging around the grotesque form of a large statue—their snake-god, perhaps. And they were *eating*!

Not daring to look at what they used for food, I unlimbered my bow and crept forward. They did not see me until I was quite near. Then, as one of them let out a cry, I drowned it with a fearsome howl and let fly with my arrows.

It was like killing a herd of calves. Not within their memory, either, had conflict between our races occurred. We, outside, remained hunters and warriors. They, safe within the caverns, fed by the grace of my own people's folly, had degenerated.

Oh, they tried to make a fight of it. They rushed me with knives grabbed up from their loathsome feast, but I retreated gradually, picking off the closest ones until they ran screaming in utter panic.

Coldly, I continued to fit arrows to my bow and shoot, until, as I groped for another, I realized my quiver was empty.

Moving closer to a group of them huddling in one corner, I flung my spear at them, and it transfixed two of the creatures at once.

Their cries were pitiful, but I had no pity. I used my sword on the rest. A few of them drew courage from the fact that I had no more arrows; now I would have to fight hand-to-hand. They had unearthed weapons, old swords of bronze and bone that once had served their ancestors in another age. But the magic sword my father had given me slashed through bone and bronze and deep into the soft skulls of these folk, sending them squirming in death to the ground.

My own death was due to trickery.

One of them had feigned injury. When my back was turned, he arose with one of my own poisoned arrows in his tentacles, torn roughly from the body of his neighbor, and plunged it deeply into my shoulder.

I cursed, stumbled, dropping the sword, and then, with my last ounce of strength, I plunged my dagger deep into his vitals.

And that is the tale of how I fought and killed the people of the snake, and ended their tyranny over my tribe.

At the last I dragged myself from the cave, painfully traversing the road I had come by. The arrow had been partially washed in the blood, if it be blood, of the snake-man, so it was not as deadly as a fresh arrow. I did not die at once, but was able to crawl back out of the cave, to take to my people the message that the dwellers within were all dead by my hand.

My father vowed that the cave would be forever sealed off, and that no more sacrifices would be made to an ancient foe.

It was with gladness that I embraced death, hoping to be again with my beloved Chaila, if indeed there were aught of life after mortal demise.

Jill looked at me with quite a different expression than I recalled the last time I had told my story.

She shuddered.

"That's what they were: giant snakes in the form of men. I remember being forced into that cave, and then the sly rustling all about me…" Her voice broke off into a sob, and I held her tightly.

I was dumbfounded.

"I'm sorry, my Jill," I said. "I hadn't thought it out—of course you remembered *her,* not *him.*"

The next morning, after sleeping dreamlessly in each other's arms the rest of the night, we arose and had breakfast, just as though it were any other morning of any normal day. We wasted a little water so Jill could wash the dried tears from her cheeks. We had both recovered a bit from the ordeal of the previous hours.

"I never believed your story," she admitted. "I thought perhaps you had heard a rumor about me, how I once found Emma's gold watch when she lost it somewhere on campus. I wanted to believe you, I wanted to so much, but I couldn't."

I comforted her. I assured her it was quite all right. After all, a man my age has to marry sometime, even if he never does quite settle down, and if she didn't mind being fifteen years younger than a slightly overused husband, I certainly didn't mind. Not the most romantic proposal in the world, but inevitable. Or I guess it was inevitable. I guess Danay and Danny were the same people thousands of years apart, and so were Jill and Chaila. Not much of an idea to swallow in the aftermath of the visions we had both had, with their utter reality and feeling of actual participation. Of course we won't ever have proof of that. But we had no doubts.

Now we were determined to find the mouth of the ancient cavern. This was not an area known for earthquakes, so there was no reason to think that any sort of landslide had occurred, but Jill did suggest that perhaps the tribe had closed off the cave entrance by piling boulders in front. We looked for a wall of worn boulders that might have been the ancient cavern mouth. And in the late afternoon we found it. I could see just where the forest had ended, and in my mind's eye I pictured Danay in leather harness and loincloth toiling with his arrows and his spear and his iron sword along that path toward the cave. "You can see it too," whispered Jill.

"Almost," I whispered back.

We decided to make an opening in the rocks. I had brought some sticks of dynamite along for that very purpose. But it was late. So we camped again, this time using only one tent, and I made love to Jill that night for the first time, feeling as if I were really Danay and might have no more time to spare. Then we took double doses of sleeping powder and slept peacefully the remainder of the night.

In the morning I set the charges and blasted open a part of the hillside. We had been right; the wall of rocks came tumbling down and an opening showed behind. I equipped myself with a long-lasting flashlight, and gave a second one to Jill. As an afterthought, I strapped a revolver to my belt.

She gave a little frown, and said, "You don't expect to find them still in there? You killed them all. If they ever really existed."

I shook my head, "They existed. And Danay, whoever he was, did kill them. I am just being very foolish. But I feel better having it."

We clambered over the rubble into the cavern.

"It hasn't changed at all," said Gillian, echoing in words what I had been thinking. "No. It's just as I saw it. Then."

We moved forward. The once-dank caverns were now dry. I aimed the flashlight into the corners of the cave, where I recalled in my vision having seen bones. There were a few grey piles of dust, but nothing recognizable.

"Let's switch off the lights for a second," I suggested. Jill clicked off her flashlight and I followed suit. The greenish glow that I remembered from my life as Danay, or my memories of that life, was right there, surrounding us.

"Must be radiation," I muttered. "It may be dangerous down here, Jill. I wish you'd go back outside."

"I will if you will," she said.

The instrument I now took out of my light back-pack was a small Geiger counter, a hand-held one with a meter calibrated in numbers I had very carefully checked out with a physicist friend. If the meter went off-scale, I would have to leave with Jill. But it didn't. It registered a minimal quantity of radiation, except quite near the walls, and I decided it was safe to go on.

"You think of everything, my dear," she told me, laughing fondly. She had changed. Despite the horror of her remembered experience, and the portentous problem of what the cave might hold, she had turned merry as a child. I realized I had never really known her.

She grasped my hand and led me farther into the caves. We switched our lights back on, so that we could see better, since the natural light in the cave was dimmer than I remembered it from the dreams.

We passed the place where Danay had killed the guard. Nothing was there. But I recognized it without any doubt. We went on. Slowly as the tunnel grew wide, then narrow, then wider again, I began to recognize that we were about to debouch upon the amphitheater, the natural cave as huge as Danay's village.

I was trembling a little, but forced myself to walk normally. We entered the amphitheater.

Jill screamed.

Something struck me a blow on the shoulder and forced me to my knees. My head brushed the edge of a rock and I was dazed momentarily. I fumbled briefly at the revolver in my belt. Jill screamed again. I groped my way back up to my feet and stood staring.

It was one of *them:* ancient, scrawny, seeming old as the brooding rocks. And what he had struck me with was a sword, an ancient, rusty, brittle sword—it had cracked off as it struck the back-pack that had protected me from a nasty gash.

He was glaring at Jill, who was keeping the flashlight turned on his eyes, and he clearly could not see well in the strong light.

Jill had regained some of her composure. She saw that I was basically undamaged, and said, "How could they have survived down here?"

"Evidently Danay didn't kill them all," I said slowly. "He left one of them alive. Maybe the one from whom that poisoned arrow was plucked. Maybe that one recovered."

The flashlight drooped momentarily in her hand as she caught my meaning.

"It can't be the same one!" she exclaimed. "Not the same one, not from so many thousands of years ago…"

The sound of her voice seemed to infuriate the snake-man. He pounced at the source of the bright light—at Jill.

And I forgot myself. I forgot my scientific training. I forgot the wonder of what was happening. For that moment I was Danay, not Danny, and here was my Chaila, alive and threatened by a mortal enemy.

I shot him. I shot him five times, and he slowly sank, writhing, to the floor. And I took my Jill in my arms and she cried, softly.

We left him there. We didn't care to take a sample of his DNA. We left the huge, ugly statue in the back of the cave, the one with the tentacles on its face as well as arms. We left all the rest of those artifacts that might have meant a Nobel Prize some day.

I dug out my dynamite, what was left of it, and blew it off above the cave opening we had made. And a new landslide sealed up the cave again.

Perhaps there are some things the world is better off not remembering. My scientific training tells me that is wrong. If so, I leave, at least, this tale, for whoever will follow.

But after that day, though we went on other digs, all around the world, neither I nor my wife Gillian went anywhere near that place, that ancient place, where Danay had finally completed his vengeance on the snake men, and—maybe—found happiness with his Chaila in an afterlife, or 20,000 years in the future, or in someone else's mad dreams.

FORERUNNERS OF DOOM

Life is queer, sometimes—most times, maybe. Five days earlier I was a stinking beggar in an obscure Colombian village, with only the faintest hope of making it as far north as Mexico, let alone Canada (of which I am a citizen on the purest of technicalities, having been born between flights at the Toronto airport, back in 1939).

How I ended up there, in those circumstances…that's another story.

Suddenly, by a curious turn of luck, my lot was transformed. The luck amounted to running into an old school-mate…Marv Grensham, the archeologist. Seems that he had just lost a pilot. I am a pilot, and a darn good one. And now, here I was, nursing an old Cessna 150 (lightened as much as possible because of the high Altitude in the region of the Andes) through the bluest of blue skies in southern Colombia. I'm Carl Hanson. The Carl is actually for Carlos—although Hanson is Swedish, of course. But my father was born in the Islands, and was a little bit of everything, including oriental, and my mother was Mexican, a lovely combination of Castilian, and Indian, with a dash of Masai. I'm a typical example of what the zoologists could call hybrid vigor—six feet four if I'm an inch, healthy as a mule and twice as stubborn (as dad used to say).

I grew up in Mexico at first, then the Islands, and later went to school in the states. My close family's been dead and gone for some years, now, and I kicked over the traces a long time ago. I'm thirty-eight, and five days ago I felt old as the hills, much older in fact than the jagged peaks we were flying near at the moment. However, I was fast recovering…but enough about me.

I was keeping one eye on my hand-drawn, battered map (not exactly a standard aviation chart) and one on the ground. The aircraft wasn't working too efficiently at this altitude (it would never make it over some of the larger mountains in the Andean chain), but the engine sounded in reasonable shape, and I had no real worries about it. Marv, not an experienced flier at all, was mildly nervous, as he showed by glancing at the instrument panel a little too often, and then at me, as if he were not quite sure that he shouldn't have left me back in that village and gotten a real pilot. Nuts—when you have done the kind of flying I have, jockeying a little 150 around is something you can do almost blindfolded, even if you've been grounded for a year or two.

"I think your map's off a bit, Marv," I said, finally, after a long silence.

I pointed toward the mountain chain, rising up almost as though to meet us. "We'll never get this crate over that ridge ahead, and the map doesn't show such a high chain of mountains this near your city."

"It could very well be off," he replied. "As you are well aware. After all, it was drawn by the fellow from memory, and even if he did know this region fairly well, still, memory can be tricky."

I dipped the wings into a shallow right turn. Too sharp a turn at present height and we'd lose considerable lift and considerable altitude, too, and I didn't like those high peaks ahead of us.

"We won't give up yet," I said. "We've got another hour or so of fuel to spare. Let's try to find that lake he indicates. This time of year the streams should be mostly dried up. Maybe the lake, too, if it's shallow and isn't fed by underground rivers. But the beds should be visible. I'll try to gain a bit more altitude. It's such a clear day; we ought to be able to see quite a distance, especially out here away from the haze and smoke of an industrial complex."

Marv looked at me oddly, as I sent the airplane crawling upward at a slight angle, the engine straining. I adjusted the fuel mixture slightly when the engine sound roughened, and we managed to gain another two thousand feet. Then I leveled off, and sent it into a slight circular arc somewhat paralleling our original flight path.

"Carl," he finally said, "what in god's name were you doing in that damned village, *begging?*"

That was about the third time he had asked me, in the five days since we met. His forbearance was only one of his good qualities. Still he was only human.

"Tell you about it some time. Not now, though, Marv. Keep your eyes peeled. You can't miss seeing the lake, if it's not dry.

The river beds might look like ribbons of clay through the undergrowth, but more likely, if they're dry, they'll be overgrown. Look for a swath of greener vegetation than the rest of the terrain, maybe even a double line of bushes or trees."

He nodded and we both got down to business, concentrating on the terrain below.

My predecessor, who had drunkenly crashed his car over a bridge into a gulley, had flown the route several times, and had mentioned causally to friends that he had noticed what seemed to be the ruins of an ancient city. The rumor had crept northward, where it reached the attention of a group of archeologists and university students, working primarily out of Mexico City—something of a cosmopolitan or international group of people. One of them was Marv, and he was caught up by the idea that this city was an ancient Incan temple city, never before investigated, and particularly interesting because if he were right, it was the farthest north of any that was known.

He had seemed to me to be a bit potty on the subject, but he was a perfectly respectable college professor with a good deal of experience in his field, so maybe I wasn't a competent judge. It had taken him six months, but he had managed to wangle rather sizable grants from two or three foundations, and had organized a small expedition. The first step was to find the damn city. Then the other members of the party could follow by jeep. They could hunt for a hundred years on the ground without coming across the place, though, unless they stumbled on it by pure accident. The jungle was expert at demolishing and concealing the works of men. But even when you couldn't spot artificial structures on the ground, the aerial view was often a dead giveaway. Small changes in the terrain, not noticeable from close by, could combine to produce a distinct pattern over a wide region, a pattern easily visible from several thousand feet above ground level. Many discoveries have been made by this same method, but no one had looked this far north for evidences of the Inca empire.

Marv had bent my ear on this subject since we had met (not unagreeably, for I found his passion for the ancient cities of the south at least mildly interesting).

"See here, Carl," he would say, shaking his balding head at me, his steel-rimmed glasses glinting in the firelight, "What do we really know of this old Inca empire, anyway? On the surface we know a lot. Why, even the language, and many of the customs, still survive. Roughly half the population of Peru still speaks Quechua. The conquistadors were fascinated by the Incan empire itself, nearly as much as by the tons of gold that it yielded to them. The son of one of these Spaniards was a nephew of the Inca, I mean Garcilaso de la Vega, and wrote of the customs and of the history of the Incas."

"I know something about these people Marv," I would remind him. "I might even be part Inca myself."

"You're part everything," he would laugh. "Even my mongrel dog wouldn't associate with you; he's comparatively pure-bred."

"Then he's a damned bigot," I would always retort. "You ought to get a new dog. But hell, Marv, that history of the Incas is so much pure bull. And you know it. That stuff about being descended from the sun god, who created the first Inca—Manco Capac, or something like that, isn't it?—to bring the blessings of civilization to the benighted villagers. Pure swill, for the suckers. Sons of the sun. I've heard that kind of junk before, a lot more recently, too!"

Marv was absolutely beautiful. He would get up and pace about wildly, plucking his steel-rimmed glasses from his nose and gesturing with them as he made his point. (I would guess that his students worshipped him, whenever he managed to take the time to go back to his university and teach classes for a while.)

"That's the point, Carl, that's the very point I am making. The Incas concealed their true history, and the history of the peoples they governed. At the time the Spaniards conquered them, only the official version was extant. All of their historians—the "rememberers," who knew the genealogy and the history of the nation by rote, and could recall it perfectly with the aid of those clever mnemonic devices, the knotted cords that served in lieu of history books—all of them not only spouted the official line, but quite possibly believed it; and so did the inner circle of rulers, the Inca, the sons of the Inca, and the sons-by-merit, who administered that fabulous empire."

"So?"

"Why? Why did they do it?"

"Why are the Soviets re-writing their own history. They invented everything including Tom Edison himself, you know. OR so they used to claim. Pure inferiority complex, I suppose."

Marv would shake his head in disgust.

"Yes, that is an official line of our own. But I am certain it must be wrong. I am certain there must be some reason why the Inca rulers completely erased the history of the foundation of their empire and replaced it with the myth of the sun kings. I am sure there is a secret there, perhaps a dreadful secret. Something so hideous that those fearless warriors buried it completely under fairy tales."

"What could it be?" I had laughed. "I can't even guess."

"There. There."

The words burst into my reverie. Marv was excitedly pointing off toward the horizon on the right. I followed his line of sight and spotted what he had seen. It was a blinding flash of light, the sort of flash that might come from a large lake, illuminated by the bright afternoon sunlight. The plane had lost a bit of headway during my musings, so I put the nose down into a gliding right turn to gather speed as we headed for the lake. The oil temperature was a bit high, and the greater speed would help cool off the engine, which had been laboring at the high altitudes, as well as bringing us to our destination more quickly.

"It's the lake all right, Marv," I said, "There, you can see the beds of two or three of the mountain streams."

"It's pretty close to the mountain range," Marv commented.

"Not the high peaks we saw before though. We can probably fly over these, if we have to, but I'd rather not fight the winds. The city is on the other side of the lake, according to the map, and it must be right up against the face of the mountain… Yes, there it is—see it?"

He strained his eyes, shook his head and muttered, "Don't know how you can make out any details that far away."

"Practice," I explained. "When you do enough VFR navigating you learn to make out everything on the ground that can possibly be seen. We'll get in as close as we can at this altitude, and then drop down."

A few more minutes brought us over the lake and the site of the ancient ruins. Indeed they did extend from the lake to the mountain, and I saw that the mountainside itself was sheer, so that it acted almost as an impenetrable wall—impregnable in case of attack. I put the airplane into a tight turn about two thousand feet above ground, and took my first good look at the ruins.

It was a shock.

I had never experienced its like. For a moment I had absolutely no idea what was wrong with me. I sat rigid in my seat, staring at the growth-infested ruins.

They were familiar! Not familiar in the sense that I had seen similar aerial views of similar ruins, but familiar in a personal way—the way something in your own life is familiar, maybe something you have tried to forget but could not, and are faced with suddenly when it is least expected.

I heard, distinctly, the rumble of drums and the chant of many voices, and I smelled a scent of deep musk, an inhuman scent that caused a thrill of terror to course down my spine.

I seemed to see the people of that ancient city. They had gathered outside an imposing building, as if worshipping—and they were filled with a sense of expectancy. I could feel it. I could feel the electric stirring in the crowd, and I sensed the overtones of fear…

And there was something else—something that I did not want to see. Almost frantically I jerked myself away from that vision, and the ruins became just ruins again—only a set of crumbled buildings lying right at the edge of the steep mountainside.

Then I heard what seemed like another distant sound…a voice…it was the sound of Marv's voice, and it was not distant at all, because he was shouting in my ear at the top of his lungs.

"Carl! Carl! For god's sake, Carl!"

I snapped back to a full realization of my surroundings. We were diving earth-ward at a shallow angle and Marv was shaking me. Had we been pointed a little more to our left, we would have piled up, straight into the side of the mountain, and the wreckage of our plane would have joined the ancient Incan rubble there on the ground.

"I'm okay," I croaked, and I levelled off the plane. These modern light planes like the Cessna 150 are difficult to put into a stall anyway, and will even fly themselves if you give them half a chance. Nevertheless, we had lost 1500 feet of our 2000 feet of altitude, and a small bead of sweat rolled down my brow as I put us into a shallow climb at full throttle.

It wasn't until we got back to the meadow, outside of the small village of Cuejaro that I began to tremble.

Marv wasted no time with recriminations. We pin-pointed the position of the lake on an accurate map and gave instructions to the rest of the party. We ourselves would fly back and land in a spot that had looked good to me—a clay riverbed that was baked dry and was not overrun with growth. They would follow us, requiring perhaps three days or more to rendezvous with us. It says something for Marv's courage, maybe, that he was willing to go back up with me in that plane after my little exhibition of day-dreaming.

That night, over the campfire in the open space where the group had pitched tents, and near where the jeeps and the truck with supplies were parked, I told Marv in low tones what had happened, as precisely as I could describe it.

He was excited.

"I am no crackpot," he disclaimed, "but I am not ready to argue against clairvoyance or telepathy. Racial memory isn't a scientific concept at the present time, but it will take a long while before we know the ultimate capabilities of the brain, let alone of a single DNA molecule. And I've seen a few other odd things along this line. You said you were part Indian…from what part of South America…from the Andes?"

"It sounds a little fantastic, but I suppose I could be. Don't really know for sure. But I don't believe that bull about racial memory, Marv. Are you trying to say that some of my own ancestors lived in that city, centuries ago, and that I remembered a scene out of one of their lives? Crap!"

I guess I was reacting, even over-reacting, against the entire concept.

"Maybe so, maybe so," said Marv calmly. "You must admit that the sight of the place had a profound influence on you, Carl. And you saw things—smelled them, too that just were not there, or possible to see from our height even if they were there. Have you ever experienced such a trance-vision before this?"

"No!" I said shortly.

And that ended the conversation for the time being. I brooded, watching the flames for another couple of hours, till I was ready to turn in.

We flew over the city again, next day. Marv wanted to see if I would repeat my previous reaction, and I had coached him on what to do to keep the plane level if I should go haywire again. But nothing happened. The city looked just like any similar set of ruins—and there are a lot of old ruins in Central and South America. No magic scents, no feelings, no sights. Just a pile of old ruins.

"It seems smaller than I'd have thought," I said, casting my mind back to a few of the other such sites I had seen as a tourist in other years.

"It is," said Marv. "That's one of the reasons I am so intrigued."

I flew back a few miles until I reached the riverbed where I proposed to land. There I made a couple of trial swoops, looking for piles of rocks or other debris, and then landed in what looked to be the best place. It was a lot like coming in at JFK; smooth and gentle, with what seemed like miles of runway still to go, ahead of us.

After I taxied the plane off the riverbed itself, we got out, pegged the airplane down, and gathered our back packs which held supplies for the next few days.

We'd figured it would take us half a day to hike the distance to the ruins, and it was already nearly noon; so we got started as soon as possible, halting only to take a very brief lunch. It turned out that our estimate was a little optimistic. I had not quite fully recovered from the privations I had endured prior to meeting Marv and his party. Marv, on his part, had not been in the field for several months and was not fully hardened to travel on foot. Moreover, the terrain between us and the ruins of the old city was not exactly mountainous, but it was not flat either; the going was rough.

By nightfall we had just made it to within sight of the ruins, and we decided to pitch camp there and continue in the morning. The campsite was located on a slight upgrade. The land sloped gently down from where we stood, rising abruptly again near the city, which was constructed partly on the incline, and seemed to go right into the mountain. Most Incan cities are built on such steep mountainsides, though none actually does continue on into the mountain itself. But I could not escape the feeling that this one was different.

For a few seconds I heard those drums and muted tambourines, and sniffed the scent of musk. But I shook my head and the sounds and odors vanished. I must have imagined them.

We made camp, had dinner, turned in. Both of us were quite exhausted from the trek, and beginning to ache a little in nearly every leg muscle, but exhaustion prevailed and we slept. It would be in the romantic tradition to report that we experienced mysterious dreams. But if Marv had any, he kept them to himself, and I slept like a whole pile of logs.

In the morning I could hardly move for the aching, and Marv

said he felt the same, only twice as bad; but after getting up and surrounding a good breakfast—something about clean air and exertion makes you very hungry, especially mountain air—we both felt better. The day was bright, the sky was a clear blue and we could see the ruins almost as if they were only a hundred feet away. In reality they were still a good three hours trek from where we had camped; so we were soon on our way. It was nearly all down hill and we made good time.

I couldn't help noticing, as we neared the outskirts of the ruined city, that the vegetable kingdom had not entirely encroached upon the site. I remarked upon this fact, and Marv replied:

"Almost as if someone—or something—had been tending the place, eh?"

Then, at the look I gave him, he grinned. "Or perhaps it is just bad soil. Their farms were located on the other ridge of that mountain. I could see remains of the terracing when we were flying over it yesterday morning."

We came to an old road, much overgrown with weeds at this distance, and not much better than a strip of rubble. But the going was easier, there, and it led directly down to the city.

The layout of Incan cities follows a single overall pattern— their city planners apparently were not encouraged to be original or creative. Marv recognized the purpose of various ruined buildings—many of which still towered over us in their crumbling magnificence—and voiced a running commentary which I won't try to reproduce here because I would probably quote it all wrong anyway.

The road got a little better as we actually entered the "city limits," and seemed to be leading us directly toward the towering mountain cliffside. As we approached I realized that a huge pile of rubble at the base of the mountain represented all that was left of the one primary structure in the entire city. Marv had realized it a few minutes earlier; all he said when I burst out with the thought was:

"Yes, I've seen that. Very strange."

Why was the most imposing structure of them all completely demolished? "Could they have had a landslide of major proportions here?" I wondered aloud. Marv nodded impatiently. I could see this was something that interested him greatly. We did not pause to examine any of the more intact structures, but headed straight for the end of the road.

Suddenly a sharp spasm took hold of me and I stumbled momentarily, although I did not fall. Everything had gone purple for an instant. But then I could see again and had my balance back. I must have tripped over a loose rock. I kicked the rock nonchalantly off the otherwise smooth road and looked ahead at the temple.

I was nervous. I had been trained ever since the age of three to be a temple priest. My life had been dedicated to Ixtahuatl from the moment my special abilities had been unearthed by the mage Zochlan. As possessor of a heritage found only too seldom among my kind, I had been encouraged since the onset of puberty to mate with a large number of women; now, not a parting thought for even one of them entered my mind, not a single stray longing; there had been too many of them in too short a time.

Zochlan, my tutor, had recently died of old age, and I could not remember my parents very clearly. There was nothing about my life to want to cling to, despite the fact that I was giving up all I had ever known; yet somewhere within me there was a touch of rebellion. Perhaps it was a natural desire of youth to live and grow, for I was still only nineteen years of age at that time. But the feeling was easily stifled, trained as I had been to view my future heritage as a duty and a privilege.

I walked slowly toward the imposing temple doors and I was certain that I would never walk out again.

The guards and lesser servants of the god bowed respectfully as I passed. I was aware that there was muttering among the laity against this tradition—I would have been deaf indeed had I not known that much—for the god took many of the people to his service, always the young and strong. But here in the temple no one questioned the rightness of these practices, least of all I.

Many times before had I entered these doors. But now I was to walk along the narrow corridor all the way to the back and out that black stone exit that led into the caves of the god. From there, it is said, he had come centuries before and, having breathed life into the clay figures of men and women that he had molded, then showed us how to speak, and till the fields, gave us laws, taught us the rules of the planets and the patterns of the days and seasons. Most important, of all, he chose from among us those suited to him and, through their offices, brought us to the worship of his godhead. Ixtahuatl was god, and he was good; from him came all things to give us life, and from him came all punishments.

All who looked on were respectful. My last sight of the priests of the temple was the bowed, shaven heads of the guardians as they closed the black gate behind me. It creaked a little on its huge hinges, made of hardened gold. At first when it closed I thought I was in a totally dark chamber, but soon my eyes made out faintly the contours of my surroundings. The walls seemed to glow with a soft, golden light that, while nebulous, was just sufficient to see by…although not distinctly.

All about me I felt rather than heard a soft melody, unlike the tribal chants or the crooning of a mother to her baby. It was music like honey, cloying and clinging, soothing my senses. I was already at peace with myself, and my resignation to my allotted fate was only partly responsible. I had drunk the sacred drink of the coca plant, mingled with other herbal elements known only to the inner priesthood. It alerted the senses, but muted the emotions.

I began to walk along the passageway. For a short space it was made of builded stone, presumably cut and fitted by human masons. But then it ended in a rough cavern that led on into the mountain. The walls continued to emit the faint luminescence by which I had groped my way along. Now, however, they were rough and slimy. There were slender spears of rock hanging down from the ceiling, much like icicles that form on the high mountainsides in winter. Yet the faint sense of music surrounded me, and now I began to smell the trace of an essence of musk. I knew it intuitively for what it was: the odor of godhead. I was not frightened; on the contrary, I was glad. I walked a trifle faster, eager to meet my god and to lay myself, and my service, at his feet.

There were two schools of thought among the priests of Ixtahuatl, one of which was considered heretical and was only discussed in private. One school pictured him in the shape of a man, though he could take on the attributes of birds or fish if he wished to do so, flying at heights beyond man's seeing, or swimming far out into the depths of the waters. This was the accepted tradition, and was taught to the people.

The second viewpoint was widespread although no one actually admitted to espousing it. The god was not human at all, but was shapeless; a huge, shapeless mound. It was said that in the first days of the tribe, men had come at the god's behest into his caverns, and there the god had taught them and given them instructions on how to build his city and worship him. And the early folk did worship him, a mound of malleable flesh, as the supreme god Ixtahuatl. This was considered a blasphemy, but if spoken in the confines of the temple, rather than in the hearing of the laity, there was no severe punishment. Now, I wondered, idly, about the two conflicting views, and thought to myself that soon I would know the truth.

Another young priest, Quecchlon, had gone to serve the god only the day before. Never in recent memory had two of us been prepared for this service so close to each other in time. But no one thought anything of it; Quecchlon had been one of my few friends, and I longed to see him, to hear what had befallen him. Some emotions still remained to me; perhaps the cup I'd quaffed had lacked an essential ingredient, used up the day before for Quecchlon; or perhaps I was more resistant than he, being larger and stronger not only than he but larger and stronger than anyone else in the entire community. I looked forward to serving the god, and to seeing my friend Quecchlon.

Now the cavern widened gradually into a huge underground chamber, which extended as far as I could see in that dim illumination. The path led through a sort of boulder-jungle, consisting of knife-edged granite and crystalline growths of great beauty. Once I fell, and sliced my left arm within the jagged garden of rocks, but I ignored the pain and continued on my way through this splendid subterranean architecture of nature.

The music in my head ballooned to a crescendo as I peered around a tumbled pile of rocks at the god of our people.

He manifested himself in the shape of a huge mound, but as I approached, ready to abase myself, I saw that his substance was moving in a bizarre lapping motion. Curiosity (even in the drugged and semi-hypnotic state that held me) led me to move in more closely for a view of what lay on the flat, altar-like rock directly behind him.

The horror that flooded through me blotted out the sound of music; it raised my hackles and pushed away all my simple devotion.

What sprawled there before me was the body of my friend, Quecchlon, his legs and part of his torso entirely gone. And the god was lapping at the raw wound as a cat would lap at a spilled pool of milk.

I turned and fled. The god had not even been aware of my presence. He had apparently not expected to receive a second votary within the space of two days, and I knew not what obscure astrological motive had caused the high priest to break with tradition in this way. It would have been better for me had I not screamed out of terror as I ran, for the god might not have realized that a second tasty meal had ventured forth when the first was hardly half-consumed.

I reached the portal that led to the temple. I pounded upon it madly, frantically, although with little expectation that it would be opened. In the memory of our people, no one had ever departed from the abode of the god.

Suddenly it struck me as a very real possibility that the high priest and his followers knew very well what manner of Thing lurked within. That shapeless mound was indeed the god I had worshipped and sworn to serve; had it not been for simple chance, I would have blindly permitted the god to murder me as, a day before, he had killed my friend.

At every instant I expected to hear a thump-thump as the great mound that was our god travelled back through the tunnel in pursuit of me.

But the god did not need to pursue. As I lay helplessly against the doorway to the temple, exhausted, there came to me again the sound of the music, stronger this time, purposeful; and I heard a sweet voice calling me. Yes, even though I stopped my ears, the voice came…

To my astonishment I discovered that I had risen and was walking slowly into the cavern toward that place of horror deep within the mountain. Without my own volition, my limbs were carrying me back to that monster god that my people worshipped.

As I neared the bulk of the mound-god, the unholy attraction strengthened gradually. But when I laid eyes upon him, the horror and revulsion I had felt swiftly returned, and I was able to move freely—again, as before, I sped frantically toward the outer portion of the tunnel, toward that gate to sanctuary that no one would open for me.

It was then, as I stared hopelessly at the solid unyielding door, that I was saved. It may have been pure chance, but I am now certain that it was through the intervention of another deity—and the only other god who could possess such awesome power was the god I had occasionally heard of, who was worshipped in secret by the common people of the street, and acknowledged as a minor deity even by the priests of our own temple. I speak, now of the sun god.

Whatever its true origin, what succored me was an earthquake. As I lay helplessly against the portal, I felt the stone beneath me suddenly shiver. A low rumbling sound began to increase steadily, like a giant landslide rolling nearer and nearer. The music of the mound-god had vanished.

The door suddenly burst asunder and I fell sprawling into the temple. The room was occupied by a number of the superior priests, mostly scattered about upon the floor as a result of the shock to the earth.

The High Priest alone had maintained his balance, and his visage became black with anger when he caught sight of me.

He strode forward and struck wildly at me with the staff by which he conducted services—a magical shaft of gilded hardwood about three inches in diameter and three feet in length But I was totally free of the compulsion, now, and of the drugs I had consumed. I grabbed the stick away from the maddened priest and struck him once, hard, about the head. He fell like a rotten tree pierced by a lightning bolt.

The earth seemed to me to be spinning like a top, but I used the sacred stick to help balance myself and scrambled out of the room and through the temple as fast as I could. No one laid a hand upon me, although startled eyes jerked in my direction as I ran.

When I stepped from the temple and lurched out into the street, I heard behind me the fearsome sound of destruction. I turned to stare. The entire temple was collapsing like a toy house of clay when a child stamps it into the ground.

For an instant I seemed to envision, behind the wall of the mountain and the rubble of the temple, a baffled angry mound, the god of our people, glaring at the cavern mouth now choked by tons of debris. Then a falling rock must have grazed my head; for with a sharp surge of pain I fell unconscious.

Now, as I told the story of my vision, I kept looking at my hands, the bleeding brown fingernails that showed only too clearly how I had scraped and scrabbled at the rock that covered the entrance into the mountain.

Marv had explained that I had suddenly dashed ahead of him

toward the mountain, toward the ruins of the great temple, and begun single-mindedly trying to tear my way through with my bare hands.

When I did not respond to his pleas and his shouts, he had chosen a hypodermic needle from his medical pouch, filled it with a soporific, and injected the full load straightaway into my thigh. I had slept the entire afternoon and night, and had awakened the next morning, perfectly clear-minded, except that for an instant I was astonished to be Carl Hansen again and not a man of the ancient Incas.

"It's in there still, Marv; I know it sounds ridiculous to you, a scientist; but I know it's in there. It *called* to me. These experiences aren't just ancestral memory. They're triggered off by the real thing—some sort of mind-touch."

I let him know as much as I had been able to deduce in the short time I'd had for introspection. "Those men who were sent into the god's cavern were specially picked—as men whose minds were highly susceptible to the influence of their beastly god."

He started to protest, but I held my hand up and continued: "Marv, back in high school—one of the several I attended back in my teens—I played football. Once I received a bad head injury, and the doctors kept me in hospital for several days. One thing they did while I was in there was to give me what they called an EEG."

"An electro-encephalogram," Marv muttered.

"A brainwave test," I said. "They found something a little weird—my brain seemed to run with a natural rhythm considerably higher than normal. At first they were worried and attributed it to my accident; but I healed rapidly and their measurements of my rhythm stayed the same."

"I see what you are driving at, but I refuse to believe it," Marv responded.

"All I know is that I want to get as far away from here as I can."

But he persuaded me to stay.

The visions did not recur. Within a few days, the rest of the expedition arrived overland, in those jeeps loaded with supplies. They consisted of four young men and two young women, Mexicans and Norteamericanos, all archeologists out to make names for themselves and discover lost civilizations. Marv did not tell them the entire story of what had happened to me, but he did explain a part of it. They were not deterred; if anything, they were even more eager to open up a path through the rubble in order to see if a cave really existed behind it.

Since the ruins had to be uncovered slowly, and with care, so that there would be a record of each shard and pebble, it required a considerable length of time for a trench to be cleared.

At first I remained aloof. They hadn't expected any assistance from me; I was only the pilot. Their other pilot would have refused indignantly to soil his dainty hands with manual labor. But when my bruised and torn fingers started to heal and my brain continued to stay on an even keel, I offered my assistance. Possibly I did this in a purely scientific spirit of investigation. But more likely I did it because I had my eye on the younger of the two females, a rather attractive if leather-skinned graduate student from Amarillo, Texas, who seemed to look at me (whenever she was around) with a peculiar kind of disdain or even loathing. You've got to admit that I bounce back easily from adversity. The experiences with the visions or hallucinations or whatever they were had really shattered me for a while, but a few days later I had recovered sufficiently to be thinking of making a pass at an attractive woman.

The days passed and the supplies dwindled almost to half by the time we had tunneled through to the point where the cave opening was visible.

It was there. Just as I had insisted it would be. I caught the eye of Miss Amanda Wilkins glaring at me speculatively, the look of disdain somewhat muted now, and I grinned at her.

"If there's a monster god in there," I told her, "a little dynamite ought to take good care of it." We had brought a few sticks of dynamite to aid in moving large boulders, but it had remained stored in one of the jeeps.

We cleared away the rubble inside the cave after a day or so. Unlike my memory of the place, the interior was entirely dark; but we had Coleman lanterns for prolonged night work, and we carried two of them in with us. Marv had agreed that I need not enter the cave if we did eventually find it—I was still as spooked as I was in my vision—but when Wilkins volunteered to accompany Marv on the first foray into the cave, I reached back into my own personal history for a spoonful of whatever manhood I could dredge up. Maybe it was merely bravado. Still, I, Carl Hanson, was a product of many adventures and considerable danger. I was quite different from my putative ancestor, the terrified and naive young priest who had escaped only by a miracle from that bestial god-thing. Or so I told myself.

In the end, the three of us went in, Marv leading, Wilkins next, and I the rear guard. As a precaution, we unravelled a ball of yarn behind us so that we could find our way out if the cavern became something of a maze. My memory had indicated that the way was simple; but they were not taking my memory as a dependable guide just yet. The ball of yarn had come from a rather worn old sweater of Wilkins'—she unravelled it the evening before when our plans were solidified.

The cavern seemed much as I recalled it; except that in the stark glow from the Coleman lanterns the rock formations took on a much more grotesque appearance, and the variety of colors in the crystal formations was breath-taking.

"What a tourist attraction this would make!" whispered the indomitable Miss Wilkins.

We passed through the region of widening walls and entered the huge natural amphitheater that I recalled from my vision—it was still littered with odd formations of stone, but I pointed out that the path I had followed centuries ago was still there, and the two were visibly shaken for just a moment.

At that instant it happened—just as my memory had depicted. The sound of incredibly gorgeous music, the scent of musk—and the urgent need to move swiftly forward, along the path of sacrifice...

Wilkins told me later that I took off like a fullback rushing through a hole in the opposing defensive line, bowling her over and practically stomping on poor Marv in my efforts to teach the stone slab where the god awaited me, hungrily.

What I myself recall is nebulous. I seemed to see the mound shape, although at first it appeared tiny, hardly the size of a caterpillar—then I saw it enlarge, swell up, until it was huger than the height of two men... I put out my hand to ward it off, I think, and then fell unconscious.

When they got me back to camp I was delirious. My temperature rose to well over 104 degrees F. The aspirin and antibiotics they carried did little for me at first. But eventually my skin cooled to a normal level and my state of unconsciousness gradually turned to normal deep slumber.

When I woke, my right hand was bandaged and there was an abominable pain in my right thumb. At first they did not want to tell me what had really happened. They were afraid it would disturb me. But Wilkins had the insight to grasp the fact that I was already so disturbed that the truth, as far as they knew it, would only serve to ease my frantic curiosity.

She had served as nurse and watch-dog while I lay in a coma; and now she actually sat and held my hand (my left, unbandaged one) as Marv explained things.

He and Wilkins had rushed after me as soon as they recovered from my unexpected onslaught. They found me stretched out on the ground beside the large stone altar. At first I looked unconscious but in no particular danger—then Wilkins gave a scream and pointed at a spot next to my right hand.

A creature that they recognized as the mound god—just as I had described it to them, except for size—lapped at my flesh, his own substance shuddering in waves as he fed. The only difference between this reality and my original vision was that this manifestation of the grotesque mound god was only two inches high. But the sight of it seemed as convincing and horrifying to them as the ten or twelve foot image I had seen in my vision would have been.

It was gorging itself on my right thumb.

They stared at it, fascinated, for as much as a minute before they fully realized what was happening. By then it had essentially finished my thumb and was starting on the rest of my hand. And, or so they thought, it had started to *grow larger.*

I shuddered when Marv said this, and Wilkins squeezed my hand as tightly as she could. I smiled at her, gulped, and said, "How did you stop the thing?"

"If your theory about being on its mental wavelength is true, and now I have no particular reason to doubt it," Marv replied pedantically, "you, or anyone with the same heredity as you, would ultimately be helpless to fight it. Possibly all of the priests or rulers of that ancient Incan cult were so constituted. But I'm just a crude American with a perfectly ordinary brain; and to me it was just a little leech more voracious than most. I did what anyone might do. I stomped down on it as hard as I could, with the heel of my boot."

Wilkins giggled nervously. "It went *squish!*" she exclaimed. "There was blood and slime all over the rock."

"I wonder…" I began, nervously She forestalled my thought.

"We shut off a Coleman lantern and poured some of the gasoline out over the remains and lit it. Maybe it survived centuries in that cave without food; but nothing could have survived the treatment I gave it."

"No wonder," Marv commented, after a moment's silence... "No wonder the Incas forsook this city and migrated south, after the earthquake, to invade other lands. No wonder they expunged all trace of their origins and invoked the sun god as their Savior!"

It turned out that Marv now credited my visions completely and utterly; and his theory of the situation was that the huge mound-god was simply some sort of giant amoeba spawned within the darkness of the caverns; as the centuries passed without food it had simply shrunk to minuscule size Had we left it undisturbed for another millenium or so it might have dwindled to nothing at all, he suggested.

I could never persuade him of my own theory; and he was now convinced that the area was safe for exploration. On the other hand, said he, there was no longer any reason for me to stay around, and if I so liked I could take the airplane and fly it back to civilization together with some of the more interesting specimens that they had already found and catalogued. Marv planned to stay, but Wilkins volunteered to come out with me and make arrangements for the samples to be sent on to the university. She would also arrange for the plane to be sent back, with another pilot and a load of supplies, so that the expedition could remain in the field somewhat longer.

This certainly met with my approval and four of us left early next morning by jeep to return to the airplane—two of them to help carry samples, plus Wilkins and me. By that time I was calling her Amanda and she was calling me darling.

To me it was as satisfactory an ending as I could hope for; and although I did dream of that unearthly music and that musk scent each night for the first week or so, these were simple, uncomplicated, ordinary nightmares...from which I awoke, unharmed and safe in Miss Amanda Wilkins' small apartment in Mexico City, and in fact, in Miss Amanda Wilkins' very bed, next to the soft and soothing figure of Miss Amanda Wilkins herself.

In the end, though, Mexico City seemed much too close for comfort to that accursed archeological site; so I took my paychecks from the work for the expedition and blew them on two one-way plane tickets to Hawaii.

I wanted an ocean between myself and that cavern of evil.

Marv's theory seems perfectly sound. Perhaps the mound-god did outlast the centuries by shrinking and shrinking until it was hardly the size of a small mouse. But whether through ancestral memory, or shear intuition, I knew differently. Or at least I had a different theory.

When that monstrosity of a god was locked inside the caverns by the fortuitous landslide, it went into a form of suspension, something like a chrysalis, but functionally different. I had seen the true size of the mound-god in its prime, and could not believe for a moment that such a being might simply wither into a two-inch sized mote.

Instead, what I believed happened to it was what often happened to other forms of life at a crisis, a time when food is unobtainable. It died. And in dying, it spawned a litter of young ones, waiting only for the propinquity of appropriate prey to be born.

There was little doubt in my own mind that the diminutive monster that had attacked my thumb was only a growing baby; and I had no reason to suppose that there were not half a hundred other immature mound gods lurking in the dim crevices of that dungeon.

I was safe, now, and I had persuaded my lovely Amanda not to return to the site, though her instincts as a scholar pressed her in that direction.

I only wish I could have persuaded Marv and the others to dynamite shut that abominable cavern and erase it from the memory of mankind.

I believe (as if my mental contact with the monsters had somehow resulted in a transfer of information betwixt them and my unconscious mind) that the larva of the mound-god are adaptable enough to alter their mental rhythms to match those of the majority of their natural prey. Unless this intuitive knowledge is spurious, there will arise new and improved mound-gods, relicts of the fearsome demons of antiquity, to prey upon mankind. And I, of all people on earth, would be helpless to prevent it.

This time no sun-god would send an earthquake to save us. We'll have to save ourselves. Mankind will have to meet the challenge alone, or go the way of the dinosaurs.

THE CUBE OF XANXES

PART ONE: THE FINGER OF XANXES

Axxar, who had been apprenticed to Marawi, crouched in a corner of Marawi's workshop and tried to make himself inconspicuous. It was difficult, for he was a tall, handsome youth of eighteen or twenty, muscular of form and firm of mouth.

Manariam the Magician, who had bested Axxar's master by cunning and had taken possession of all of his domains and his talismans, stood at a cluttered work bench across the room, peering through a microscope at a crystalline cube.

With a grunt, Manariam turned away and surveyed the youth.

"Axxar, attend well!"

"Yes, noble Lord," said the lad.

"You are familiar with the rules of conquest and the laws by which I may make disposition of you. How much do you know of the black arts?"

Axxar's face fell, and he mumbled his reply. "Little, my Lord."

"Come now. Do not lie. Did you not serve that fool, Marawi, and did he not impart to you some of the secrets, the lesser secrets, of the mysteries?"

"No, my Lord." He shook his head, ruefully. "Many were the times he would cuff me to the floor in despair, calling me thick-headed. But I could not master even the simplest spell. I have not the talent."

"Interesting," muttered the magician under his breath.

Animation suddenly came over the youth. "But I am dexterous with sword and dirk, and know many of the secret holds—"

Manariam spat three curt syllables and waved his right hand in a half-ellipse. Axxar's protest was cut short. Before him materialized the figure of a scaled dragon, belching fire and smoke. Coughing and sweating, he lurched backward. Then he heard the magician speak again, completing the ellipse with his hand. The creature vanished, leaving behind a trace of fumes and sooty air.

"Do you think, then, that I have need of a bodyguard?" queried the master sardonically.

Gasping and wheezing, the youth replied with a strangled, "No, Lord."

"Nonetheless," said the thaumaturge, "I do believe there may exist a task which you could be able to perform for me…if you would escape the slave block or the pit…"

Axxar waited expectantly, his face broadcasting his innermost qualms.

"It is not an easy task, but you possess certain qualifications for it."

"What are they, my Lord?" he asked with surprise.

"Physical strength and dexterity, total inability to comprehend the basis of magic,—and a determination to escape the inevitable fate which awaits you if you should refuse!"

The magician paused, measuring Axxar with his bleak eyes, and then continued.

"Do you know by what means I bested Marawi? And before him, Zenoxian and Pericomeon?"

The boy shook his head, eyes bulging with respect.

"'Twas done with that cube that I have been examining—the Cube of Xanxes. It was unearthed by Pericomeon a thousand years ago, in the ruined city of Bhanticum, which had perished under volcanic ash. He sought it, and found it—and I watched through the Mirror of Leagues as he met his fate, the inevitable fate of untutored curiosity. I resisted such curiosity. Instead of directly attempting to probe the mystery of the cube, I merely sent it in turn to Zenoxian and to Marawi; and in turn, they too perished of curiosity."

"What is the cube, my Lord?"

"It is a trap, of sorts. Inside that cube, placed there through lost arts by the ancient genius Xanxes, perhaps a million years ago, is a different world. Yes, a whole world, peopled by men and monsters. The various spells by which one may enter it are relatively simple. However, there is a *caveat!*—those same spells of entrance should suffice for the exit as well…but apparently they do not. At least, no one has ever been known to return."

Axxar crept closer. He could see the tiny cube: no bigger than an inch on a side. "A world?" he queried hesitantly.

"You doubt, boy? Then come closer still. No, fear not. This instrument is passive; its magic is harmless." He gestured toward the microscope. "With it one can magnify things by a million times."

Gingerly, the youth approached the microscope. Then he peered through the eyepiece lens, as instructed. After a moment, a scene swam into focus. He could hardly believe that he was staring into an inch-sided cube. What he saw looked like the world might look from a vast height. He saw forests, streams, a lake, a castle…

The magnification was not strong enough, however, to reveal the forms of animals or men.

The wonder of it showed on his face as he stepped back.

"I believe the world of the cube is inhabited by men. Possibly they are descendants of those who entered the trap, or were forced to enter, long ago. Possibly Xanxes simply created them. I care not."

Manariam shook his head, impatiently.

"I believe that the transition from our world to that world creates a reversal of magic powers. That is why the magicians who entered could not return. In the world of the cube they are stripped of all power. But if one entered who was totally without talent for the black arts, Axxar, one such as you…"

The youth stepped back in dismay.

"This is what I wish. I believe that Xanxes, himself, fell at last into his own trap of curiosity, and entered that world. Such a hypothesis explains both his mysterious disappearance at the height of his power, and also the strange vanishing of his possessions… for he would certainly have taken with him his talismans of power, such as the Eye and the Finger of Xanxes. And he might even have taken with him his Book of Spells, which has been forever lost since his disappearance. I want them. You can get them for me."

Axxar was stunned. "But how…but how could one such as I succeed where apparently Xanxes himself, and my own former master, Marawi, have failed?"

"You possess two advantages. The first is that you are strong, you can use a sword and dirk, and you know some of the secret holds—or so you told me but moments ago…"

Axxar nodded.

"The second is that you know no magic and have proved unable to learn any. However, if I am correct, then within the cube world there will be a pattern reversal, and you will discover that you are able to learn and wield the power. Of course, your strength and skill at arms you will still retain!"

Axxar shook his head.

"But I will not know any magic to use, even if I should miraculously gain such talent!"

"By my arts, I can store within your mind unconscious knowledge of several spells, including the Spell of Return. When you are in dire extremity you will remember one of them, not before. I believe that they will not themselves be subject to the reversal of magic, because they are merely memories." The eyes of the mage burned into his. "But I shall be honest with you. I am not altogether certain that this is true. It is a theory—extremely likely, but as yet unproved."

Axxar shook his head again and started to speak.

The magician forestalled him: "I shall also implant, deep in your mind, a familiarity with what you are seeking. When you see it, in any form, you will know it. The Eye of Xanxes, other baubles of Xanxes, and most important, the Book of Spells. You will know them if you see them—even if they should be disguised."

Axxar stared at the Cube much as a tethered lamb might look at a growling lion.

"Finally, I shall install a compulsion in your innermost mind, a compulsion to seek out the various possessions of Xanxes for me. Should you turn aside from this quest, you will be afflicted. Otherwise, you could simply remain in that world of the Cube, where my powers cannot reach you, and merely laugh at my threats."

Axxar frowned, unhappily into the malignant bearded face of his new master.

"'Tis that or the pit," threatened Manariam. Reluctantly, Axxar agreed.

Axxar experienced a falling sensation. He was surrounded by millions of scintillating stars. Then came oblivion. After a time he felt pain, dull pain, and sunlight against his eyelids. Stifling a groan, Axxar opened his eyes and blinked.

He lay upon a lush greensward. The sun hung low in the sky. To one side loomed a thick forest, to the other a rolling hill. Like a toy on a velvet slope, a castle was visible in the distance. He stared at it in awe. He was certain it was the same castle whose miniature form he had discerned using the microscope.

Groaning under his breath, Axxar rose to his feet and tottered uncertainly, staring at the castle. Gradually a semblance of strength was returning to him, although the whiplash from Manariam's spell had left him weak and shuddering. He was dressed in loose garments that concealed a light chain-mail jacket. At his belt he wore a dirk and a longsword, forged by a master from tempered spring steel. He was capless, his short-cut dark hair pointing in all directions like porcupine quills.

He recalled in vivid detail the instructions he'd had from Manariam, up to the instant when the magician had blanketed his senses by flinging a pinch of queer dust at his nostrils. No trace could he find, though he racked his brain, of the spells that were to have been implanted within his memory. Had the passage to this world of the cube left them untouched? If not, could he use them here? Well, he might discover that sooner than he liked, if he found strangers to be unwelcome in this place.

Axxar began trudging toward the castle. As he went, the aches eased from his muscles and his body waxed stronger. His spirits lightened a trifle. After all, in his own country strangers were not welcomed, certainly, but a lone man was rarely set upon except by robbers or madmen, and adventurers might even turn up to offer themselves as mercenaries in the army of a duke or a king.

As he went, the sun settled down toward the horizon, and his shadow lengthened. Slowly he grew puzzled. He had estimated the castle to be at most half an hour's walk distant, but he did not appear to be getting much nearer, if nearer at all. And the forest behind him seemed almost to be advancing with him. A few quick glances backwards filled him with foreboding. He did not like the appearance of that forest, although just what aspect of it repelled him he could not decide.

Though young, Axxar was tall and strong, and he was indeed highly skilled in both armed and unarmed combat. While his brothers and his few friends had spent a portion of their time practicing the arts of war, as befitted the sons of noblemen, they had also delved deeply into the studies of thaumaturgy, for most men possessed at least some talent at wizardry, and many possessed more than mere talent. But Axxar's free time, until about a year ago, had been almost entirely devoted to warlike games.

He had been magic-deaf, as some men are tone-deaf. Moreover, he had a natural affinity for weapons and for physical sports such as wrestling and horsemanship. While a warrior could not ordinarily overcome a practiced wizard unaided, lack of talent for magic is actually a defense against certain forms of it. Finally, a year previously, his father—desperately attempting to instill in his second son a semblance of magical skill—had apprenticed him to Marawi. But even that sage could teach him nothing, though he had continued to try until Manariam's trap had swallowed him. During Axxar's apprenticeship he had continued to develop his fighting skills, and the wise (though too curious) Marawi had not gainsaid him.

So it was that although Axxar scented wizardry in the aspect of the forest, and in the reluctance of the castle to let him draw near, he could do little but place a hapless hand on the hilt of his sword and mutter curses. He tried to put his faith in Manariam's hypnotically-implanted spells, but he found it difficult.

Axxar increased his pace almost to a trot. He did not like the forest, and he did not like the queer way his own shadow bobbed and weaved as he strode. The sun drifted lower and lower…the castle drew nearer, ever nearer, but very slowly. That worse creatures might dwell within the castle than without did not occur to the youth.

At long last, Axxar approached the walls of the castle. There was no moat, nothing but an imposing bronze gate set solidly into the huge stone slabs of which the structure was composed. To one side dangled a pull-rope which apparently activated an alarm. As he reached for the cord, he heard a rustling noise behind him, and whirled. The next instant his sword was out and he had set his back against the great bronze gate.

The sun's disc had crawled behind the brooding black hills to the west, but light still spattered the sky, and in the blood-red twilight, Axxar spied a horde of hairy grey creatures loping swiftly toward him.

They were as large as dogs, but they were not dogs. They were rats: giant, tailless rats, identical in every other aspect but size to the rodents he had often, as a child, killed with sling and pebbles in the back yards and stables of his homeland.

When they saw him turn at bay, they chattered to one another in squeaky voices. He felt the horrible certainty that they possessed intelligence, that the squeaks represented a language, although he could not comprehend it.

The foremost rat arced toward his throat with a smooth and terrible leap. Only reflex made his arm come sharply up to slice with the iron sword, so mazed was he at sight of the creatures. But when the blade bit easily into the fleshy neck of his attacker, and red blood spurted forth, and the rat collapsed with a feeble kick, his demeanor changed. Creatures of magic they might be, or natural denizens of this strange world…he knew not. But he now knew they could be killed.

Like a berserker, Axxar wielded his weapons of destruction, bloody sword in his right hand and the dirk, with a blade fully fifteen inches long, in his left. Although they could attack him from three sides, his back was protected in the shallow niche made by the inset bronze door, and the marauders were not as quick as ordinary smaller rats would be. As the last rays of twilight were disappearing, Axxar stood panting in the midst of a sea of red blood and a veritable graveyard of carcasses. Many scratches on his arms and a few bites on his legs were his only wounds. In their initial frenzy to reach him, the creatures had gotten in one another's way, and afterward the bodies of the first to die had formed a partial blockade against a too-easy leap for his throat.

As he gasped for breath, and pushed back the sweat on his forehead with his bloody arm, a chill swept over him. In the dim light of the half-risen moon, and the afterglow of the twilight, he could see the bodies slowly beginning to disappear. One by one, they vanished into nothingness. He gritted his teeth, fully expecting the whole horde to wolf down upon him once more, revitalized and revivified. But nothing happened. The silence was unbroken.

"By Verinon!" swore Axxar. "They were real, I know they were real, but now…"

But now in the dim illumination, his night-sharp eyes saw that neither a single corpse, nor a single drop of rat blood, remained. He shuddered.

Resolutely, he turned, senses alert, and reached for the pull cord. It was hard to believe that the inhabitants of the castle had not heard the sounds of battle, though suddenly he wondered if there had really been a battle after all. Only the nagging irritation of his wounds remained as proof. He grasped the cord, and started to apply a mighty yank, when again his heart leaped.

The gate was opening. Ponderously, the bronze gate turned on its creaking hinges until there was a space large enough for three men to enter abreast. Then it paused, seeming to wait.

Mustering his courage in the face of what might be more wizardry, he entered slowly. With a feeling akin to horror he heard the gate creep shut again. The lock clanged. He looked about him.

He stood in an alcove at one end of a huge hall, the central room of the castle. The room was lighted by thick wax candles mounted in chandeliers holding a hundred each. The floor was bare stone. To his left and right, doors opened onto what he supposed were cloakrooms, and kitchens, and servants' quarters. Straight ahead, far across the gigantic room, was a grandiose staircase leading to the upper chambers of the castle. To each side of the staircase, dimly lit corridors led to the rear of the castle.

Simultaneously from right and left came two swordsmen. They were tall warriors and bore bronze swords of a design he had never seen before. Their hair was light grey. They were dressed in red cloaks, and by their slightly awkward but practiced motion, Axxar concluded that they too wore body armor. He laid a hand upon the sword he had sheathed, but did not draw it.

"How have you come here and what is your mission in the castle of Greybear?" growled one of the men.

Axxar was not surprised that he could understand the man's language, for in his own land all men spoke a common tongue, except for certain religious ceremonies and festivals.

"I seek shelter for the night and information about the countryside. I have traveled far. If you have need of men-at-arms, I am willing to stay and prove myself."

The second man laughed.

"We have no cause to enlist demons or spies in our armies, rash fool." The first one added: "Dead men cannot fight for anyone," and with that, thrust his sword at Axxar, who danced out of the way and toward the center of the room. The two men converged upon him, grinning in anticipation of the sport they were to have. Axxar unsheathed the iron sword, and held his dirk poised in his left hand. He had partially recovered from the encounter with the dream rats, but he retreated, moving slowly backward so that the two men remained in front of him.

Grunting, the men crossed swords with him. Axxar fended them off partly by skill, partly by luck, and mostly by continuing to move away from them.

Almost by intuition he knew when he had reached the staircase, and he backed up five or six steps, angling toward one railing. Neither his sword nor theirs had tasted blood. Suddenly Axxar vaulted the rail and sprinted headlong toward the back of the castle. Here the corridor was dark and narrow, and he hugged the wall.

"After him!" cried one of the swordsmen, suiting action to words.

Axxar smiled, grimly. He might defend himself against two men for a time, or even beat them, if they were not good swordsmen; but presumably these men were professionals. On the other hand, if one of them came in pursuit far enough ahead of the other one, Axxar might have a tiny chance to survive.

Thus it happened. The man who had shouted evidently believed Axxar was in full flight, and he was incautious. Axxar whirled and leapt at him from the shadows with sword and dirk. Desperately batting away the other's sword, he moved in close and brought up the dirk in a sharp and accurate arc. The man's astounded grunt bubbled away with his life blood, as he flailed backward, throat cut. Then his companion rushed forward with upraised sword.

There, in the dim alcove behind the stairs, the two men fought. Axxar's second opponent was big and brawny. His sword was a trifle longer than Axxar's, and he was seemingly without fear or wariness. Axxar's previous fight with the rats, and his body-wracking transmigration from one world to another, had taken inevitable toll of his stamina. Now he found himself breathing in raw gasps, and battling on the defensive. Twice, three times, he avoided death by a whisper. He was faster than the big man—it seemed his only advantage. But as he fought on, even that edge seemed to be slipping away.

Was this dire extremity? Would one of the spells of Manariam appear in his mind, released by that strange hypnotic geas? Axxar expected nothing; but he hoped. Still, metal crashed against metal, and the fight continued.

Finally he was trapped in a corner, no longer able to use his frail edge of speed and agility. Twice he essayed to escape, and twice the man drove him back with flashing swordplay. But Axxar retaliated with a furious combination of desperate strength and brilliant improvisation, as old Westerley the court guard had taught him in a childhood that now seemed like centuries ago.

Cursing him in the name of *Klulu* and *Azathoth*, his opponent fell back momentarily, then pressed forward again. Desperately

Axxar feinted, then threw the dirk with his left hand. This left-handed toss was a move he had practiced since he was was barely old enough to walk, and the knife sped true for his enemy's throat. But the man was quick, quick enough to dodge. Axxar had anticipated this, however, and the feint with his sword became instead a true stroke, a stroke that severed his opponent's right hand at the wrist.

Spouting blood, his hand and sword bouncing on the floor, the man screamed curses. But he did not yield even in extremity. As Axxar's iron sword cleft his pate clean and true, he was still groping for the fallen sword with his left hand, and as he fell dead, his fingers spasmodically grasped and held it. Then they relaxed.

Axxar's first action, after sweeping his surroundings with a quick glance and finding no other enemy, was to reclaim his dirk and wipe both sword and dirk on the mantle of his fallen foe.

Then he stood back, lips pursed, trying to decide on a plan of action.

He could not go back outside, for he knew intuitively that worse dangers than giant rats were lurking out in that moon-drenched wilderness. On the other hand, he could not fight an entire castle garrison of soldiers. Even two had taxed his endurance to the limit. And he no longer could have hopes of being treated courteously by the rest after he had killed two of their number.

He tarried for five full minutes, crouched in the dimly lit alcove behind the stairwell, without reaching any conclusion. The only bright spot in the whole affair, other than the fact that he was still alive and relatively unhurt, was the fact that the sounds of battle had brought no other persons to investigate. And that was almost beyond belief.

Axxar tried desperately to formulate a plan. Any plan, even a feeble one, was better than cringing in the shadows.

He would have to remove the evidence. He felt certain that there was one place to put the bodies of the guards where no one would ever find them.

Outside. He was positive that by morning the corpses would have been dragged off by wild animals, if he could get them outside. He was afraid to open the great bronze door, but it was a chance he decided must be taken.

Resolutely he turned back from the shadowy alcove, then stopped—and gaped in astonishment.

The bodies had vanished.

The blood of the fallen men still stained the stone floor, but their bodies had vanished. Even the severed hand had disappeared, though the sword remained. He looked around, slowly. No one was in sight. He was alone.

He breathed deeply. The silence pressed in upon him like a fog of blood.

For a moment he could hear nothing but the pounding of his own pulse. Then soft footsteps slithered on the staircase. He was so shaken by the succession of events that he did not stir. He merely watched as the figure of a woman appeared on the landing. She slowly descended, approaching him as he stood motionless beside the staircase, next to the pool of congealing blood.

The woman halted, five steps from the bottom. She smiled at Axxar. Her expression denoted triumph, interest, disdain. She spoke:

"When he returns, Lord Greybear will welcome you, champion knight."

She took three more steps and moved to the railing. She surveyed him calmly. "Follow me."

Then she turned and began to ascend.

Her hair was sweet-corn yellow, her eyes blue, and her skin like the purest ivory. She was about five feet eight or nine inches tall (she looked even taller, standing on the upper stairs), and dressed in a purple and gold robe that covered her figure without concealing its voluptuousness. In her left hand she clutched an object that he could not see clearly.

Axxar had half-drawn his sword without realizing it. Regaining some of his poise, he shoved it angrily back into the scabbard and mounted the stairway, determined to find out what was going on even though further dangers awaited where the lady led. Danger, after all, seemed to lurk everywhere he went.

She had nearly reached the top of the staircase before he moved, but she dawdled to let him catch up, and then led him through a richly adorned hallway to a large and sumptuous room, from which several doors led to other rooms. This room was empty but for the two.

"I am Luna," said the straw-haired woman, "daughter of Lord Greybear."

He bowed to acknowledge her statement. "I am Axxar of Arichna, second son of Lord Daymoor of the Silver Gauntlet."

"Ah!" she breathed. "A nobleman. But I do not recollect having heard of a Lord Daymoor. Does he reside nearby?"

"Far away my lady."

"How very intriguing," she murmured. "We seldom receive visitors from afar."

Axxar remained silent, and the two stood eyeing each other for a few moments.

"I observe that you are wounded," said she finally.

"I was beset by rodents outside the castle," he replied evasively.

"And inside?" she asked.

He made no answer.

Luna laughed merrily.

"Well, it is of no consequence. I see you are not one of those 'gainst whom I must be on guard. You mean me no harm, do you, my bold knight?"

From somewhere in the depths of the castle, Axxar thought he could discern the echo of a sword blade striking stone.

"Harm? Mean you harm? Not at all," was Axxar's reply. "I mean no one harm."

"Unless you are provoked?" she added suggestively.

He said nothing. He listened, but the sounds of the sword were not repeated.

"Hear me!" she demanded, her manner shifting, her eyes imperious. "Lord Greybear and the garrison are absent. They have been away for over a week. Only the two knights downstairs were left to guard me, and...one other. In addition, I have only my maid and the kitchen slaves. You have, through no evil intent of your own, robbed me of my guards."

"I regret that, my Lady Luna," said Axxar.

"I request that you take their place. It is your duty, if you are a civilized and honest man, as you seem to be. We shall discuss your payment at a later time."

She made as if to turn away.

"I require no payment. I would serve you freely," he responded.

She turned back gracefully and laughed.

"He is gallant, too, my young champion. Very well; I shall hold you to that. Come, are you hungry? I was about to eat. Join me."

Axxar followed her into one of the adjacent rooms, a small

alcove furnished with a table and chairs.

"Come sit," she offered. They waited, motionless, for a moment. Then another door opened and a girl entered, bearing a tray. Luna ordered her to set a second place, and soon the two were dining. Axxar was intrigued by the food, which resembled nothing quite like the cuisine with which he was familiar. Here was a roast that tasted like duck but looked like beef, and there were several vegetables and fruits that were entirely strange to him, though she called them by familiar names like granates and pares. She tried to induce him to tell her of his home, and how he had travelled to her castle, but he recounted nothing concrete, and she did not insist on details.

He ate slowly and carefully, but the profusion of strange scents and tastes would have made it impossible for him to discern a poison or a drug, had anyone wished to administer such a potion to him. So gradually he shoved this possibility from his conscious mind and concentrated on studying the two woman—Luna and the servant girl, whom she called Usana.

The Lady Luna was a self-assured and self-possessed young woman who seemed about twenty-eight or thirty. Upon sitting, she had thrown off her outer robes to reveal a green and gold blouse, cut low over a jutting bosom, and a full skirt of grey and gold that blossomed out from an unbelievably narrow waist. Her features were nordic, her chin regal. Her voice was low and rich. She ate daintily.

Usana, the slave girl, was nearly as tall as Luna and slight of build, though her figure was delicately pleasing. Her hands were capable and her arms, though smooth and attractive, were well muscled for a girl. He estimated her age at about sixteen or eighteen years. She wore a white garment that showed part of her thigh as she strode. Her hair was cut very short, and was almost as red as blood. She possessed the freckled skin that most real redheads do. Her green eyes seemed always to stare at him as she walked around the table, serving them. She moved as though in a trance, and she never spoke.

He glanced around the room. It was illuminated by candles set in several small wall lamps. Curious paintings hung on the walls. They were not paintings at all, he realized—they were mosaics of metal fragments like copper, silver, and gold, and pieces of colored gemstones, such as jade and sapphire, glued to wooden slabs. They depicted scenes of subtle terror: maidens pursued by dragon-like beasts, seduction scenes in which a man possessed the head of a horse, or a woman the body of a serpent. One scene showed a forest which seemed to brood like a violent storm, though nothing was visible but trees of copper and jade.

Dessert was followed by a generous portion of brandy, which made him light-headed. The room seemed to swim about him. At first he was sure the food or the brandy had been drugged, but he came to realize that the events of the past few hours had taken a significant toll of his strength. He rose to his feet, and tottered there dazedly.

Luna seemed to comprehend his plight.

"You may sleep now," she said. "Later I shall have a need for your assistance."

She led him to a sumptuous bedroom.

"Come," she told him. "Sleep here. I will care for your sword and other weapons if you wish."

He stifled a yawn.

"I keep my weapons by my side, even in bed," he said. Then he collapsed upon the bed, instantaneously asleep.

But he remained faintly conscious of her imperious figure bending over him, beside the bed. He thought he could hear her mutter, "An ill-mannered lout, but a handsome one." Her arm reached out and gently touched his belt, whereupon his right hand instinctively fell to his sword. She straightened again, stood gazing at him for a few moments, then departed. He heard the click of the lock, dimly, as he lay in a stupor.

He slept, deeply, amidst the glow of candles that flickered on their wall-mounts.

Once he woke briefly and almost unconsciously divested himself of his garments, burying his dirk under the pillows and placing his sword beside the bed, near the far wall. Then he slept again.

The lights burned low.

He groaned in his slumber, and turned fitfully.

He dreamed. He dreamed that a figure entered his chamber through a wall panel, and snuffed out the candles. He dreamed that a darkness settled over the room. He nearly awoke, again, when the figure of a girl seemed to glide to the bed and settle on it next to him. He felt (or dreamed that he felt) gentle fingers on his body. In his dream, he reached out and clasped a soft female form close to his own.

In the dream, his voluptuous visitor had long, blonde hair, and he called her Luna.

But when he awoke, in the light of morning, the three strands of hair that he found on the otherwise empty pillow next to his were short and red.

He shook his head, wonderingly, and rose, dressing hastily. He recalled clearly the events of the preceding evening, if not those of the night, and it was in his mind to ignore his half-promised offer to serve Luna and flee from the castle while daylight prevailed.

As he turned to depart, his blood chilled.

The echo of a scream resounded through the castle. It was repeated, again and again. Cursing, he grasped his sword and determined to follow the sound. He thought he recognized the voice as one he had heard in a dream.

He found the chamber door to be bolted shut. But it was only the work of a moment to pry the lock apart with the blade of his sword. He stepped outside.

He saw no one. Down the broad stairway he went, following the sound of screams and moans. Back among the shady corridors behind the stairway was another stairway leading down into a damp passageway. The screams grew louder as he hurried down the stone steps and throughout the narrow entrance way to a large room.

He cried out. In the center of the room was red-haired Usana, her hands fastened to heavy ropes dangling from iron rings in the stone ceiling; her body, clothed in tatters, hung loosely, her feet a few inches from the floor.

Behind Usana stood a long heavy table, upon which rested a series of huge bell-jars. Some of them seemed to contain the entrails and organs of humans. With a start of horror, Axxar recognized in one of them the heads of the two guards he had killed. For a moment his attention was riveted on these.

Luna stood a few paces in front of Usana, laughing grimly as a whip came crashing down upon Usana's nude body. At the sound of Axxar's entrance, Luna turned to glare at him angrily but did not stop laughing.

Axxar stared dumbfounded at the girl who shrieked and moaned as the whip crashed down upon her. Again and again the whip came down upon her soft skin, engraving ugly red slashes.

The whip was wielded by no one. It hung alone in thin air.

"Come join us, dear friend," cooed Luna. Again she held something Axxar could not discern in her left hand. When she gestured with it, the whip hung slackly in mid-air.

"What does this mean?" Axxar burst out.

"It means your death, foolish man, and hers as well, as horrible a death as I can mete out."

"I do not understand. Why? What is it all about?"

"Very well—I shall explain, you foul dog." Luna made a left-handed gesture and the whip raised itself and smote Usana once more, then clattered to the floor as though suddenly lifeless.

"I took you at your word, when you represented yourself as a stranger. Though you murdered Ardanath, my lover, I forgave you that—he, too, was a fool. But when you repulsed me, and then spent the night in dalliance with this, my slave—as I discovered early this morning—then you committed a heinous sin in my eyes, foolish Axxar.

"You could have been mine, had you wished. You could have been master of Castle Greybear, and more—but you and she, whom I thought totally in my power, have made it impossible for me to ferret out the secret of Lord Greybear's treasure. So I shall at least have revenge upon your foul carcasses."

"What secret?" cried Axxar, his intellect grasping upon the few words in Luna's tirade that made any sense whatsoever.

"Lord Greybear is gone!" burst out the red-haired wench defiantly. "I—I am his daughter, not this witch."

The blonde Luna grimaced. Seemingly by itself, the whip rose and slashed Usana again.

"I would have had the secret, for there is a monstrous rite, that few wizards know of, for calling back the dead to make them speak the truth. But it requires one special ingredient—a direct female descendant of the dead man, whose spirit can be poured into the body of the sacrifice—her body would have served as a vessel for the shade of her grandfather.

Axxar stared blankly.

"But to serve that purpose, she must be a virgin, foul knave!"

The vague, dream-like memory of the previous night returned to Axxar, and he stared dumbly at the tortured Usana, then back at Luna, then at Usana again.

"It was not a dream, then," he murmured, and began to realize how the desperate Usana had tricked and thwarted her captor.

"Fool! Fool! Villain!" cried the blonde beauty. She gestured savagely with her left hand. Axxar turned toward the whip, expecting to see it rise to life once again, but it was dormant. Then Usana screamed. He turned.

Slashing toward him in a wild and savage arc was a bronze sword half again as long and heavy as his own.

Only his instinctive reaction prevented immediate disembowlment. He raised his own sword to parry. Even so, he felt the hot sharp pain as the point of the bronze sword sliced across his left arm. But he hardly noticed the wound. His mind was stunned by the fact that the sword which opposed him was borne by nothing visible. The sword, like the whip, seemed to be imbued with a life of its own. In thin air it whirled, flashed, parried, and thrust.

He backed away toward the bound and bleeding Usana, on the defensive against the slashing, whirling sword that fought by itself. How else could he battle, except defensively? He could discern no opponent whom he could attack. And the brilliance of his strange foe was devastating. Axxar was a master swordsman—though not a veteran, he ranked as an expert among experts, or so old Westerley had claimed. And yesterday he had been blooded. But the wielder of the sword (if wielder there were) was also a master; and the utter strangeness of his invisible foe worked against Axxar.

The eyes, the muscular movements, even of seasoned swordsman, always give some slight indication to the expert eye of the incipient slash or the planned parry; but in this case Axxar fought only a mute and enigmatic blade.

After only a few minutes he had been slashed several times, once badly on the rib cage. He had a sinking feeling that the wielder of the sword was but toying with him, and could dispatch him at any time. Still he fought, fought while his breath was wheezing and his legs rubbery. And ever he heard ringing in his ears the hideous laughter of angry Luna, the blonde witch.

He retreated again, but the sword followed, imbued with devilish life of its own. Once or twice Axxar attempted a riposte, searching with his sword blade for the wielder's flesh, invisible though it might be, behind that mad sword. But his blade sliced only air.

Following a particularly spectacular display of defensive swordsmanship, after which even the ponderous blade backed off, spent for a brief moment, Axxar leapt back toward the bound girl and with a wild swing cut through the heavy ropes that held her. She dropped with a dull groan and a thud, but when he returned to the fray he was a second too late to avoid a cunning thrust that opened a bad gash on his sword arm.

Even as he continued to struggle, he knew that he had met a better swordsman than he, whether human or elemental. The pattern of attack was intricate and cleverly woven, and his defense was becoming more and more haphazard, incapable of sustaining itself against the ultimate sweep of his opponent's attack pattern. Like a chess player who sees certain defeat impending, he could almost foresee the final strokes that he would be unable to parry. He watched the fatal thrust in the making.

Desperately he drew his dirk and hurled it toward the place where a man's heart would be if the sword wielder were human. But it passed through empty space and beyond, shattering a huge bell jar which had housed a homunculus.

Luna cursed and laughed sardonically.

Then her laughter turned, suddenly, to a cry of rage, as Usana leaped upon her, screaming to Axxar, "Lay hold of her *wand*. Your one chance to live is to kill her and retain it."

He heard the clink of an object striking the ground, and the intricate pattern of swordplay before him faltered. He risked a swift glance at the snarling women, and then caught his first clear view of Luna's *wand*. She had been holding it tightly in her left fist, until Usana had knocked it loose, and she was now trying to grasp it with her other hand.

That one fleeting glimpse of the talisman snapped a synapse in his brain, and data flowed swiftly into his conscious mind from the hidden storage place where Manariam had placed it.

"Behold: *The Finger of Xanxes!*"

As the words of an ancient spell tumbled into Axxar's consciousness, he automatically spoke those words aloud. As the words came forth, the stricken Luna screamed with rage and fear.

The sword that opposed Axxar made a supreme effort to slash him to bloody ribbons. Then it clattered to the floor and vanished. Usana shrieked.

Dazed, he stared at the spot where the blade had disappeared. Then he turned toward the girl. Usana was half-sitting, half-lying on the stone floor, a comical expression of astonishment on her face. Luna had vanished like the sword. So too had the Finger of

Xanxes.

With a supreme effort, the spent Axxar picked up Usana and carried her upstairs. Gently he bound the wounds caused by the whipping and the scratches and bruises made by Luna's nails and teeth.

All the time he was thinking: it was a Spell of Returning. I saw The Finger of Xanxes and spoke the Spell of Returning. But it was not I, but The Finger, that vanished, and its mistress with it, swept back to the real world.

All the time he was thinking: had I realized, I could have grasped the Finger while I spoke the spell; thus I, too, could have returned home.

Then, through the cloud of homesickness, he stared at the slim body of Usana. She was smiling up at him through her pain. Though not as voluptuous in figure as the blonde Luna, she was an attractive wench. He thought of the previous night, but could not remember it clearly. Perhaps there would soon be other such nights, similar ones. These he would remember.

He smiled, then. And Usana laughed through her tears. Then he, too, laughed. Suddenly he was thinking of sardonic Manariam, and wondering whether his expression of calm superiority and his spells for summoning green-scaled dragons would be sufficient to tame the small package of blonde vindictiveness that he, Axxar, had inadvertently sent him as a present. He chuckled. They deserved each other. He reached out a gentle hand and stroked the flaming short hair of his new friend.

THE CUBE OF XANXES

PART TWO: THE CITY OF JOY

Axxar reined his telope to a sudden halt and sat staring ahead at the city. He and his steed perched scarcely a foot from a sharp precipice which, farther to the east, smoothed down into merely a steep slope. About a mile beyond rose the spires of Alanandamon, the fabulous City of Joy.

Beyond the city were high mountains and arid wastelands. The location was a natural fortress, accessible only from the front. And yet there were no walls, no forts, no gates, no moats, no obstructions of any kind. A broad stream flowed past, but it was shallow and easily forded.

In a world where all castles have moats and all towns have walls, here was an open city, a city that seemed to beckon to all: *Come to me, taste of my pleasures… I fear you not, for I am willing to give you all you desire.*

He had arrived by a devious route, for he had been hotly pursued by Lord Greybear's soldiers. True, Lord Greybear was grateful to Axxar for protecting his daughter Usana from the machinations of the witch, Luna, who had planned to use her as a virgin sacrifice to her evil godling. But he was not so grateful that he did not resent an unplanned-for grandchild. And he regarded the marriage of his daughter to an unknown wanderer as unthinkable.

Usana had warned Axxar to avoid the City of Joy, but her father's soldiers had blocked every other avenue of escape.

Some of those soldiers were so near that he could hear the faint clop of hooves and clink of armor from the jungle trail behind him. The sounds broke his brief reverie and made him hasten his queer mount along the precipice and toward the valley Gwondar, where lay Alanandamon. He had hoped to avoid it, but now it was his only chance of safety, so he had to find a trail down the slope or a sufficiently gentle place to descend, and he had to do it soon.

After a few minutes, Axxar's one-horned mount was picking its way cautiously down the weedy escarpment, while ahead of him the last rays of the setting sun were burning the tops of the city spires. Behind him he heard loud curses as his pursuers dashed out into the clearing in front of the cliff and scrambled to a sudden stop. He urged his telope to greater speed, and was rewarded with a surge of fright as the animal responded by a seemingly reckless plunge down the slope. But of all beasts in this strange world, Axxar had found that the telope was the most sure-footed. They survived the descent, breathless, and set out at a trot toward the city. Axxar turned his head to look back at his foes at the top of the cliff.

They sat their horses, eight of them, making no effort to follow. They saw and understood his destination. And they knew they could not catch up to him before he reached it. They just watched, and waited, making sure that he actually entered the city.

They would not follow him farther. Usana had explained that no man of the region would enter the city of Alanandamon even under pain of death.

Alanandamon was haunted by ghouls and devils. Axxar shivered. But he continued to ride forward.

The sun had set, now, and the moon was rising. Its light was tinted red, and the landscape seemed to shiver in the dusk. Ahead, the city shimmered in a gold green halo that grew brighter as he approached. *Ghost light,* he thought, but he had no place to go but forward.

The streets were wide and clean, and the buildings, set back from the streets, were small. As he continued past the outskirts of the city, the size of the buildings gradually increased until they seemed like man-made mountains. Never had he beheld such a city.

As he rode he watched carefully for inhabitants. But he saw no one.

Yet, even as he went, lights flickered on and off behind strangely-colored window panes, and occasional humming sounds emanated from the buildings.

He had a definite feeling of being followed. The telope, too, was nervous. Evidently it sensed something out of the ordinary. Yet, though he often cast quick glances around him, no living thing was visible.

Gradually the streets grew broader, the buildings still larger. The green gold light seemed to pour out of the very walls themselves, providing a serviceable illumination, now that the tall buildings had blocked out the moon's rays.

Once or twice he stopped to listen, but heard nothing other than the occasional humming sounds, the dripping of water, or the noise of his own breathing.

As he continued, he passed by hitching posts and watering places for steeds. All were vacant, but seemed in good condition, as though they had been used as early as yesterday. At one of them, when he tarried awhile to let the telope drink, he dismounted and tasted the water. It was pure, clear, and cold.

Only moments after he had again mounted his telope, the animal reared back, mewling in fright, and he reined it in firmly.

Crowds suddenly appeared all around him and he heard the sounds of people and animals. The roar of it momentarily deafened him. The people were so numerous that they seemed to buffet and jostle against the telope.

The odors were exotic. Spices, there were; foods and fruit being hawked by street vendors; the stale odor of excrement and garbage; the pungent overlay of sweat.

Languages abounded. Here and there he heard cries in various tongues that were totally foreign to him. He now understood two spoken languages, in addition to the written language of wizardry, but most of what he now overheard was unintelligible. Here and there he could detect fragments of sentences that were comprehensible. The variety of accents was bewildering—startlingly high-pitched voices, speech like musical notes, gutturals almost like those of an ape, all intermingled in a panorama of sound that was overwhelming.

Imperceptibly the background illumination had grown stronger. Colors were abundant. The dress of the people was as varied as their accents, from a coal-black cape employed by a dour-looking oldster to flowing crimson and azure ribbons worn by some of the women. A few people were nearly nude, except for leather harnesses inset with gold and jewels. Others were entirely robed, even to their faces, in rich-textured cloth. Some wore chain mail.

Not one of this throng seemed to be paying the least attention to Axxar, who sat his telope pensively and surveyed the amazing sight.

Most were on foot, but a few rode horses, and others were carried in litters by slaves or servants garbed in brown. Some rode in wagons. Axxar gaped long at one white-haired oldster, garbed only in a scant loincloth, who sat calmly in the center of a rich tapestry which glided forward in a stately manner seven feet above the ground.

Reflexively Axxar's hand had slowly crept to the hilt of his steel sword, which protruded from his saddlebags, as his mouth dropped wide open in astonishment. For he had suddenly become aware that among this crowd, a tiny but distinct proportion of the individuals surrounding him were not human.

Although vaguely human in shape and size, these individuals were clearly demons. All were identically garbed in green and gold folds of cloth tightly woven about their torsos. Atop their bare heads were antennae, and their arms ended not in hands and fingers but in a multiplicity of tiny tendrils like the roots of a flower.

A few people had jostled Axxar's mount, as he stared at the strange beings, then moved off ignoring him entirely. But suddenly a huge man on horseback cannoned into him from the other side. He was saved from falling only because his telope had partly anticipated the collision and had braced itself, mewling.

Like the others, the man seemed to ignore Axxar as a person, casually reaching out to brush him from his path with a huge hand.

Angrily, Axxar grabbed the man's arm and dragged him from the horse.

The man wore no sword, no dagger. Axxar leapt from from his mount, leaving his own sword in his saddlebags, and turned toward his assailant.

Even as he did so, he noticed that no one else watched them or shouted at them. They might have been in a deserted necropolis, for all the impression they made on the rest of the population.

"Cursed demon," snarled the man. "I'll smash you and your devil-city to pieces."

He stood half a head taller than Axxar, who was himself quite tall. He outweighed Axxar by forty or fifty pounds, and it all looked like muscle. Axxar was beginning to think himself imprudent for abandoning his sword. But he felt better when he saw that his opponent merely clenched his hands and rushed at him.

The huge man evidently knew nothing of the secret stances and holds of unarmed combat.

Easily Axxar evaded his rush, neatly tripping him. He fell, sprawling and cursing.

"Who are you and what is this all about!" Axxar shouted.

But fury prevented the man from replying. Like a wolf he was up and roaring toward Axxar.

He leapt upon Axxar like a bear, arms circled, muscles bulging. Calmly, Axxar sliced at his arm with a hand made calloused by long hours of practice. There came a surprise grunt, and the man's right arm suddenly dangled, numb and useless.

However, almost in the same instant, the man's left arm swung wildly toward Axxar's body and caught him squarely on the chest. The force behind the blow was astonishing. Axxar felt as if a manglewood tree had collapsed on him. The breath sobbed from his lungs and he felt himself plunging head-over-heels on the glassy surface of the roadway.

But long training brought him into a tumble and back to his feet, though coughing and wheezing, before his foe could continue the attack.

Now Axxar was more cautious. At the man's next rush, Axaar grasped his other arm and flipped the man over his head and onto the pavement with the full force of the man's weight falling on the numbed arm. There was a snapping sound.

He lay there, still cursing.

Axxar looked about, swiftly. A wide region had opened up around the battling men. To this extent the crowd had deferred to their existence. But there were no onlookers. They were both being ignored, still.

Axxar moved over to the telope, retrieved his sword, and lashed the heavy leather scabbard about his waist.

His opponent sprawled on the ground, groaning—hurt but evidently even more astonished than hurt. He positively gaped up at Axxar as though he could not believe his own eyes.

"You're human!" he gasped. "And you're real. Real." The madness, the frenzy, had not abated from his eyes. Axaar stared at him for moment, then replied.

"Of course I'm real. How could you doubt such a thing?"

"You're from Outside!"

He groaned again holding his arm.

"You're from Outside," he said again. "But no one has dared

approach this place, no human at least, for hundreds of years."

Axxar chuckled. It sounded hollow to him. He wondered how it sounded to the other man.

"What of you, then?" he responded. "How did you get here?"

The man grimaced. "I have been here longer than that, I think. Time passes, here."

Axxar was incredulous.

"A thousand years or more, I think," the man added.

"A thousand years!"

He nodded. "My name is Ul-balthor. I was King in Shemnaz-zoth, the great city that lies to the west. When my people revolted in support of my brother, Om-balthor, I was compelled to flee, and this was necessarily the only haven I could find."

As Axxar stared, speechless, Ul-balthor added, "But one day I shall return to Shemnazzoth as King. Oh, yes, I shall return one day soon."

Axxar recalled Shemnazzoth. He had passed the great city on his way to Alanandamon—or, rather, its ruins. The site of Shem-nazzoth was one of the landmarks on the path from Lord Grey-bear's castle. Usana had once recounted briefly how it had been destroyed in a great rebellion, in which the king had been de-posed—not one but ten thousand years before. The ensuing civil war against the new monarch had resulted in a gigantic fire that destroyed the city and most of its populace. Axxar shivered uncon-trollably as he gazed upon the face of Ul-balthor, the last lawful King of fallen Shemnazzoth. "But time passes, here," the King was saying. "It passes. It passes."

"What—what of the people of this city," he stammered. "The people of Alanandamon. Would they not aid you to recapture your domains?"

King Ul-balthor laughed. He laughed long and maniacally and horribly.

Finally he stopped, gasping, and said with still another horrid cackle, "There are no people in this city."

Axxar gaped at him. But having drawn close he suddenly found himself grasped violently and dragged to the ground, Ul-balthor's good arm clenched about him.

"And you, who have dared to lay murderous hands upon the sacred person of Ul-balthor the King—you must die!"

Frantically, without conscious intention, Axxar drove a killing blow to the vulnerable spot where the bridge of the nose meets the skull. There was a sharp crack, as bone fragments dug into the man's brain. The muscle-riving hold on Axxar was released. Ul-balthor trembled slightly in death, then lay still.

Shuddering, Axxar rose gasping to his feet.

And he found that at last he had gained an interested audience.

The people of the city might well be shadows, figments of his imagination—such was his reading of the king's remark. But this demonic creature with tendrils for hands was real. It stared impassively at Axxar from the edge of the unseeing crowd, dressed in the gold and green folds of cloth like the others.

Axxar's voice cracked slightly. His hand went back, automatically, to the hilt of his sword. He shouted, "Who are you? What are you? What hellish place is this?"

The answer came, softly, across the short distance that separated them:

"This is Alanandamon, man. The City of Joy. I am your servant. I am Andemus. I am here to obey your every wish. What is your greatest desire? Ask, and it shall be yours."

Axxar's thoughts whirled wildly. He pointed to his dead foe. "Life," he said, defiantly. "If you can obey my every wish, then obey that one. Restore him to life." He laughed a little shakily. "I have killed him without meaning to. I do not think he was sane."

"It shall be done," said the thing calmly. "And he shall be restored to sanity."

Three more demons, indistinguishable from the first, appeared with a cart and lifted the corpse of Ul-balthor into it, then departed quickly.

"In the morning he shall live again," Andemus said.

Axxar stared at him for a long minute Then he spoke slowly: "What are you?"

"I am Andemus, as I have said. I am your loyal servant. I am a servant of Alanandamon. Ask and I shall give."

"A tavern," Axxar finally choked out. "Food. Wine. And accommodations for myself and my mount. We have been long on the road."

"Come," gestured the green-gold-garbed monster. He pointed out a building off to the side of the square, where three smaller alleys conjoined.

"You will be well cared-for at the Inn of the Three Worlds."

Axxar's night was not dreamless. It rarely was. Vaguely, just beyond the surface of his conscious mind, monstrous knowledge lurked. And in his dreams he knew more than he did in the waking world.

This night he dreamed the old dream. He had been an apprentice to Manariam, greatest wizard of his day. But he had possessed no skill for magic—like a person who is tone-deaf, he seemed magic-deaf. But Manariam did not seem to mind. Instead he taught the boy other things, skills of combat with and without armament. And every few days he put Axxar into a deep hypnotic sleep and trained his mind to hold secret knowledge.

The dream skipped. He recalled the strange silvery Cube of Xanxes. He recalled some of Manariam's instructions. He would be forced into the Cube—which was not a real Cube but a gateway into a mirror universe. Xanxes (the greatest wizard of all time) had done the same, but he had never returned. With him Xanxes had taken his famous amulets—the Eye of Xanxes, the Finger of Xanxes, the Ikon of Xanxes—most important, the Tome of Xanxes, that magical book that contains the lost spells of the Times Past History.

Manariam wanted those things But he would not, could not, seek them himself. For he had deduced that in the mirror world, his magic would be powerless. In that world, a magician would be a dullard, and a dullard would become a magician. That was why Xanxes had never returned. He had lost his powers. But in that world, a dullard like Axxar could be—

* * * *

Axxar awoke, sweating, in the darkness. His dream whirled about him. He remembered a little. He remembered, too, having conquered the Witch, Luna, with a strange magic incantation that had powered up and out of his unconscious mind, when it was needed. That incantation had sent the Finger of Xanxes—together with the Witch, Luna—back to the other universe, to the world of Manarium. Afterward he had forgotten it once more.

He slept again, fitfully. The hypnotic suggestions implanted by Manariam stirred in his brain, perhaps disturbed by the wizardry surrounding Axxar here in the magical site of Alanandamon. His dreams were grotesque, but he forgot most of them upon awakening.

In the morning he was still half-asleep. Lying there he tried to get his bearings. He remembered Andemus, shivered a little. Would the King be revived as promised?

The tavern to which Andemus had led him seemed reasonably normal, except that the barkeep's assistant was another of the green-gold demons. It was crowded by men of all kinds. Many dandled whores or female slaves upon their knees, others sang or quaffed strange-looking brews. Tired, aching for a retreat from mystery, Axxar had quickly eaten and drunk. By now he was somewhat accustomed to the presence of Andemus.

He had then ordered a room for the night, paying for it with good silver coin that Usana had given him. For a moment it seemed to Axxar that the tavern-keeper's assistant had hesitated. Then he had picked up the money, stared down at it with distatste, and stowed it away beneath the bar. Axxar was so weary that he had barely stumbled to his room and to his pallet, falling on it without even taking time to remove his garments.

He opened his eyes at a slight noise and saw that Andemus had entered the room. "Are you well rested, Master?" the creature asked.

Axxar nodded.

"Several times you shouted aloud in your sleep, Master—I am curious as to what you meant—you shouted of the baubles of Xanxes?"

"An ancient wizard, Xanxes," replied Axxar. "But I rarely remember much of my dreaming…"

Andemus nodded, beckoned to someone behind him. The other figure stepped into Axxar's room. It was Ul-balthor, the King of forgotten Shemnazzoth.

The King seemed affable.

"Good morn to you noble Axxar," he said. "May I enter?"

Axxar rubbed the sleep from his eyes, but Ul-balthor did not disappear. He was really standing there. "Enter, then."

Axxar rose and crossed over to Ul-balthor, a little hesitantly, as if expecting a renewal of the other's fury. But the King remained passive. Gently, Axxar touched his shoulder.

"It *is* you. You live."

"Thanks to you, noble one," replied the King. "Ah—I assume that you do indeed belong to the nobility of your land?"

The green grey eyes of the King bore into Axxar's. He nodded.

"I am the second son of Lord Daymoor of Arichna, your majesty. But sit with me and eat and tell me of this place. I am most curious."

As they were speaking, Andemus and another demon were bringing breakfast trays and a small portable table which they set up for the two men. The meal of bizarre fruit, small delicious cakes swimming in butter, and baked roc's eggs, was strange but satisfying. As the meal progressed, Axxar learned from his companion the history of the City of Joy.

Alanandamon had been founded so long ago that even the pre-history of modern mankind postdated it. No one knew its origin, but it was rumored to have been created by a race of wizards who wished a city all to themselves. These wizards, in order to achieve immortality, had denied themselves the capability to reproduce their own kind, and therefore they welcomed other people into their city, selecting the noblest and finest of their visitors to repopulate the city as, through accidents or weariness with existence, members of the original group died or left. To fill their own immortal lives with wonder and joy, and to stimulate others to join them, they created the fabulous Palace of Life which comprised the entire heart of the city. In the Palace of Life, all was possible. Death and resurrection, love and hatred, base sin and noble sacrifice, all were to be found.

To be sure, the wizards of Alanandamon possessed unique powers, but it had not usually been necessary to defend the city from attack. Why defend, when you offer freely whatever the attacker may most heartily desire? When you can offer freely so much more than any conqueror could try to take, no other defense should be necessary.

Gradually, however, fewer and fewer newcomers appeared. As the millennia passed, it become evident to the outside world that no one ever returned from a journey to Alanandamon. The rumor began to circulate that Alanandamon was dangerous, that its inhabitants offered not joy but death—and that only the foolish and naive would enter expecting a pleasant welcome.

Husbands had forsaken their beloved wives and children forever; armies and generals had left their homelands to conquer Alanandamon, and remained, never to return to their kin. Kings had come and never departed. Wizards as potent as any who had existed in times past journeyed to try their skills against the folk of

Alanandamon, and were never heard from again. Entire towns and even cities in its vicinity had been depopulated, first by mass migrations into the City of Joy, then later by reverse migrations away from the fearsome place.

Gradually Alanandamon became a myth in the present day, shunned by wayfarers, and isolated in a region of the continent that was no longer well-travelled save by fugitives.

Ul-balthor's recital persisted long after the last crumbs of breakfast had vanished. At its conclusion, Andemus brought a bottle of pale yellow wine, decanting a small glassful for each of the men.

Axxar nodded his head at the servant, otherwise ignoring him. Thus does familiarity lead to contempt.

"Are these creatures then," he asked Ul-balthor, "what remain of the race of wizards who built the city?"

Ul-balthor laughed heartily, sipping at the wine, which was more potent than the finest brandy.

"These? These were their servants, created by them (or brought by them from some nether region, I know not) to service this city. Many of the wizards sleep. Some have slept for centuries or millennia in the Palace of Life, and therefore they require faithful attendants. I myself have never beheld one of these wizards, sleeping or awake."

Axxar gestured toward the window. A throng already crowded the market place, even though the hour was till early. The noise of the people was muted within the room, but it was still clearly discernible.

"And those—what are they? You said before that there are no people in this city."

Ul-balthor waited for Andemus to pour more of the fiery wine, then drank it off. He laughed. "They are shadows."

"Shadows?"

"Aye, shadows. True, they seem solid enough, you can feel them and see them and hear them—and even smell them. But they are shadows." He grinned shamelessly.

"Such a shadow I thought you to be, yestereve, in the square, when we fought. Then he laughed again, gulping more wine. "Not true, not entirely true. At first I thought you a shadow—but the shadows ignore real men for the most part, and they never speak to us, let alone pull us off a horse! I guess that then I thought you were one of the Qaichai, like Andemus, here. Perhaps disguised. Occasionally one of them runs wild and goes amuck. Occasionally the ancient spells put upon their race by the ancient wizards will fail, and then they revert to their normal state. I have killed several."

Axxar lowered his voice. "Dare we speak of this in their presence?"

Ul-balthor snorted. "Certainly. They would themselves assist us in subduing one of their fellows if he should revert to the wild state. But it does not happen often."

"Well, then!" Axxar stood up, stretched, looked about, then said, "It appears as though I may have a long stay, here in Alanandamon. It should be interesting to see this city. Lead on, then, if you will, oh Ul-balthor!"

Even so, Axxar had some slight hesitation at thus following the man he had once killed, the man who had been so mysteriously raised from death by the Qaichai. But he quaffed the remainder of his goblet of wine and put this thought resolutely from him.

Although the men and women in the street were but shadows unable to react to Axxar's presence, they were a pleasant enough background. Sometimes he could even forget their non-existence and make himself believe that he resided in a normal city of normal people.

Days and weeks passed by rapidly.

His acquaintance with Ul-balthor quickly palled upon him. They had never actually become friends, for the King seemed in his own way a creature as strange as the servants of Alanandamon. He was a man raised from the dead, first of all. And he was hundreds or even thousands of years old, at that. Often Axxar shunned his company in favor of the strange Andemus and his kindred, now become wholly familiar by longer acquaintance.

Most often, Axxar would spend his time alone (but for the shades and shapes that thronged Alanandamon), drinking fiery brandies in the solitude of a comfortable booth in one of the many taverns of the city. He would sit and sip the wine and watch the beauty of the shadow women who danced and sang for the other less substantial customers. He never even consciously noticed the fact that each bartender had a Qaichai as an assistant.

At times the songs were in the language of Usana's people, as was only to be expected, since they lived not overly distant from

Alanandamon. Usually the languages were alien, obscure; and even the music—often bizarre music, with different scales and a different conception of tonality—meant little to him. But on occasion he heard a song in the language of his own people—the people of the other world—and he wondered at that. He had rarely heard one of these songs before, so ancient were they but he could always grasp their meaning. Sometimes he wept a little when they sang such a song, always reminding himself that none here could see him, for there were no real people here.

Rarely, when he became really intoxicated, he would try to pick fights with some of the shadow men, and try to make love to some of the shadow women. They never resisted, but always seemed to melt away from him and dissolve into the night-mist. Then he would return to his drink until oblivion struck him, and he would wake in the morning in a room at the nearest Inn.

And then he would hunt through the city for Ul-balthor, who at least was real, or would call for Andemus and several of his kind and spend hours discussing mundane matters, or ask questions on more arcane subjects, connected with the city. Most of the questions were evaded.

He never slept soundly, except when thoroughly drunk. Always the magic stored in his brain warred with the magic that surrounded him. Always there were troubled dreams, and the voice of Manariam the magician calling from afar: *Seek the baubles, seek the baubles of Xanxes!*

Axxar could see several choices before him. He could commit suicide—if the post-hypnotic commands of Manariam would permit that. He could return to the castle of Lord Greybear in search of Usana, his beloved. This path might mean death, but he no longer feared Azhotep the death-god after his time in Alanandamon. He could attempt to escape from the city across the desolate plains or across the sharp-peaked mountains of ice. Since none had ever left Alanandamon, these choices might not even be feasible, but he could try.

Or, he could remain in the city, living as he was. That had been Ul-balthor's choice, to exist as long as the city might stand, waiting for the outside world to come to him or to forget him. That, indeed, was his current status. But the example of Ul-balthor was not a stimulating one.

That a choice needed to be made soon was clear to him. The

strongest reason was the geas placed upon him by Manariam—to search, search, search the world for the baubles of Xanxes.

The last choice was the most dangerous of all. He could relinquish his passive existence in the City of Joy, and enter into the Palace of Life. If no one had ever left the city of Alanandamon, it was most likely to be because they all, sooner or later, entered the Palace of Life. And from there, truly, none returned—or so it seemed.

"In the Palace of Life," Andemus told him, "repose the Masters of the city, bathed in dreams of far places. In the Palace of Life, anything is possible. There, the mind, through the combined effects of drugs and magic spells, may be severed from the mortal form and the world in which we exist, and sent to roam through any universe of imagination. Most of the Masters, tiring of the real universe, now journey in worlds of their own creation. Even the youngest of these has remained dormant for over seventy thousand years, and the oldest has been there for hundreds of thousands of years."

Axxar was stunned as the concept became clearer—a race of dreamers lay without death, dreaming in the immensity of their imagination.

"Don't any of them exist in the real universe, this universe of ours?" Even as he said this, he wondered which universe really was his and whether either one was truly real!

"A few are what we denote as reality dreamers. They have remained true to their original ideals of searching and exploring this universe. But even at the speed of thought, which is a considerable speed, a million years is hardly time enough to examine more than a minute portion of this immense world."

Often the memory of that conversation with Andemus returned to Axxar as he contemplated the ultimate choice, the Palace of Life.

But, as Ul-balthor had told him, Time passes in the City of Joy. Time passes. And he had not yet made a decision.

He could have anything and everything, Andemus had emphasized. He could regain the life he had given up for lost, when Manariam had sent him through Xanxes' Cube, to this world of Ancient Earth. Or he could have a lifetime with Usana on this world. He could have both—a multiplicity of lives, all new and different, all real to him.

"Out there," Andemus pointed toward the distant mountains,

"man lives but one minuscule lifetime. They wither. They grow old, in what seems to us in this city like a few weeks or a few months. Then they die. But here, you can live eternally. You could have that old life of yours yet, the life you would have known if Manariam had not sent you here. And then you could turn about and live it over again, if you wished, like rehearsing an old Play once more. Then you could live another. And another. You could explore, gain knowledge, travel back into the past and learn again the secrets of the ancients. Or you could enter worlds that exist only in idle tales. Whatever you might desire, that would be re-ality…your reality…but it would indeed be real. Real. Real. In-deed," Andemus looked at him slyly, "Indeed, how can you know even now that you are not already lying there, in the Palace of Life, dreaming over again your previous existence."

Upset, Axxar could not resist responding briefly: "Or how could you know that you yourself are not there in the Palace, dreaming?"

This seemed to disconcert Andemus, and he did not at once reply.

Here, Axxar thought, was a concept to reckon with. Even in a drunken stupor on his pallet at night, Axxar was taken aback with the very idea!

Life. Life eternal. Lives re-run like tales re-told. Real lives. Or real-seeming. Whatever that might mean…is this what he wanted? Magic warred against magic. Magic rebelled against magic. Outer magic pressed inward against inner magic. The forces of wizardry, installed in his brain by Manariam, seeped near the point of release into his conscious mind, as if thrust there by dire necessity.

Solidly implanted was the geas of obedience: stronger and stronger came the urge to quit the city, to follow unknown path-ways to far continents in search of the talismans brought here by the wizard Xanxes. Closer and closer to consciousness seeped the command; harder and harder to resist.

On a dark evening, months after he had entered Alananda-mon, Axxar was awakened from a reverie by distant shouts and the clank of swords. For a moment he listened, puzzled. Another shadow play by the shadow people of the city?

Suddenly another sound intruded. The door to his room burst open, and Ul-balthor rushed in, followed by Andemus.

"The city has been invaded by an army of swordsmen," Ul-balthor announced. "They are garbed much as you were when you entered the city. They attempt to fight the shadow-people, and will not listen to the Qaichai, but slay them."

"Usana's father," muttered Axxar. "They must have followed me. It took them a long time to gain the courage, perhaps."

"Not in my memory has such a thing happened," Ul-balthor told him. "Do you wish to escape them or fight them?"

Axxar fingered his sword hilt; he had never stopped wearing that weapon. "Can we raise an army? The Qaichai?"

Ul-balthor shook his head. "They do not fight. There are no defenses in the outer part of the city. Alanandamon is not defended at all, since all joys are freely given to those who come. Gold? Jewels? What care we for those, when we can make them from light and air? The supply is inexhaustible. We have no defenses and there are no places to conceal ourselves. But there is one solution to your problem."

"And that?"

"The Palace of Life!"

Axxar shivered.

"The Palace of Life is the only fortified structure in the city—it has to be, to protect the dreamers against madmen who might try to harm them. And the defenses are magical—impenetrable. Come, we shall be safe there."

Axxar followed him out into the street and toward the center of the city, Andemus silently trailing the two men.

"But can we conceal ourselves in the Palace of Life without becoming dreamers ourselves?"

Ul-balthor shook his head. "No. But I have made my decision at last—to join the dreamers for a few months cannot do any harm."

"A few months?" They were passing the great gates that led to the Park of Pleasure, at the center of which towered the thick and gleaming Palace of Life.

Axxar went on: "But all the other dreamers have stayed to dream forever. How can we return to reality after a few weeks or months?"

Ul-balthor seemed certain of his knowledge. "Any time a dreamer wishes to return, he need but will it so, and he will awaken."

"Why do none return, then?"

"Presumably they do not wish to. Perhaps they have left no ties to bind them to mundane existence. But you have your woman—and I have my desire to reconquer my beloved city of Shemnazzoth!"

Axxar remained prudently silent.

Andemus conducted them to a small entrance at the side of the main building, pressed a hidden button, and preceded them through the doorway that opened in response. A smooth expanse of hallway, absolutely dust free and highly polished, led on interminably. But they walked only a short distance, then were gestured by Andemus into a small antechamber. The chamber was a waiting room for a series of elevators. One of these whisked them to a subterranean chamber, far below ground level, after which they walked to a small office where another of the Qaichai sat waiting for them.

He looked exactly like all of the others—the bartenders, the waiters, even Andemus.

"Your will, gentlemen?"

Ul-balthor spoke first. "I shall dream of my kingdom. I shall live again in the days of glory when I ruled Shemnazzoth, and this time 'twill be I who triumph!" His eyes began to light with a red glow of madness.

"It shall be done," said the Qaichai calmly. He pushed a few buttons and summoned another of his kind to lead Ul-balthor away.

"Farewell, good friend," said the King to Axxar. "When we awaken I shall relate my dream life to you, and we shall drink wine and laugh."

"Farewell, O King." Axxar waved his hand in a salute.

Andemus grunted, almost a human sound.

"What is it?" Axxar turned to the now-familiar monstrosity, brow furrowed. "What are you thinking?"

"I am thinking that never again will you behold Ul-balthor the King in this world of reality, even should you yourself decide, Noble Axxar, to return. He will never do so. He should have taken to the Palace of Life long long ago."

Axxar nodded. "I think you are right about him."

"But then what are paltry years in the eternal life of the city of Alanandamon?"

Axxar had no reply.

"And your will, noble sir?" spoke up the Qaichai behind the desk.

Axxar opened his mouth to speak, but suddenly his vocal cords constricted.

The geas implanted in his brain came forth strongly—*"Search,"* it said silently to him, *"Search this world for the baubles of Xanxes. You may not retire to dream! You must search..."*

It seemed almost as if the voice of Manariam the magician was literally speaking to him from a universe away. Axxar responded—aloud.

"If I become a reality dreamer, I can search this world, this universe, better than I could do any other way." The compulsion of the geas continued for another moment, then vanished.

"It is your wish to dream of reality? That can be done." The Qaichai called another attendant—perhaps the same one who had led Ul-balthor away, perhaps not. Axxar followed.

Led into a small chamber containing a bed, Axxar was told to disrobe. His clothes were placed on a hook mounted on the wall. His sword and scabbard he himself placed beneath the bed. All around him he felt the raw force of pure power. He was still fearful, but his decision and been made, and he literally could no longer back out. The geas was now operating to keep him to this path, almost as if a replica of Manariam resided in his brain and was amenable to logical argument.

"I shall come back," he told himself. "I shall. Whatever I find out there, I shall return to real life and to Usana and our child. God, perhaps the child has already been born! How long have I been in this place?"

A slight sound of hissing drew his thoughts away. Moments later he detected a bitter odor in the small cubicle. He grew faint. Belatedly following the instructions he had been given, he flopped down upon the bed and composed himself. He was just in time. Instantly a dark veil of unconsciousness descended upon him.

Then, seemingly in the very next instant, he was again aware.

He seemed to be awake with all his senses tingling.

He stood up. He peered about. The room was the same as before. Exactly the same. Soft illumination poured from the gold green walls. The hissing sound had ceased. He could no longer detect that queer odor in the atmosphere.

On the bed lay the naked body of a man.

At first he wondered who the fellow could be—another human being in this desolate city! Then he knew!—*the body was his own!*

A shock went through him. He still possessed a body of sorts, apparently identical to his real one. It was naked, like his real body. He compared his hand to the hand of the body on the bed, his chest, his legs—all were the same. It was so! He was now truly a reality-dreamer.

Suddenly his nakedness bothered him. He did not stop to think that no mortal could see him in this state, so it mattered not whether in his dream state he was bare or accoutered like a king. He *felt* naked and helpless. He wanted clothes. He wanted his weapon.

And with the thought, they appeared. His clothes were on his body as though he had never removed them; the sword in his hand, solid to him as a real one. He was shaken. What was reality and what was dream? He sheathed the sword in the scabbard that immediately materialized, bound about his waist.

Continually he stole side-glances at his true body, lying on the bed in the small cell. If anything could be said to be real, it was that.

He tried the door, cautiously, but it gave way before him like smoke and he found himself in the corridor. He willed himself to be back at the desk where the Qaichai sat. In a twinkling he was there. Andemus was there, too, conversing in low tones with his colleague. They spoke in the language of this city, the language of Usana.

He shouted at them: "Andemus! Andemus!" They ignored him.

A chill went through him. As far as they were concerned, he was but a shadow, much like the shadow-people of Alanandamon. Worse than that!—he was less than a shadow, for they could not even perceive his existence. To them, indeed, he did not exist at all.

He tried shouting again, willed with every iota of his being for Andemus to hear him. And the Qaichai flicked an antenna, and a slight puzzled frown appeared upon his face. But still he ignored Axxar.

This, then, was a taste of reality-dreaming. He could not affect his surroundings when he dreamed of reality. No doubt in fantasy-dreaming, the dreamer was a part of his world and could function normally in that world. But here he was merely an observer, necessarily aloof from all action. No wonder most of the other dreamers had switched from reality-dreaming to an existence in fantasy worlds.

Reality-dreaming was a lonely experience. But perhaps other

such dreamers would be able to communicate with him, if he could discover any of them.

Tentatively he walked toward the wall and found that it offered no resistance at all. He passed through. Then he floated upward at command of his own will, passing through ceilings and floors, through hundreds of cubicles. All those he encountered were empty, as if waiting for occupants. Through a hundred such layers he passed, then emerged through the rooftop into the grey night.

Darkness had settled over the city. The lights of the city had been dimmed, perhaps to confuse the invading army. He willed his dream body to be more sensitive to what light still existed. He smiled—he could see.

Now he knew that while he could not affect material beings, he could affect the manner in which his body responded to them. He could walk on a floor as if it were solid or pass through it as though it were a mist. He could see in the dimness of the city—perhaps he could even see in the absence of any visible light at all.

The army. He must go at once to investigate the invading forces. Perhaps they had not come from Usana's father after all. Perhaps they were not hunting him down. He willed himself toward the outskirts of the city; and there they were.

Stop! This was no army. It was a mere dozen men, and they were led by Usana herself. She had come to find him. There was no fighting. They held their swords at the ready, but there was no one for them to fight. From the looks on their faces, and the way they whispered, Axxar thought they were frightened almost beyond human sanity. Only Usana seemed more determined than frightened. Axxar divined that the men had only come into the city because they refused to be shamed by a mere girl, and she would let nothing short of death deter her.

Was this the so-called invading army? Where were the swordsman whose clanging and clashing he had heard.

Of a sudden, as the pieces of a puzzle might suddenly mesh to form a united whole, the answer came to him. He had been fooled. Fooled by the Qaichai. They had known he would leave with Usana, had he known of her presence. And they had tricked him into a situation where he would choose the bed of dreams instead. Why had they not simply murdered him in his sleep? He did not know. Nor did he think long about it.

Angrily he wheeled and went soaring back to the Palace of

Life.

The Qaichai still sat at his desk, but he was alone. Andemus had left. Axxar growled at him, fingering his sword, but desisted, knowing that to the Qaichai that sword was less than the most tenuous vapor. Then he willed himself to the cubicle where his body lay.

Had they lied to him about the awakening, too? Could he really awaken himself if he wished to? He came to the realization that no one had given him any sort of instructions about the awakening process. Cursing under his breath, he tried willing himself to awaken, as he had willed himself to move from one place to another. Nothing happened.

He tried grasping his own arm (his real arm) and pulling himself awake. Nothing happened. He resolutely lay his dream body directly atop his real body, attempting to match the forms precisely, and willed himself awake. (A little shudder went through his frame. The body on the bed twitched, once. But nothing else happened.) No matter how frantically he tried and willed and wished himself awake, nothing happened. He was impotent, a spirit, a dream wraith.

Was he dead? He looked carefully at the body in the bed. Once, twice, three times in a minute the chest rose slightly and fell. No, he was not dead. Now he willed himself back to Usana's small expeditionary force. He willed himself to stand beside his lovely mistress. Her soft red hair, grown longer since the Witch, Luna, had shorn it, gleamed in the starlight, which to Axxar was as bright as day. He saw lines on her face—new lines caused by the suffering she had undergone in the months of his absence. The childbirth. The longing for her lover. And he saw etched there the fierce determination to find the man she loved.

If only she could hear him, see him, feel him—sense him. He felt a moment of total despair. He felt cold, he who was but a spirit or less than that. Then he saw her head rise. She stared about. The men watched her, sullenly, fearfully.

"I—seem to hear him. He seems near. Axxar?"

Axxar felt as if a miracle had happened. Somehow she could sense him.

He recalled Andemus' antennae twitching a little when he had tried to communicate. And Usana—Usana was his beloved. There was a bond of love between them—and the bond of the child of their union, as well.

He willed it as hard as he knew how. He willed her to hear him, and he shouted her name and shouted of his love for her?

Was it that bond alone? Or were the spells of Manariam, locked in his physical brain, a source of power? He did not know. But she responded.

"I hear you. Where are you, Axxar?"

Quickly he explained. "I am here next to you Usana, and at the same time I lie on a bed in the Palace of Life. Do you understand? It is my spirit that stands here, but my flesh is in the Palace of Life."

She appeared shocked.

"Not dead, not dead. Dreaming. I am dreaming, in the Palace of Life. It is the huge central building of the city. Take care. Flee while you may. I am trapped here, perhaps forever. Be careful of the demons that throng the city. The people you see here are shadows, less actual than I, but the monsters, the Qaichai, are real. The green-gold ones are not to be trusted. They have tricked me into becoming a dreamer. Leave. Leave and be safe."

The eyes of the soldiers bugged out as she repeated Axxar's words aloud. "Can you not awaken?"

"I do not know how. None of the dreamers had ever woken in the memory of man—or demon. Perhaps they cannot.

Usana bit her lip. The blood came. Was she imagining these things, overwrought by her ordeal? Or was she really conversing with the disembodied soul of her lover? The thing was incredible, but in the city of the wizards one would expect the incredible to be commonplace.

"Axxar. Listen. Are there many other dreamers, then?"

"All the wizards who founded this damned city are here, dreaming, or so the Qaichai told me. Most are living millions of fantasy lives in their dreams, but they say a few still roam the universe of reality, learning and studying."

"Ah!" Usana stamped her pretty foot. "Then perhaps one of those ancient wizards will know the means by which you can be awakened. Can you find them?"

Axxar suddenly felt faint stirrings of hope.

"I know not. I can only try. I shall try. But promise me that you will return home. If I am successful, I shall try to come to you. It is unsafe here for you."

Usana shook her head.

"No! I am going to the Palace of Life, as you call it. Perhaps there will be another way to free you—through my sword." She tapped the hilt of her slender blade. "And the swords of my brave men."

Axxar had learned better than to argue with this particular red-haired wench. A smile crept over his features as he examined the visages of her brave men—they looked ready to turn into piles of quivering jelly. But they followed her as she went onward toward the heart of the city.

"Be careful," Axxar told her, feeling his futility. "Do not succumb to the temptation to be one of the dreamers. I go now, to seek the wizards who dream of reality."

"Go with the knowledge, my beloved, that you have fathered a healthy son, and that my sire is resigned to my choice of you as husband. Since the Witch, Luna, looted the kingdom of its wealth, there is little remaining to make a dowry for me. And none other desires me now." She laughed. "And he is beginning to show affection for his grandchild, after all."

With uplifted spirits and new determination, Axxar's dream body shot back toward the Palace of Life.

Again he found himself standing in the little chamber where his body lay. He studied it carefully, again. Very slight rise and fall of chest but only twice or thrice per minute. He put his ear over his heart: that mighty pump was nearly still, but he did detect a small tremor that showed him blood still flowed.

Again he willed himself to wake, with no results, as before. His body continued to lie almost as still as death.

From curiosity he sought the cell of Ul-balthor. He had supposed that the King would be in an adjoining cell, and the thought had struck him that possibly he could make contact with the King, since the King was the most recent of the other dreamers. True, he dreamed in a fantasy world, but it seemed worth a try.

However, he found the cell on one side to be vacant. The cell on the other side was occupied by a man with coal black skin and grey hair. How long, he wondered, had that form lain in dream? Was there any way to know? Not a speck of dust remained in these cells to tell of the passage of centuries.

He went out into the corridor, beside the door to the black man's cell. There he saw a nameplate fastened to the door. It was incised in an archaic language, similar to the wizards' tongue, which he had learned first from Manariam and later from the scrolls left behind by the Witch, Luna. The nameplate read: AGROTOSH, CHIEF OF THE BULILOMO, followed by a numeral that seemed to be 213487, although Axxar was not certain of the number system for such a magnitude. Was this numeral a date in some archaic system? Or could it represent the number of dreamers? He sped to the door outside his own cell. There was a new nameplate in the same antique tongue, which read AXXAR, LORD DAYMOOR, 213488.

The number must represent the totality of dreamers in the Palace of Life. He was awe-struck. So many lay here wrapt in an eternal life of dream…over two hundred thousand. But something else puzzled him. If this were indeed a consecutive ordering of dreamers, why was the next cell vacant? Where was King Ul-balthor?

He shook his head in wonderment, but then turned his mind to the task at hand…the search for the ancient wizards whose dream bodies roamed the true universe. How might he learn who and where they were, and even if he could locate them, how could he converse with them in disembodied form? The difficulties seemed insurmountable. Nevertheless, he decided to proceed with the search by studying the Palace of Life in more detail. Since he now knew the cells above him were all vacant, he dove downward.

As he willed himself to sink through tier upon tier of subterranean cubicles, he was amazed at the sheer immensity of the numbers of occupied chambers. The figure 213488 etched upon his own door had been but a label, a collection of symbols, an abstraction. Now, faced with sleeper after sleeper in multitudes of floors, each with dozens or hundreds of chambers, his amazement knew no bounds and he came to have a dim appreciation of the true magnitude of that simple abstract number.

He was no longer surprised that the city of Alanandamon was peopled by shadows of the past—the true populace lay here in the stillness of their eternal sleep.

At times he paused outside the doors of the cubicles to read the nameplates. "Anthemides of Ntarranos, 116841," "Polonux of Shemnazzoth, 91364," "Gremnatorith of Hopthath, 18639," he read as he willed his essence lower and lower into the truly terrifying edifice. The Palace of Life was a gigantic tomb of the living!

Occasionally he tarried to examine the inhabitant of a room.

In most instances these resembled the shadow figures who populated the city, for those forms had apparently derived from real people, from the population of Alanandamon as it had varied over the millenia. Both men and women lay sleeping in these honeycomb cells. He saw thick-set hairy men with muscles like steel tendons, and soft and delicate men from highly civilized environs; men with beards, mustaches, hair cut long and hair cut short, and heads shaved bald. He saw women fragile and tiny as opals in a gold-lace setting, soft-skinned blondes and swarthy dark-haired lasses, women young and voluptuous with proud jutting breasts, and painted nipples, and women old and shrunken, skinny and bloated. In some cubicles were even children of ten or twelve, smooth-bodied boys and undeveloped girls.

The panorama was magnificent. In his dream state, Axxar felt no pangs of sexual desire for the female beauties he saw, but could view all as a true philosopher might see it, lovely and remote. Even the ugly old women and the scar-torn warriors with amputated limbs were beautiful in their own way.

Down went Axxar, down, past the multitudes. He thought he might be nearing the center of the earth, so long had he passed by on his journey. But he noticed that the numbers on the nameplates were becoming relatively small. "Radosh Yumakil, Alanandamon, 2845," read one, and "Kantosse Perimultean, Ypktnil, 1762," read another. So he continued from tier to tier.

What impulse drove him to seek all the way to the nadir? How might he know which were the powerful wizards, which perhaps victims or dupes or visitors beguiled by the opportunities of the dream world? He could not know. But he was impelled by an urge to survey all there was to see, to understand, in hopes of gaining some slight clue as to what further course to take.

At long last Axxar floated to a stop before the door of the lowest cubicle. He had nearly missed it, and had found it necessary to search carefully to locate it, for the bottom-most tier consisted of but a single cell. The Palace of Life had apparently been designed in the shape of an inverted pyramid or a gigantic needle, with the point being driven deeply into the bedrock of the earth.

And Axxar then gasped aloud as he stared at the name plate on that lowest cubicle. He almost reeled in sheer astonishment. Never once had he thought to hazard a guess who the chief wizard of this wizard clan might have been...

XANXES OF UDDABON, 1—thus read the nameplate in the ancient language of wizards.

The full impact of Manariam's geas struck him like physical blow despite the fact that he lay in dream—that the physical brain upon which Manariam had laid his post-hypnotic commandments lay miles above.

"Xanxes," he gasped aloud. "I must find Xanxes!"

Added to his other compelling reasons for locating one of the ancient wizards—dwarfing those reasons, subjugating them entirely—was this magical compulsion enacted by Manariam. He forgot Usana, forgot his plight, forgot all but one command: *find Xanxes!*

His dream-body hovered indecisively in the tiny room which contained the physical form of Xanxes. Xanxes appeared to be a man of about forty, small of stature and slightly corpulent, but not at all repulsive in appearance. He differed from all the other sleepers Axxar had examined in one single aspect. Unlike the others, Xanxes wore about his neck a golden amulet.

At the sight of the amulet, Axxar's brain produced one of the potent spells concealed in its depths by Manariam. It was the spell of sending-back, the same one he had used on the Witch, Luna, and the Finger of Xanxes. And other information trickled into his conscious mind. This amulet, he now understood, was a powerful tool, called the Ikon of Xanxes. Its capabilities were generally unknown to Manariam, but it was supposed to confer immortality, at least, upon its wearer.

Unable to desist—even as he came to an understanding of the situation—Axxar found his lips shaping the words of the incantation designed by Manariam to retrieve any of Xanxes' baubles that might turn up. The Finger (and the Witch, Luna, who held it) had proved highly susceptible to this spell, and had been whisked at once back to the other-world laboratory of Manariam. But this time, the spell met resistance.

Xanxes' medallion flickered for an instant, and then began to glow with a bright blue aura. It did not disappear—it remained securely attached on its golden necklace to the body of Xanxes, Xanxes the wizard who had vanished from Axxar's home world hundreds of thousands of years ago.

With the glow came an incredible pulse of sheer power. Axxar, in his disembodied state, felt the backlash of that power, and an overwhelming surge of terror made him tremble.

Then it passed, and Axxar waited…waited for something to happen. He knew not what it would be. But he knew that something would happen. After minutes of time-stopping silence, it came.

The vibrant voice penetrated incredible years and incredible distances. It was the voice of Xanxes, unused these many millennia, and it cried out:

"Who disturbs me in my eternal search for knowledge? Come to me. I command it. Come to me whoever and wherever you may be. By the Ikon I place upon you an irresistible geas. Come!"

Axxar felt the gentlest of breezes tug at his dream-self, impelling him toward the top of the world.

Wherever Xanxes might have gone, it must be far. The force that plucked at Axxar was evidently meant to be overwhelming, meant to sweep the intruder violently and bodily from this chamber into the presence of Xanxes. But it did not do so—it was only as strong as the pull of a spiderweb. Xanxes must have travelled on a great journey for his irresistible command thus to dwindle to a sad suggestion.

But the other geas still drove him. He must find Xanxes. He did not need an additional compulsion—only a guide to follow.

He directed a thought, backed by all the force of his will, toward the Ikon of Xanxes, hoping that it would be delivered to the soul of the wizard:

"I have sought you and I have found you. And I come."

Then he willed himself into the presence of Xanxes of Uddabon. The result was unlike his earlier experiences. The passage was not instantaneous, as it had been in his previous astral travels. So long was the distance in time, and so far in space, that the projection of his dream self from one place to another could not happen at once. It would take—an appreciable length of time.

Axxar felt the cold ether winds of remote space tug at his soul-stuff, felt vertigo and violent fear, as his dream body lurched through space on its far journey. Above and beyond him he saw grotesque shapes, like hounds, only monstrous in form. They were the awful hounds of Tindalos, and they rode the ether winds; when they spied Axxar they moved swiftly toward him, shrieking in soundless space.

But his speed was increasing and soon he left those awful hounds behind, together with the earth and, soon afterward, the sun. Now he saw what he had never before envisioned—that the earth was not infinite and flat, but a small round sphere of cloud and sea and green land. And the sun was not a small orb of light, but a huge roiling mass of hot gases. Was it the same in his home universe, the mirror universe to this? He did not know.

Soon he realized that the sun was but another star, and with it came the understanding that all the other stars he saw were also suns, many with planets like Sol's. And he was filled with a great wonder at the immensity of the galaxy of suns, the uncountable billions of them. And then he grew even more astonished as he traversed the Milky Way galaxy and saw it for what it was—a gigantic pinwheel of suns, but finite in extent, glowing like a godling's toy there behind him. And then he left the galaxy itself behind, moving ever faster—faster than the speed of light, faster than the speed of any physical body, fast as thought.

From the sun, located near the outer edge of the galaxy he had ranged through the entire star group and past it, into intergalactic space. Gradually the mass of stars became a spot smaller to him than his fingernail, hardly visible in the blackness of space. Gone was his adopted planet earth, gone was Sol, and now—gone was the Milky Way Galaxy. His fear grew to utter terror. He perceived that he was totally lost in the immensity of space—an immensity he had never dreamed of before this experience.

Gradually a mass of light appeared ahead of him, growing from a softly glowing mist to a larger pinwheel shape. He was approaching near to the galaxy of Andromeda, another group of stars that was twin to the home galaxy. But he soon saw from the direction of his motion that he would bypass this new island-universe entirely. Soon his speed had increased so much that the galaxies behind him had turned a pale red hue, while the new ones that appeared in front were dark blue, then violet, then finally went off the visible scale altogether. After a moment of panic he willed himself to perceive them, and they swam back into sight again.

Galaxy after galaxy flashed by like glowworms. Some were shaped like Andromeda and the Milky Way. But some were spherical or elliptical, others were shaped irregularly, and here and there were several galaxies that had come together, as if colliding, and he saw great plumes of star-destroying plasma roaring out from these regions like mad tongues of flame.

He cried out feebly, "Xanxes, where are you? Xanxes! I am lost, lost!"

Was it the voice of Xanxes that he heard, exhorting him to be calm and to watch the spectacular display spread out before him?—or only the whisper of the plasma-winds that buffeted him.

Axxar's only contact with his home galaxy was the direction of the unchanging line in which his dream-self was moving. Should he stop without gaining his bearings, he would be utterly lost, here, in the remoteness of the universe. Had something like this, indeed, happened to the other dreamers? Did this explain why none of the reality dreamers had ever awakened? Were those dreamers now scattered in far-flung portions of this immense universe, unable to find their way homeward? He felt a thrill of terror at the thought. He resolved to watch carefully for landmarks at journey's end.

And now at last his journey did draw to an abrupt halt. He entered a large galaxy, spherical in shape, packed with an incredible density of blue-white stars, and hurtled straight along a radius of the gigantic galactic ball toward the center. He was slowing down drastically, now. In horror he watched what he was approaching— it was a quasar, a gigantic mass of colliding suns which emitted as much light as thousands of normal galaxies. It was the mind-shattering nucleus of this star-packed galaxy.

To his astonishment—he was now beyond mere horror—he plunged right through the roiling surface of the monstrous mass, down into the unimaginably hot depths, into the very center, where the temperature was so high as to be beyond the very concept of temperature.

But his dream-self was untouched by the physical hell in which he found himself. His perception in the nucleon gas that made up the interior became almost nil, but he willed himself to perceive more clearly and he did—though not by detecting light or any normal radiation.

He found himself floating in the center of the quasar. About three feet away hovered the imposing figure of Xanxes.

Axxar recognized him at once, though his dream self had taken on a somewhat different shape from that of the body left behind in the lowest cubicle of the Palace of Life. He appeared much younger, taller, more muscular; he was blond of hair and wore a short blond beard. He was garbed in golden robes and his eyes, golden eyes with golden irises, stared coldly into Axxar's.

At sight of him, Axxar felt once more the hypnotically implanted spells of Manariam rise to consciousness, felt himself automatically impelled to speak out the spell of captive enchantment.

Then blackness and peace descended upon him for a time. And he could neither see nor hear.

He found himself dreaming in his dream. At first he did not comprehend; then he realized that a more powerful mentality held his own mind in its grip, compelling him to remember the salient details of his past life and to explain the purpose of his visit.

How long the period of mental enmeshment lasted he was unable to estimate. He was never sure that time was the same, here, as it was back on earth. Again he pictured in his mind the scene in which Manariam had thrust him into the Cube world, armed with spells placed in his unconscious mind. Again he pictured his encounter with Luna and Usana, his search for the baubles of Xanxes, his flight from Usana's father, his life in the City of Joy. Finally he re-lived the last moments in which he came to realize the manner in which the Qaichai had tricked him into becoming a dreamer, and resolved to seek out the great wizards of Alanandamon for aid in his endeavors; and the last moment of amazement when he stood before the door to Xanxes' chamber and read the Master's name.

There followed a time of utter peace, in which his mind rested and healed. It was a little like dreaming about being asleep, but it served a similar purpose.

Then, in a sudden transition from night to day, he was again floating fully aware, in the center of the quasar, with the figure of Xanxes before him. The amber eyes were kinder, now, as they gazed upon his young visitor.

"I have considered what course of action to take, and have decided to help you. You, in turn, will assist me."

"Am I—you understand my…" Axxar could only gasp.

"I have studied you. I have followed closely your actions, and understand most thoroughly. I have already excised the geas of Manariam from your mind, and the spell of returning. You will no longer be a captive to that magician from the mirror world—our home world. As long as you remain in this universe, you will be safe from his enchantments."

Axxar tried to stammer his thanks, then added—"But Usana—she is in dire peril in that city, and I must return to life. I cannot remain here."

"Neither of us shall remain here," was the reply. "First, however I wish to explain to you those things that you need to know.

"First," Xanxes went on, after a short pause, "know that Manariam was right—in passing from one of the mirror worlds to the other, a magician loses his power of magic. The reason is quite obscure and almost impossible to explain to you. Imagine, however, that in the cells that make up the human brain are little parts shaped something like tiny coils of hair, and that these are either attuned or not attuned to the secret powers of the universe. If they are so attuned, the cells of the brain, if properly organized, can exert a powerful compulsion upon the material of that universe. The proper spells, talismans, or prayers constitute such a means of organization. But if the cells are not attuned, but are wound in an opposing sense, they cannot directly influence the universal ylem."

Axxar's mind, totally ignorant even of the basic concept of DNA, reeled; but he continued to listen, gamely.

"The talisman which you call the Cube of Xanxes is not another world, but a gateway between worlds—a gateway between the two mirror universes. Thus a man such as I, attuned to the one, a magician, will lose his powers when he crosses to the other, unless he takes special precautions. A man like you, without magical powers in the one universe, will (as Manariam postulated) gain such abilities in the other."

"But I am no wizard!"

"You are a most powerful wizard," retorted Xanxes in a friendly tone. "In the dream state your powers are weaker, whereas mine are unaffected. And you are untutored. But the unconscious spells absorbed by your brain from Manariam were nevertheless extremely effective. I seriously doubt whether this world contains any other magician who could match you if you study the art for a few centuries."

"Centuries!"

"And of course the Qaichai sensed your abilities, which gives ample reason for their behavior toward you. They dared not confront you directly, so they sought to exile you in the Palace of Life."

"Centuries," mused Axxar quietly.

"I, of course," continued Xanxes, "knew of these facts when I entered this world. But I was bored in my own universe, and wished to explore the mirror worlds. Thus I evolved a plan to avoid losing my own powers. It consisted of storing, if you understand me, certain magical energy within some of my talismans, which I carried with me. I made one serious error of judgment, however, for I discovered that these stores of magical power were not sufficient to return me to my own world."

Axxar listened with amazement and deep interest.

"My error was in not setting up an appropriate spell operating from the other world—that is the method by which your Mananriam operates. The spell by which you can return things to our home world simply triggers the master spell that operates from back there. They aren't sent back, but drawn back."

Xanxes nodded with satisfaction.

"In any event, I was able to solve the major problem of recharging my amulet. To do it I created a confederation of wizards and trained them properly. Before I arrived in this mirror-world, there was hardly any wizardry worthy of the name. And we constructed the city of Alanandamon to house them. In a very real sense, the city and the society of magicians are my tool for maintaining my supply of power. Or at least—they were."

"But how could they do so, lying in their state of dream? All of them seem to be there, with the Qaichai ruling the ghost population in a ghost city."

"Yes," Xanxes nodded. "The Qaichai were denizens of a nearby world.

"We bewitched them and compelled them to act as our servants. They were primitives. But they have been unfaithful. The strongest command implanted in their minds was never to kill, and that apparently still survives. Even though self-interest has caused them to forget their proper duties, and to permit all the dreamers of the city to remain in the dream state."

"You are saying that they can revive us?"

"Certainly. Various of the dreamers are supposed to awaken for an interval of a few weeks or months, as they choose. We never intended to allow the Qaichai to have all responsibility for maintaining the city. The mechanism for revival consists of a revivifying gas, an antidote to the one that originally sent you to sleep. Without its presence no dreamer, however much he wills himself to wake, can do so."

"How can we operate this mechanism?"

"We cannot. We shall require outside assistance. None of us has ever been able to make contact with entities in the physical state. But with your help, there may be hope—for both of us. You have already succeeded in doing this. There is a special bond betwixt you and your woman, a bond of such a kind as we have not been able to forge. Of course, if the Qaichai have had time to overwhelm her, to make her a dreamer too…"

"Let's hurry!"

"We are returning at once!"

Of a sudden, the nucleus of the quasar no longer engulfed them. It receded swiftly, diminished to a tiny spot, and was lost in galaxies of stars behind them. Together the dream shapes returned along the path Axxar had originally taken.

"There is always a tenuous connection between the body and the dream spirit, even at a tremendous distance. But from here the connection is so tenuous that you would be lost forever in the immensity of space without me as a guide."

Xanxes continued to converse with Axxar as they sped earthward.

"There is another situation that must be dealt with. No doubt other dreamers have roamed nearly as far as I and are lost beyond their capabilities."

"In your case, the medallion did the trick, is that it?" Axxar guessed.

"Exactly. However, since I have learned to use the excess energies of suns to sustain myself on my journeying, I have not needed to tap the stored energy. So it remains for our use."

"So that's it!" exclaimed Axxar. "That's why you were inside that hellish mass of…whatever…that pit of flame. I wondered."

"I needed maximum power to face you, a natural magician, with your added link to Manariam."

Onward they flew… Through galaxies of weird wild shapes… Through the vastness beyond imagining of intergalactic void… Swiftly buffeting the ether winds on the geodesic toward home…

Now Axxar was no longer frightened of the starry immensity. He gave it all his attention. It amazed him with its beauty and variety. As they passed by some of the galactic islands, Xanxes told him of many planets he had visited that circled such far suns. He had spent hundreds of thousands of years exploring them in quest of knowledge, but knew not whether his quest would ever reach an end.

Then, in a twinkling, they were standing outside the cubicle of

Xanxes. He pointed out a panel in the wall next to the door. This panel opened, he explained, with a touch of the button in its center, exposing to sight two valves. The left hand valve permitted the sleep gas to enter the cubical, and the right hand valve controlled the restorative.

"What must I do?" Axxar asked.

"We must restore you first," said the mage. "We shall hope that the restoration unit has not been dismantled. You must tell Usana to go to your cubicle, open the panel, and turn the right hand valve."

"Wonderful!" exclaimed Axxar enthusiastically. "But you— should we not try to restore you first? You can destroy them or reduce them to submission with magic. Then would be time enough to revive me. All I have is my sword, whereas you…"

Xanxes smiled grimly. "My source of magical power is not inexhaustible. In using it as a beacon to return us to Alanandamon I have reduced my powers to a dangerously low point. In this mirror universe I am no magician, save by virtue of the Ikon. I cannot use the many spells I know. Whereas you, Axxar, are the magician, untutored though you are. When you awaken, and feel that sword of yours in your hand, do not forget this in your lust for battle."

Axxar was dismayed. "But the only spells I've had are the ones Manariam gave me, and you have removed them from my mind. I never knew them consciously, anyway…"

"No." Xanxes spoke firmly. "I only removed the geas, not the knowledge of useful spells. And I have added to them a spell of dissolution which will be effective only against the Qaichai. In effect, it will not really dissolve them, but will return them unharmed to their own world."

Axxar searched his memory but it was blank.

Xanxes smiled more broadly at that.

"Knowledge will come to you when you need it," he said simply.

Axxar, followed by Xanxes, willed himself to the corridor outside his own cubicle. He had vague plans of finding Usana and explaining that in some way she must come to this chamber and turn the valve. But he was astonished to find her already there, just exiting the tiny room. She was flanked by two of the Qaichi, but she still wore her slender sword. On her features was a look of sadness, almost of defeat.

"Now," spoke one of the Qaichai, "you have seen him, seen

that he still lives and dreams."

Axxar gaped. Following Usana out of his chamber was Ul-balthor, King of ancient Shemazzoth. The King was not a dreamer, then; that explained why Axxar had not found a cubicle given over to his body.

"There, Usana," he said, soothingly. "You can see there is no danger of any kind. I can assure you that I have dreamed many times, and have awakened fully and with no bad effects."

Usana shook her head sadly, as though unable to reach a conclusion.

"Should you choose to dream of reality you should be able to find Axxar's dream self, and with him explore all the universes, a lifetime of mutual satisfaction and intellectual excitement."

"But how can one waken? How is it done?"

The traitor smiled and said, "It is done merely by willing yourself awake." Clearly Usana was confused, but Axxar gave her no chance to reach a decision.

"Usana!" he shrieked. "If you can hear me, do not let them know it, and do not reply. Just smile.

Usana started slightly, then forced herself to relax. She smiled sweetly. "They are lying to you. Here is what you must do to release me. See the tiny button in the wall next to the door?" Usanas eyes moved over to the panel and she nodded, once, briefly. "Push that button, and when the small panel opens, turn the right hand valve. Be sure it's the right hand one, not the other. This will awaken me."

Immediately, Usana turned to Ul-balthor.

"I agree," she said decisively. "I shall become a dreamer, and shall do so at once."

King Ul-balthor smiled, and the two Qaichai seemed to relax slightly.

"But I wish to commune at his bedside for a few moments. I want to compose myself and pray to the gods of my people. May I be alone for those few moments?"

Reluctantly the King agreed, and Usana turned back and re-entered Axxar's cubicle, where she slowly knelt next to the bed.

"Can you tell me, Axxar? Are they leaving?" She whispered the words under her breath.

Axxar moved out to the corridor. Ul-balthor and one of the Qaichai were leaving, satisfied now that Usana would be no further problem. Axxar wondered what had happened to her guardsmen. The other Qaichai reminded on guard outside the door.

When the two had gone, Axxar relayed the information to Usana, who drew her sword and stepped to the doorway.

"Tell her," Xanxes spoke from behind them, "that a sword in the exact center of its body is the best way to kill it."

Usana nodded, as Axxar passed on this advice. She stepped into the corridor with a sudden twist, confronting the Qaichai. Before it could move or speak, the small blade was thrust directly into its middle: once, twice, three times. Green ichor spouted forth, splashing on her sleeves, and the feature slumped back, writhing on the floor.

Axxar said, "Quickly, the panel, the panel."

She heard him. Still holding the wet, dripping sword, she pressed the button with her left hand. The panel opened smoothly and silently. She grasped the valve and tried to turn it. It resisted her efforts. Angrily, she tore a piece of cloth from her skirt, wiped the green ichor from her hands, and from the valve handle, and then grasped it with both hands, letting the sword clatter to the floor. With a supreme effort, she twisted at it, grunting. Nothing happened for a long moment, and then it finally gave way with an audible rasp.

Within the room, the hiss of gas came from the corners, invisible and almost inaudible.

Usana, acting on Xanxes' instructions as relayed by Axxar, closed the door, remaining on guard outside with sword in hand to guard the panel.

Axxar willed himself within, crouched next to his body and put his dream self in close contact with his true self. He slid within his body effortlessly. "Awaken!" he commanded himself. "Awaken!"

The slight odor of the gas made his nostrils tingle. The hissing continued.

Outside the door, Axxar heard the clank of swords. Usana screamed, "No!" Then a moment of darkness descended.

The body of Axxar began to stir, opened its eyes, breathed deeply.

He lay on the bed in the room. He heard the continued hiss of gas entering the chamber. Had he dreamed? Or had he indeed traversed the limitless reaches of intergalactic space?

The clash of swords continued outside the door of the room.

Axxar suddenly came fully awake. With an oath he leapt to his feet, swayed giddily for a moment, then found his balance. He drew his sword from the scabbard he had left beneath the bed. It seemed unaccustomedly heavy in his hand. He shoved open the door.

Three of the Qaichai, together with Ul-balthor the King, were confronting Usana, who was defending herself with her small sword against all four assailants.

Already they had forced her away from the panel, and one of them was closing the valve of the right-hand control, and trying to reopen the left hand valve.

"Traitor!" roared Axxar, and weak though he felt, he swung his sword in a wobbly arc toward Ul-balthor. Too astonished to parry it, the King stood astounded as the great sword clawed his neck in twain. His body gave a twitch and sank to the floor.

As he stared at the body of the King, a multitude of Qaichai poured into the corridor from the elevators and stairwells; some were armed with swords, others with ropes and nets. But Axxar ignored them for a fleeting instant. For the body of King Ul-balthor was *changing*. The red of his blood, which had sluiced Axxar's sword, was turning grey, then green. The head of the King was being transmuted, and his fingers were being metamorphosed into tendrils. King Ul-balthor was not human after all: though antenna-less, he was one of the Qaichai!

In a flash, Axxar understood that the revived Ul-balthor had always been one of the Qaichai, hypnotically or magically disguised as the King of Shamazzoth. The amazed Axxar had accepted the miraculous revival of the dead King, but apparently this feat had been beyond their abilities. Even these vassals of magicians could not restore a dead man to life. He had killed the real King Ul-balthor that first day in the city, months ago, and ever since he had been comrades with a monster in human guise.

As the Qaichai rushed toward them, he felt Usana's slim body at his side. "Now we can at least die together," she cried passionately.

"No!" Axxar roared, as the spell of Xanxes, carven deep in his mind, sprang to his lips unbidden. The unaccustomed syllables of the spoken language of ancient Uddabon erupted from his throat and burst out upon the stricken Qaichai. Even as they tried to grapple with him, the spell of dissolution took hold. They seemed to disintegrate into fog or smoke, and then drifted away in a direction known to no earthly denizen—into a kind of fourth dimension of space. And were gone.

Even the green slime of the Qaichai corpses vanished with the dead bodies. The corridor was deserted, now, save for Axxar and Usana.

He clasped her to him and kissed her long and tenderly.

Then he told her something of the task remaining. They must free Xanxes the wizard from his dream state. Only then could they leave the city to Xanxes, make the trek back to Lord Greybear's castle, marry, and try to forget the horrors and wonders they had found here.

But Axxar knew he would never truly forget his flight through the farthest corridors of space, though he spared Usana this knowledge, and he felt deeply within himself that one day, perhaps many years from now, he would again return to the haunted city of Alanandamon, the City of Joy, once more to lie dreaming in the Palace of Life.

www.ingramcontent.com/pod-product-compliance
Lightning Source LLC
Chambersburg PA
CBHW021243260626
47155CB00004BA/1280